Beautifully Shattered

Beautifully Damaged Book Three

J.A. Owenby

FREE BOOK

Edited by: David Steele

Cover Art by: iheartcoverdesigns

Photographer: CJC Photography

Model: Eric Guilmette

First Edition ISBN-13: 978-1-949414-48-6

Trigger Warning

Beautifully Shattered is recommended for readers 17+.

Due to dark and mature content, graphic sex scenes, and sensitive topics, please consider this your *trigger warning*!

Chapter One

Acidic, bitter grains of dirt rolled over my tongue. I attempted to swallow, but my throat gave me a firm "fuck you." I wasn't sure how long I'd gone without water, but at this point, if I drank any, it would turn the grit in my mouth into mud.

My cheek pressed against the cold ground as tears burned down my face and melted into the soil. After nearly drowning, I'd woken up trapped in this hellhole. I'd frantically searched for a way out, clawed at my surroundings, and screamed for help until my voice was reduced to a scratchy whisper. I found nothing. I was alone. Underground, with no windows, dirt walls, and no light except an occasional sliver from above. My desperation and fear permeated the air around me. *What had I done to end up here?* I pushed off the hard dirt and sat up. A wave of fear crashed over me, and I rested my chin on my knees and cried.

Attempting to conserve energy, I curled my naked body into a ball, hoping for a bit of warmth. Instead, I was met with my cool, clammy skin. A shudder traveled through me. "Mind over matter," I said softly. I sniffled and wiped my nose with the back of my hand. Crying wouldn't accomplish anything. I needed a plan of action for when the door finally opened. *If it opens at all.* I swatted the dark thought away as though it were a wasp, waiting to sting me at the right moment.

Holden's name escaped my parted lips as I imagined his arms around me—safe, sound, and warm. We were supposed to be in our new home together and making love on every surface possible. Afterward, he would have pressed gentle kisses against the side of my head. Instead, I'd ditched Zayne after I'd stared at the pregnancy test. In my state of panic, I'd left myself vulnerable, wide-open for the sharp prick of the needle to my neck, bag over my face, and the fight for my life. If I'd only known ... but there was no reason to play the *what-if* game now. Eventually, someone would come for me, and I suspected that Logan was behind my kidnapping. He'd made it clear he would take me as payment in place of the money Dan, my piece of shit guardian, owed him. My guess was that Dan wasn't just drinking and smoking pot, he was strung out on the meth Logan so readily supplied.

An unseen critter scampered across my back, and I shivered, my skin crawling. It was most likely a spider, but not for long. I laid down, wishing it a slow death for having the nerve to touch me.

Memories of the shitty trailer I'd grown up in taunted me. The place had also been cold and bug-infested. I swore I would never live that way again. And yet here I was, worse off than before.

Light seeped through the cracks above my head, and the floor creaked with footsteps. I bolted upright and waited, my pulse beating wildly against my wrists. *Open the door. Open the fucking door.* I rubbed my throat and willed it to work. I pried my lips apart, and only hoarse, quiet choking sounds came out.

Almost as quickly as the light peeked through, it disappeared, leaving me in complete darkness.

I sank to the unforgiving floor as my thoughts drifted to Holden again. He had to be out of his mind with worry. At least he suspected his father, Tim, and Logan, who had been business partners at one time. After Tim had put his disgusting paws on me and I'd dropped him to the floor, he'd been pissed at me. I couldn't blame him. I'd made him look weak and stupid in front of his family. Once Holden, Brynn, and I had learned that Tim was an illegal weapons dealer, though, I realized he was capable of anything, including kidnapping me. Hopefully, there would be enough evidence for Holden to find me. But would it be soon enough?

A sharp pang stabbed me in the chest. Closing my eyes, I said, "I love you," but there was no sound. A brutal reminder tapped me on the skull. Even if my voice had been working, there wasn't anyone around to hear me. Whoever had been walking above had left.

Waves of nausea rolled in my belly. I scrambled across the small space and attempted to puke where I wouldn't sit or lay in it later. I wished the morning sickness were an indication that it was actually morning. At least then it would help me mark time. At this point, I had no fucking idea if I'd been in this hole for an hour or a week. My guess was a few days from the number of times I'd squatted against the wall and peed. My aim sucked, and the warm liquid had streamed down my leg instead, marking me with the pungent stench of urine. I got better at it, eventually.

I'd lived in some messed up conditions, but this ... this was quickly stripping me of my dignity and replacing it with the burn of shame. I was living like an animal. If I ever had the opportunity to shower, I suspected that tears of joy would run down my cheeks.

Fear settled in and wrapped her long fingers around my heart while she whispered that I wouldn't ever see the light of day again. I would never touch Holden's beautiful face, kiss his full lips, or tell him I loved him. I sucked in a lungful of air and clawed at the dirt, the grime caking under my fingernails. I'd come too far to lose now. Logan wouldn't win. I fucking refused to let him. I'd rebuilt my life with Holden, Brynn, and the guys ... even Catherine, Holden's mom, and I had grown closer. I loved my job at the club—missed the people, the interaction, and the sense of belonging I had.

I squeezed my eyes closed and listened to the beat of my pulse thumping rhythmically in my ears. I was alive.

Images of my abduction flickered across my mind, and I shook my head. It didn't make sense. The face of the monster that had attempted to drown me was someone I knew. I'd obviously been delirious from the drug that had been administered. I must have hallucinated because what I saw couldn't have happened.

My left calf started to cramp, and I shot up off the ground. I stretched my arms in front of me and began to walk back and forth in the small space while I swore a blue streak at the obnoxious pain. I'd learned really fucking fast that I'd break a toe or my nose since I couldn't see the walls. Once I'd figured out the layout, I'd counted steps in order to be able to move around without hurting myself. I barked out a laugh. I was naked, hungry, dirty, and freezing. I wasn't sure breaking a fucking toe would be that big of a deal. But I had to try and take care of myself, take care of my baby.

I leaned into my anger and allowed it to build. It fueled my mind and provided energy, keeping me warm. Holden had taught me to love and trust. Brynn had taught me to laugh and live. But now ... now I reached into the darkest part of my soul and fanned the flames of the fury toward Tim and Dan. It broke through the fear and the self-pity. It marked me as a different woman. In a short time, I was no longer the person who had kissed Holden and watched the furniture for our new home be delivered. Whatever stupid son of a bitch had thought taking me was a good idea ... I swore that I would destroy them if it was the last thing I did. Anyone that had any sense understood not to mess with a mama and her baby. Come hell or high water, I would be with Holden again, and I would keep our child safe ... unlike my mother.

The creak of a door opening reached my ears. I turned my head toward the sound and was blinded as a flood of light cut through the darkness. A combination of fear and hope sprung to life deep inside me. I rubbed my eyes and blinked rapidly, trying to clear the grit. I wasn't sure when I'd fallen asleep since I'd been locked away in this damned hole unable to tell time.

My stomach growled as I shielded my vision and stood slowly. I was weak and probably dehydrated.

"You can come out," a deep, husky voice said. As a ladder was lowered down, I gulped and hoped I had the strength to climb it.

I gripped the side, a sharp splinter immediately slicing the palm of my hand. Shaking it off, I placed my bare foot on the first rung and grabbed the sides. One shaky step at a time, my head finally peeked through the opening in the ceiling. I gasped as I scrambled to gather my wits and clear my muddled brain. It was daylight out, which meant I'd been in darkness for no less than twenty-four hours.

I crawled the rest of the way out of the hole, then sat down quickly, pulling my knees to my chest to shield my exposed body. My attention swept across the kitchen, and I mentally took notes. Every detail would be important to my freedom. A white refrigerator hummed in the corner next to an old farm sink. The white and blue linoleum floor was worn but clean. A man I didn't recognize sat at the white table, only a few feet away from me. He took a bite of what appeared to be a roast beef and cheese sandwich, then followed it with a long drink of water. Maybe he would share with me. Not only was I starving, but the baby needed food as well.

"W-w-who are you?" I stammered, my throat raw as I spoke. I didn't recognize the burly man in front of me. His red hair was sheared close to his head, and his beard was neatly trimmed. His biceps bulged against the navy, short-sleeved shirt that was tucked into the same color slacks. My focus landed on the gun holstered to his hip.

His dark, lusty gaze raked over my dirty, naked body. His mouth parted, and his coffee-stained tongue darted out over his bottom lip. I cringed but remained still. Antagonizing him didn't seem like a good idea, at least for the moment.

"I'm Barrett. You'll see a lot of me around here."

I nodded. "Where is 'here'?" My voice trembled.

"Training camp." He bit into his food, the crunch of the fresh lettuce and the smacking sounds of his open-mouthed chewing breaking through the silence.

My forehead creased in confusion. "Training? I don't understand."

Barrett stood and wiped the crumbs from his lap. He strode to the refrigerator and opened it, revealing well-stocked shelves. Barrett reached inside, then produced a plastic bottle of water and a half of a sandwich. "I'm under orders to feed you. Then it's shower time."

Tears of relief stung my eyes—a *shower*. I gulped and stared at the drink. Surely, Barrett couldn't be all bad if he allowed me to clean up and eat.

He closed the gap between us and squatted down. "Open your mouth."

I parted my lips slightly, the chapped skin painfully tearing. My attention remained on him as I waited while he removed the cap on the bottle, filled it with water, then dumped the small amount down my throat. I swallowed, nearly groaning from the sweet taste.

"Open." Barrett poured a bit more and fed me another two capfuls. He moved to recap it, and desperation rose quickly.

"More. Please."

"You'll fucking puke everywhere. It's why I'm only giving you a little at a time."

I met his gaze and searched for any sign of compassion. None. This was all part of the control game, and it started with water and food.

He continued to give me small doses, then set the bottle next to him. "Let's try a bite to eat." He opened the sealed sandwich baggie, and I looked at the ham and cheese eagerly. He ripped off the crust from the top of the bread. I parted my mouth like an obedient little puppy, and he placed the food on my tongue.

Once I'd chewed and struggled to swallow, he allowed me to have another drink.

He stood and returned to his seat at the table. "We wait." He

6

folded his hands across his chest and stretched his muscular legs in front of him.

Something told me he was used to waiting.

"Thank you," I whispered, unsure if he was a good guy or not. My instincts told me not to trust him, but I had no other choice in my current situation. "I'm River." If I could connect with him, maybe Barrett would tell me where I was and eventually help me leave. All I wanted was to go home and pepper Holden's face with a hundred kisses.

"I know." His brown eyes remained on me, and I wrapped my arms around my legs as I tried to cover myself the best I could.

"Do you work for Logan?"

Barrett didn't even blink at my question. His stoic expression didn't offer me a glimpse of who he took orders from.

"Why are you keeping me here?"

He answered with more silence. I struggled to understand. What did Barrett mean by training camp? What was I training for?

I studied the small room and finally realized I was still sitting beside the trap door. Barrett could easily shove me back into the dark hole. I shifted my weight and tried to scoot away, which was difficult since I didn't want to expose my breasts.

"You're not going back in the hole ... for now." He rose and approached me again. Over the next several minutes, he fed me small bites and allowed me to drink more.

Fear rippled through me at the idea of returning to the pit of darkness. Dirt streaked my legs and arms, and I reeked of urine, sweat, and vomit. I had no idea how Barrett was able to sit with me and not gag from the stench.

After I'd finished the sandwich, Barrett gave me what was left of the water, and I gulped it greedily. "Thank you," I panted, wiping the droplets from my mouth with the back of my hand.

Barrett tossed the baggie into the trash, then grabbed another bottle from the fridge. He looked at me with a smirk on his face. "Stand up."

"I don't have any clothes."

With two long steps, he closed the space between us. "I said stand up." He peered down at me.

I was nearly at eye level with his bulging cock that pressed against his pants. Barrett didn't even try to hide his arousal.

"Please. I need some clothes."

He reached down, fisted a handful of my hair, and jerked me to my feet. "I fucking told you to stand," he growled.

My legs wobbled as I found my balance, the pain shooting through my skull.

Barrett released me and stepped away. His gaze traveled over my breasts, down my flat stomach, and to my stubbled pussy. He palmed his erection through his pants and grinned. "Let's get you cleaned up."

Barrett motioned for me to walk in front of him. I crossed an arm over my chest, but before I could cover my center, he knocked my hands away.

With a shove, I stumbled to the front door. Barrett removed his pistol and pressed the cold, hard metal to my back. "Just so you don't get any big ideas."

Ragged breaths tore through me. I had a feeling that Barrett wouldn't think twice about pulling the trigger. I suspected the only thing that would stop him were orders from above.

My bare feet landed on the sidewalk outside of the house. I squinted against the harsh sunlight and inhaled slowly. Fresh air. While in the pit, I wondered if I would ever see the light of day, smell freshly cut grass, or enjoy the bright colors of flowers again.

I took mental notes of the layout of the land. Several small homes were spread across the property. The landscape was flat, with only a few trees planted here and there. Toward the back of the acreage, a large, beautiful white home with black trim stood out like a sore thumb. Next to it were four huge outbuildings.

Barrett guided me to one of them, then rang a buzzer. Within seconds, the door swung open, and I stepped foot into my new hell.

Chapter Two

Barrett led me to a corner of the vast, empty room and holstered his weapon. It looked like a warehouse with rows of cabinets on the opposite wall. The walls were a dirty white, and dark stains spotted the floor. "Don't move."

I subtly assessed the area for a way out. We were the only people in the building, which gave me a direct path to the exit. But even if I had the strength to run, Barrett would shoot me before I ever made it outside.

I eyed Barrett as he grabbed a long, brown hose that was larger than the average garden variety. Shivers shook my body as I waited to see what he had planned. I spotted the drains on the concrete floor, then it dawned on me. As soon as my terrified brain formed the thought, freezing cold water pelted against my skin, stabbing me like a million tiny needles. A scream tore from my throat as I tried to dodge the blast. I held my arms up to block the sharp spray. The son of a bitch had used some kind of power nozzle. Barrett was merciless and sneered at my pain. Tears streamed down my cheeks as I turned away, refusing to let him see me cry.

Finally, he lowered the hose and tossed a bar of soap and a small bottle of Garnier shampoo at my feet. "Hurry up," he barked.

I scrambled for the shampoo. I struggled to open it but finally squeezed the honey-colored liquid into my palm. I turned my back to him and lathered my long, dark-brown hair. I quickly ran my fingers through it the best I could while my teeth chattered violently. I retrieved the soap while peeking through strands of my wet hair in order to see if Barrett had moved any closer to me. He hadn't. I soaped up quickly, skipping the crack of my ass and lady bits. Although I was pretty sure I had dirt in all my crevices, I rejected the idea of him watching. I tossed the bar to the floor and braced myself for the next wave of the agonizing blast.

"You girls are all the same." Barrett approached and grabbed my wrist. "Wash your pussy and ass, or I will."

"Fuck you," I whispered through clenched teeth.

Barrett chuckled. "As you wish." He rinsed the suds from my hair and body. Once I was clean, he gathered the soap. He dropped the hose and lathered his hands. "Turn around, raise your arms, and spread your legs."

I wiped the droplets of water from my face and glared at him. "Don't you dare fucking touch me."

He quirked a light-colored brow. "Then you should have done what I asked and washed yourself, bitch."

In a quick move, Barrett overpowered me and smashed my cheek against the wall. His booted foot kicked at the inside of my ankle, sending pain ricocheting through my leg. He slid his soapy palms over my breasts, and I squeezed my eyes closed as I tried to block out his touch. I bucked against him, but he had me pinned, and I couldn't shake him loose.

Barrett pressed his erection into my ass as he dipped his hand between my thighs. "Oh yeah, that sweet little pussy."

"You sorry son of a bitch! Is this how you get off? Holding girls against their will?" I seethed, latching onto my anger for mental and emotional protection.

I sucked in a breath as he slammed a finger inside me, and his thumb massaged my clit. My molars ground together as I squirmed against his unwanted touch. "Stop!"

Barrett pulled my hair, forcing my head back while he continued. "You'll be on your knees begging for it soon, little girl."

"Get your fucking paws off of me!" I raked my fingernails across the back of his arm.

He met my demand with a grunt and pressed his hips against me. He grabbed my throat, cutting off my air. I clawed at his arm, mentally pleading for him to let me go. He loosened his grip, but I understood I had to stay quiet and stop fighting, or he would end my life.

I hated him. I hated myself for ditching Zayne. I hated my body for not being stronger. A whimper escaped me as he skillfully played with my sensitive flesh. I sank my teeth into my lower lip and refused to cry out. I wouldn't give him the satisfaction.

"Oh yeah. I like you," Barrett whispered against my ear.

"I hate you. I love Holden. Do you understand? No matter what you do, you'll never take that away from me," I hissed.

"It won't stop you from coming for me, darlin'."

"Fucking pig." I pushed against him, but it just encouraged Barrett to continue.

"I like the ones that have some fight to them."

"No," I whimpered, refusing to believe that my body would betray me.

Holden. Holden, I'm so sorry. I imagined it was Holden behind me, touching me. Owning me.

Barrett chuckled, his breath grazing against my ear. "You no longer own this." He gave my clit a little pinch, and my world exploded. My core clenched around his fingers as I released.

As soon as I finished, he ordered me to bend over. My tears freely flowed as I obeyed him, my shame for betraying Holden stomping all over my heart. Guilt knotted my stomach as I mentally checked out.

The cold water between my ass cheeks didn't even phase me.

This time I welcomed the sting and pain. At least it was a deterrent from what I'd done. *You slut. You just came all over a stranger's hand.* I choked on my cry.

When he was finished, Barrett spun me around. "Dry off."

I grabbed the oversized tan towel and dried myself. My nakedness no longer mattered. This monster had violated me. *And you'd enjoyed it, whore.* I shook the thought from my mind. I couldn't dwell on it right now. I'd already been stripped of my clothes and dignity. I couldn't allow my need for revenge to be stolen from me as well. I tucked the awful memory away, saving it for when I needed it to drive me forward.

Barrett took the towel before I was finished and wrapped it around me. Without a word, he led me to a row of metal cabinets that spanned across the back wall. He opened a drawer and removed something. I couldn't see well enough to understand what it was.

He tossed it at me. "Put this on."

I shook it out and realized it was a long, white, see-through dress. Slipping it over my head, I tugged it down. It hit me at mid-thigh.

Barrett removed a pair of slip-on tennis shoes from the drawer and tossed them at my feet. "They should fit."

I slid my damp foot into the right one, then the left. Afterward, he handed me a hairbrush. Over the next several minutes, I took great care to rid the tangles from my hair. Memories of when Shirley bought me a brush flickered through my mind. I pursed my lips. She and Ed had most likely betrayed me, or I wouldn't be standing here in front of this bastard. I mentally added them to my revenge list.

Barrett's lust-filled gaze never left me as he allowed me to brush my teeth over a sink near the drawers. Rust stains rimmed the edge of the basin. Or were they blood stains? I was afraid to ask. I didn't want to entertain thoughts of what Barrett and his people were capable of doing. Although I hadn't seen anyone else yet, there were at least ten homes near where I'd been held hostage.

Once I was finished, Barrett assessed me and nodded. "Better."

He grabbed my upper arm hard enough to bruise it and walked me to the exit.

I desperately wanted to ask where we were going, but I was terrified to hear the answer.

We left the building, and the sunlight warmed my skin. I hadn't realized that I was still shivering from my cold shower. At least I could feel my toes now, thanks to the shoes. *And run. Soon.* I needed a plan and to build up my strength.

Barrett walked me past two additional buildings, then stopped at the last one in the row. He opened the door and pushed me forward. My heart lodged itself in my throat as I stared at the scene in front of me.

"Move. You'll have plenty of time to adjust to your new home." A malicious grin spread across his face.

A musty odor nearly stopped me in my tracks. This wasn't a building that got a lot of fresh air. I blinked rapidly, attempting to focus on the row of empty prison cells that spanned both sides of the walls as far as I could see. A wide aisle separated them, ensuring no contact. Barrett led me to the next to last one and released my arm. He fished around in his pocket, then produced a key. The loud click of the lock echoed throughout the building.

"Go," he ordered.

My gaze narrowed, anger igniting a spark inside me. "Does this make you feel like a man? Locking someone up and playing mind games with them?" I clenched my jaw, determined that he wouldn't see any more tears from me. "Rot in hell, Barrett," I said, spittle flying from my mouth and onto his lips.

He growled and wiped his mouth with his meaty hand, then shoved me inside the cell. I went flying to the concrete floor, landing on my hip with a hard smack. The door slid closed behind me.

"I'll be back with food soon."

Barrett's booted footsteps faded, and the second the rat-bastard was out of the building, I broke into sobs. Placing my palm over my lower abdomen, I hoped the baby was okay. I slowly picked myself up and glanced at the dingy, small area. A bed, a sink, a toilet. I grabbed the blanket off the worn mattress and wrapped it around me. It was then that I realized I had a small window. I hurried to it. Pushing up on my tiptoes, I attempted to peer through the bars. Nervous energy tap danced over my ribcage. The view was expansive and overlooked hills of green grass. No houses. No people. No cars or animals. An ache traveled from my chest to my throat. Even if I had an opportunity to run, where the hell would I go? I would be shot before I made it very far.

Shivering, I crawled into bed and curled into a ball. Tears flowed fast and furious as my thoughts turned to Holden, then my body's betrayal. How would he ever forgive me? Maybe I didn't need to tell him. It was against my will, even if my body responded. I'd told Barrett to stop. I hadn't given him consent. Holden always asked. *Always.* For now, I decided to lock the shameful memory away and focus on a plan of how to escape. It was imperative that I concentrated on Holden and my future.

I rubbed my tummy. "Hang on, little one. I swear I'll get us out of here." This time, I would make good on my promise. I'd failed my baby brother, but I was older now.

I stared at the cinder blocks separating my cell from the next and forced myself to focus on the positive. I was out of the dark pit. I had a mattress and a blanket. I didn't have to crouch and pee in a corner. I had a sink. *A sink!* I shot off the bed and ran to the white porcelain bowl. I gripped the faucet and turned it on, the squeak of the handle the only sound other than my heavy breathing. *Please. Please. Please.*

A rush of water sputtered out, and I ran my fingers beneath the flow. It began to warm quickly. A cry broke free, and I tried the cold. My shoulders slumped forward with relief as it dawned on me that I had both. I cupped my hands together and filled them. Tentatively, I took a sip. I allowed it to roll over my tongue and trickle down my throat. It tasted so good. I continued to drink until I felt better. After I was done, I wiped my palms off on my thin dress. The sun had started its descent, and the darkness had begun to settle in. Still chilled, I crawled into my bed.

My mind returned to Holden. I imagined him sitting in our new penthouse, shoving his fingers through his hair, distraught. I hadn't ever regretted such a stupid choice as much as I had ditching Zayne. I should be with Holden, Brynn, Jace, and Chance, celebrating our new home together. I swallowed against the ache in my chest.

The hours passed, and the glow of the moon filtered into my cell. At least I would be able to tell the time better than in the pit.

The sound of a door creaking reached my ears, and I stood and straightened my bed. I didn't want Barrett or anyone else to know that I was using the blanket. They might take it away, and I needed it to stay warm.

A bright light filled the building, and I blinked several times in an attempt to clear my vision. With a smirk on his face, Barrett appeared with a tray of food.

"Don't look so surprised. I told you I would be back." He entered and placed the container on my bed. "And as you learned earlier, I always do what I say I will." He grinned as he raked his eyes up and down my body, then stepped out of the cell, locking me in again. "G'night, sweetheart." He winked, then walked away.

I hurried to the bars and watched him leave the building. Once he was gone, I looked at the white tray. Water, milk, fried chicken, mashed potatoes, and green beans. I grabbed the plastic spoon and napkin, then shoveled a bite of potatoes into my mouth. "Shit, that's hot!" I sucked in air, trying to cool off the food that was burning my tongue. I waved my hand around as though it would help. Finally, I was able to swallow. I immediately snatched up the bottle of water and drank several gulps, allowing the cool liquid to soothe my tongue.

I sank onto the edge of the bed and forced myself to eat my dinner slowly. Only when I'd greedily eaten every last crumb had it occurred to me that the dinner might have been drugged. I gathered the tray and placed it on the floor, hoping like hell I hadn't just killed myself or my baby. I remained standing in the middle of the room, counting to a hundred ten times. Mentally, I scanned my body for any strange feelings, chest pains, or odd symptoms. All I noticed was the sudden urge to pee. I made my way to the toilet and spotted a roll of toilet paper. I settled onto the seat, grateful I didn't have to crouch over the ground. I finished and wiped, still not feeling any alarming sensations.

With a massive sigh of relief, I climbed back into bed and nestled under the blanket and white sheet. At least the cover was thick and provided a decent amount of insulation.

Once again, I pretended that I was in Holden's arms, safe and content. Eventually, my breathing slowed, and my eyes fluttered closed.

***

The clang of a door woke me from a sound sleep, and my pulse kicked into high gear. Barrett must have been back, but it was in the middle of the night. I cringed. Maybe he'd returned to rape me again. I sat up, attempting to peer through the darkness. It wasn't my cell that had opened. Heavy footsteps slapped against the concrete floor, then nothing.

"Hello?" I whispered. "Is someone there? Barrett?"

I counted four beats of my heart, then convinced myself I'd imagined the noises. It wouldn't have been the first time I'd dreamed something and thought it was real.

I laid down, my head sinking into the small pillow.

"You're not alone. At least not for tonight," a male voice said.

Chapter Three

"Who are you?" I asked, rubbing my arms through the thin material of the dress.

A heavy sigh filled the night. "My name is Reid."

"Are you here to ... hurt me?" I chewed on my thumbnail, hating how fragile and broken I sounded.

"No. I'm one of you. I think I'm in the cell next to yours, actually." The creak of a mattress told me he'd sat or laid down.

I hopped out of bed and pressed my left cheek to the bars, trying to see the cell next to mine. "Wiggle your fingers so I can see."

A strong male hand slipped through the small opening. I inched to the side, then waved at him. "I'm River. I can see you. Well, your arm, anyway."

"A-are you all right?" Genuine worry clung to his tone.

"It depends on what you consider all right." I pondered the possibility that we might be able to touch each other, if the cells weren't too far apart. Not that it mattered. I didn't know this guy. One man assaulting me for the day was enough.

A beat of silence hung in the air. "Where am I? And what do you mean 'one of *you*'?"

"You don't have any idea why you're here?" Footfalls echoed through the hall, and I imagined that he was pacing.

"No. I was drugged and nearly drowned. I fought back, then woke up in a dark pit under Barrett's house. I have no idea for how long, but I'm guessing a few days. I was moved here today after ..." My words failed me.

"I'm sorry. I'm sorry you were hurt already, but you need to understand that it won't be the last time."

"I don't understand. Please, tell me what's happening?" An imaginary hand fisted around my heart at the thought of being hurt again.

"You've been brought to a training camp where they teach you to please people sexually. You'll either be auctioned off as a slave, or you'll stay here to be used at parties and for wealthy clients."

I didn't miss the sadness in his tone. "What?" I squeaked. I shook my head as if he could see me. "How long have you been here?"

"I'm not exactly sure, but since I was young. I've spent most of my life here."

His confession doubled me over, and I sank to my knees, the cold concrete floor biting my skin through my flimsy dress.

"River, I'm so, so sorry. I'm not going to lie and tell you that it's going to be okay because it's not. It's really not. But you'll learn to adjust."

"How can you say that?" I yelled at him, sobbing uncontrollably. "I have a boyfriend, a job, a future."

Reid remained silent as I came undone, swearing to kill anyone that touched me. My eyes burned with tears, and my chest ached. I sucked in a shaky breath. "Reid?"

"Yeah?"

"Can you just talk to me?" Even through his grief, his voice was deep and soothing. Maybe he'd help me stay sane until Holden found me. I knew that Holden would never stop searching. He'd burn the world down to save me.

"Of course. It's always hardest when you're new. Honestly, this life gets lonely, and I'm grateful to have someone to talk to."

Overwhelmed with compassion for him, I fought the urge to scream. "What do you look like?" I whispered through the darkness.

His low chuckle filled my ears. "Well ... I'm forced to work out twice a day, so I stay in really good shape. Clients don't like flabby slaves, you know."

I cringed at the word slave, still fighting to wrap my head around the fact that I would be groomed to pleasure people. I scrunched up my nose at the idea of being with a woman. Brynn was the only girl I'd even consider experimenting with, and it wasn't a physical thing on my part. I loved her. She was my best friend. I hope she knew how I felt. I cleared the thoughts as I realized I might never see her again. Grief stabbed me over and over in the chest, and I rubbed my sternum, easing the pain.

"What else?" I needed Reid to keep talking and distract me.

"I'm six foot two, dark hair, brown eyes. I have a small scar through my left eyebrow."

"The girls probably find it sexy." I pursed my lips, regretting the words that had flown from my mouth. "I'm sorry. I didn't mean ..."

"It's okay. I don't get offended easily. Especially after growing up here."

I picked at my fingernail, wondering if any questions were off-limits. "How old were you when they forced you to ... ya know."

Reid cleared his throat. "Ten."

I gasped, his confession punching me in the stomach. I grabbed the bars in order not to stumble backward.

"Shit. I don't even know how to respond other than to tell you how sorry I am." I hung my head, my long hair cloaking my face.

"You learn to make the best of it after a while. I hear staying here to serve clients is better than being sold. I'm not sure if it's true, but maybe you'll end up with someone that's not brutal." His voice trailed off with his last word.

"Brutal?" Images of Barrett pinning me in place and choking me reared their ugly head.

"I've been whipped with a riding crop until my back bled, then the client and his wife raped me, using my blood as lube for anal."

I gasped. Not only because of how Reid had been hurt but the lack of emotion in his tone. Holden wasn't brutal. We played hard, both of us liked it a little rough, but there was never a doubt in my mind that he loved and cherished me.

I quickly found myself protective of my new friend. "Who is behind all of this?" I gritted my teeth.

"I don't know. Whoever it is keeps their identity a secret. None of the kids could identify him."

Kids! Oh, God. Reid had been ten when he started.

I pressed my fists against my eyes as my thoughts somersaulted. *Shit.* I'm pregnant. What if my baby is born into this life? I rushed to the toilet, my dinner rushing up my throat, then landing noisily in the commode.

"River, are you okay?" Reid called out.

I coughed and hurled again, my body trembling as I gripped the sides of the seat. After a minute or two, I stood on wobbly legs and made my way to the sink. I rinsed my face and mouth. "I'm here," I croaked. "This is a lot to stomach." I would have laughed at my pun, but there was nothing funny about the situation.

I returned to the front of my cell. "I'm fine." I wiped my lips with the back of my hand. "Who do I need to watch out for? If I'm here, then my first order of business is figuring out how to get the hell out. Until then, how do I survive?"

"I've been trying to figure it out since I was ten. I'm twenty-three ... I think." Reid paused. "Anyway, the guards are who you want to appease. There are several and they rotate shifts. They don't give a fuck what happens to us, but they do care about themselves. Make friends, fuck them when they want it, they will take care of you, I promise. Plus, it's better to willingly have sex with them than be raped."

"I have a boyfriend," I whispered, guilt tying my heart into a million knots. "I wouldn't ever cheat on him."

"River, you're not. You're trying to survive in a world where you're stripped of your dignity. Some of the clients are kind, but most aren't. You no longer own your body, but they can't steal your mind unless you let them. Also, learn to dissociate when possible. Find those places to visit mentally when it gets bad." Reid's pain weaved through his words.

I reached through the bars, wishing I could hug him.

"Barrett." I swallowed hard, then pushed myself to talk to Reid. "He assaulted me earlier, but ... he made me ... I ... I came." A cry escaped me, and I slapped my hand over my mouth. Why had I just shared that with a total stranger?

"I wish I could tell you not to feel guilty. It's part of how they break you down. A part of you will hate what they'll do. Your body will love it. Beg for it. They want you to come in order to control you. It's a mental game. Maybe it will help now that you know it's the plan. Don't beat yourself up over a normal physical reaction."

"Have you?"

Reid snorted. "So many times."

I imagined him frowning. Hopefully, at some point, I would see his face. For now, maybe I'd found a friend to help me maneuver through this sick world until I was free. Then, I'd take him with me. He deserved that.

"You mentioned others. Where are they?" I sat on the edge of my mattress and wrapped the blanket around me.

"I'm not sure why we're here together, but I'm not complaining. Most of the time we're separated. It's another way they control us. Loneliness is a powerful tool. If it consumes you, it will control every decision you make. Don't let it. You have to fight it."

The sound of a door creaking cut off Reid.

"Hurry. Pretend you're asleep," Reid ordered.

I laid down and remained still. For whatever reason, I already trusted Reid. Maybe it was his honesty and vulnerability.

A male voice whispered, then a cell opened. I quickly identified Reid talking, then kissing noises. I suspected it was one of the guards.

21

The sound of a zipper, grunts, sucking ... I covered my ears and tried to block out the sounds. It was as good a time as any to mentally build safe places in my mind. Hearing Reid and a guard fuck was the least of my worries.

Chapter Four

The scrape of my cell opening caught my attention. I'd learned years ago to sleep with one ear open. I had Dan to thank for that.

"Wake up."

I sat up slowly and rubbed my eyes. "Barrett?"

He stepped in and yanked me out of bed and to my feet. "I like to start my morning off right." He grinned at me as he brushed a knuckle over my nipple.

I knocked his hand away, my nostrils flaring as I willed myself not to gag. Reid's warning to give the guards what they wanted appeared front and center to my brain. But I couldn't. I would fight until I died.

"I do like them feisty." With a quick tug, Barrett ripped the dress in two, leaving me naked. "We can do this nicely ... or?"

I reared my head back, then spit in his face. "That's for yesterday, asshole."

A scream tore from my throat as he spun me around and slammed me against the wall. "Stupid bitch. You'll learn soon enough." His palm traveled down my side and to my ass. He gave my butt cheek a hard squeeze.

"Why don't you crawl off somewhere and die?" Pain shot through me as he shoved my head against the rough cinder block.

Barrett's laugh echoed through my cell. Before I realized it, he grabbed my arms and pinned them behind me. The click of handcuffs reached my ears. I tugged on them, but it was too late.

"Can't have you trying to run now, can we?" He snickered as he fished around in his pocket. I glanced down and realized the bastard had another pair, but with a longer chain between them. He dropped to his knees and slipped them around my ankles.

"Bend over the bed." His voice was low and gruff as he gave the order.

I refused to move. He could beat me, rape me, or whatever other despicable thing he wanted, but I would never give it to him willingly.

He snatched a fistful of my hair and dragged me across the floor. Barrett slammed my head into the mattress and forced my legs apart.

"As I said yesterday, you don't own that pussy anymore, little girl."

To my shock, Barrett knelt, then licked the inside of my thigh. Gritting my teeth, I pretended it was Holden. Holden's hands spreading my ass apart. Holden's tongue licking up and down my slit and toying with my clit.

Tears streamed down my face while my legs trembled beneath me as I was forced to endure Barrett's assault again.

"You taste even better than I imagined," he grunted.

"Fuck you," I retorted. "I fucking hate you."

Barrett quickly stood, then the sound of his zipper echoed in the space.

Panic curled in the pit of my stomach. "No. No. Please don't. I'll do whatever you want, but not this." Tears clouded my vision as I begged and pleaded.

"Too late. You had your chance to cooperate and now I'm going to take it," Barrett growled. He ran the tip of his cock against the back of my leg.

"Stop!" I choked on the snot in my throat. "I'm pregnant. Please don't hurt me."

Complete silence filled the cell, and I slammed my eyes shut, preparing myself for Barrett to continue.

"Goddammit," Barrett said, stepping away from me. "Stand up. I have to clear everything with the boss now."

He jerked me by my hair, and I straightened as he removed the cuffs from my ankles, then my wrists. "I'll bring you more clothes later."

With that, he stomped out of my cell and left me alone. I placed my hand against my stomach. What had I done? Had my outburst just saved or killed us?

"Reid?" I called out. Only silence responded.

I snatched the useless scraps of my dress off the floor and wrapped them around my breasts. I tore another strip and hurried over to the sink. Turning on the hot water, I allowed it to warm up as I tried to gain control of my tears. Once it was ready, I wet the smallest piece of the material and scrubbed the inside of my thighs, and everywhere else that piece of shit had licked and sucked on me. "Fucking bastard," I whispered and placed my palm against the wall for balance as I cleaned the Barrett scum residue off me the best I could.

Finally feeling a little better, I used the last piece of fabric and wrapped it around my waist. It wasn't much, but at least I was covered. Scrambling into bed, I curled up on the corner of the mattress and draped the blanket around me. My breath stuttered in my throat as I realized that eventually, Barrett would be back. I stared at the prison gate and waited.

The sun had disappeared, and the moonlight filtered in through my window. Barrett hadn't shown up again, not even with the clothes he'd promised. At least I was covered and warm for the time being.

Two sets of footsteps echoed through the hall, and I cringed at the sound of a cell door scraping against the cement floor. I remained quiet but hoped Reid had returned. If so, I suspected he would wait until he was certain no one else was around before he spoke.

Sweat broke out over my skin as fresh anger coursed through my body. I wasn't property. I was a human being, not a goddamn sex slave.

"River?" Reid's deep voice floated through the air, instantly calming me.

"Reid?" It was probably stupid that I asked if it was him when I knew it was, but I had to make sure.

"I'm back." He sighed softly. "I thought about you today ... wondered if they'd started your training." The familiar creak of his mattress told me he'd probably crawled into his bed.

"I thought about you today, too. I hope you weren't hurt." The strangeness of our conversation hadn't escaped me. We'd met twenty-four hours ago, yet he was already my lifeline. I cared about what happened to him.

"It was a good day as far as that goes. What about you?"

I sniffled. "Barrett came back, but he stopped right before he raped me."

"What? I don't understand. That's really weird. I mean, don't get me wrong, I'm glad he did, but I'm a bit confused."

If I closed my eyes, I could imagine what Reid looked like from the details he'd provided me. I imagined there was a crease in his fore-head at the moment.

"I told him I'm pregnant."

A low whistle escaped Reid. "No shit?"

"I found out the day I was kidnapped and brought here. My boyfriend doesn't know. Well, he might now. I dropped my purse on the club's loading dock right before I was tossed into the back of a moving truck like a fucking Raggedy Ann doll." I questioned if Reid even knew what a rag doll was or if he'd lived in this hell for so long, he'd not even heard of her.

"That's fucked up."

"Yeah. I have no idea what that means for me now. Barrett stopped and said he had to speak to the boss. Do you know what he meant by that?" I massaged the back of my neck, where a nagging pain was beginning to throb.

"No, I don't have any friends here, River. You're it. I've not been allowed to talk to any of the girls here, so if they got pregnant, I wouldn't know anything about it. I wish I could tell you something different."

I sank my teeth into my bottom lip, wishing he had some information as well.

"There's one thing I do know," he said.

"What's that?"

"If you're here, you have to be beautiful."

A flush traveled up my neck and cheeks. Holden's warm smile came to mind, and I melted. I clutched the blanket and brought it closer to my chest, longing for Holden's arms around me.

"So ... what do you look like?" Reid asked.

"Probably like we're related." I grinned even though he couldn't see me. "I have waist length brown hair, and my eyes are blue. They're the first thing people tend to notice about me. Otherwise, I'm just average looking. I ran cross-country track in high school. I'm tall for a girl, I guess."

"Tell me more, River. Please? It's so nice to have a normal conversation, even if we are in this hellhole."

I understood what he meant. I'd only been here for a few days, and the heaviness of the isolation had nearly smothered me.

"I grew up in Montana with my guardian, Dan." An uncontrollable shiver skated down my back as images of his lifeless, bloody body assaulted my brain. I swallowed, and my stomach growled. Apparently, I'd pissed Barrett off with the news because he hadn't fed me at all.

"He wasn't a good man." I rested my palm against my lower abdomen, wondering if the baby was okay.

"What happened to your mom?" Reid's tone was soft and gentle.

"I don't know. I mean, she had a drug problem, and she would leave ..." I wasn't ready to talk about my baby brother. Not yet. "She'd leave me alone in our apartment for days at a time. Eventually she never came home. Child Services said I'd tried to claw my way through the door to get out."

"You're a survivor already, River."

Instead of him feeling sorry for me, he'd immediately pointed out the fact I'd made it through those horrible days. I hadn't thought about it like that, but Reid was right.

"I've never had a choice." I waited for him to ask another question, but he didn't. "Do you have any memories before you were brought here?" I questioned if it would be easier if he said no, or if it had left an enormous hole inside of him he'd never been able to fill.

"Not really. I think when I was taken, my brain protected me and blocked out the life I'd had before. Hell, I don't even recall how old I was. I just remember waking up in a strange bed, scared shitless. A nice man fed me and told me that my parents had died in a car accident. I honestly have no idea if they did or not. All I know is that I never saw them again." A long pause filled the air. "I don't even remember what they looked like."

Saying nothing, I waited for Reid to continue while my heart looped around itself, rolling into a pile of painful knots. I hoped there was a special place in Hell for people who stole and harmed children. I scrubbed my face with my hands, searching for something to say.

My stomach growled loudly again.

"Is that your stomach?"

"Sorry. I haven't eaten today."

"That's not good for you and the baby. Hang on." The sound of plastic rustled before Reid spoke again. "I'm going to try to slide this to you."

Frowning, I jumped out of bed. "What is it?"

"It's not much. Since I'm extra nice to the guard, he brings me snacks that I hide beneath my mattress. It's a blueberry muffin."

"Reid, save it. You ... earned it." I cringed. What a shitty thing to say. No one should ever have to earn food by providing sex. A little whisper in my head reminded me I would most likely be doing the same soon.

"River, I'm not growing a baby inside of me. I'll get more, I swear." Reid's arm poked through the bottom of the cell. "I'm going to slide it and hope it gets close enough for you to grab."

Smashing my forehead against the iron bars, I reached my hand through and waited for the item to come my way. The plastic scraped the floor, then it landed in my palm. "I got it!" Never in a million years would I have thought I would be excited about a partially smashed muffin. Without hesitation, I ripped the bag open and took a bite. "Oh my God. Reid, it's so good." Tears burned my eyes. "Thank you."

"You're welcome. I wish I could hug you and tell you everything is going to be all right."

I leaned my head against the door. "I know. You, too." Savoring every bite, since I had no idea when I'd eat again, I nibbled slowly on my dinner. "Hey, Reid?"

"Yeah?"

"Do you think we can touch? I mean if we stretch our arms, do you think we might be able to?" I moved to the closest corner of my tiny room and waited for his reply.

"I've never tried because I'm usually alone in here."

I set my muffin down on the bed, then stuck my arm through the bars. "Here, let's try."

Reid's arm popped out, and he crooked it in my direction. It was hard as hell to see, but our fingertips grazed. "Is that you?" I asked, breathless from smashing my body against the unforgiving iron bars.

Reid's fingers found mine. "Hi, River," he whispered. "It's nice to officially meet you." He squeezed my hand in his.

I held on, refusing to let him go. "When I get out of here, you're coming with me. If neither of us have a biological family, then you'll be a part of mine." Reid deserved a real life. One filled with laughter, love, and friends. He'd already shown me compassion. I had no doubt in my mind that he could recover and build something wonderful out of his life. Crazily enough, if I could have hope for Reid, I had hope for my own recovery.

"I like the sound of that. What will your boyfriend think, though? I'm pretty good-looking. It might make him uncomfortable." I could hear the smile in his voice.

"He'll love you. He'll love you for being here for me. For checking up on me and sharing your muffin." I giggled. "You'll love Brynn. She's my best friend and stunningly beautiful. Men literally trip over themselves when she walks by. She's smart and funny. So are Chance and Jace. I have a feeling you'll fit right in. More than that, you'll be safe from anyone who wants to hurt you again." I trailed off, hoping he would get the impact of my statement. "We can even spend holidays together." Even though Reid had been forced to live behind these walls most of his life, I'd lived as a prisoner in my own home with Dan. Other than the few holiday celebrations at school, I hadn't ever had a real Thanksgiving or Christmas. Addison and her family drove to see relatives every year. Everything that I mentioned to Reid, I wanted, too. I would've had it with Holden, Brynn, Chance, and Jace if I hadn't gotten myself kidnapped.

A rush of overwhelming anger rose inside me, and I gritted my teeth. There was no use wasting my energy being angry at myself when it was impossible to reverse time. I had to stay focused on surviving and protecting my baby.

A sniffle came from Reid's direction, breaking through my thoughts as his thumb stroked the back of my hand. "You're the first family I've had since I was little," he whispered.

And I promptly burst into tears. "Well, now you've gone and done it. You're stuck with me. And from now on, I'll do everything in my power to protect my brother."

"And I'll do the same for you. Thanks, River. That's the kindest thing anyone has ever done for me."

I smiled. "Get used to it."

We remained silent as I marveled over the bond we'd formed so quickly. I just hoped like hell my words weren't lies. I knew deep down I would do anything to help him, which gave me something to hold onto—that, and seeing Holden again.

"We should try to get some sleep." Reid dropped his arm.

"Night, Reid." Without another word, I gathered my muffin and crawled back into my bed. At least I wasn't alone in this terrifying camp anymore.

Chapter Five

The following day, Reid's cell opened, and I tracked two sets of footsteps. There must have been another entrance at the end of the building because they never walked by me.

I stretched, then placed my feet on the ground. I'd slept with my shoes on in order to keep my toes warm. Plus, I wanted to be prepared for any opportunity to run.

Every muscle in my body ached from Barrett jerking me around the day before. I wondered if he would return with food and clothes, or if the portion I'd saved of the blueberry muffin last night would be my only meal for the foreseeable future.

Walking around the small room, I realized I should be exercising. Sit-ups, planks, pushups, running in place. Anything to keep my muscles active and in shape, because when the opportunity presented itself, I would have to haul ass across the field I'd seen when Barrett brought me here.

Since I literally had nothing else to do, I dropped to the floor and started the indoor routine I'd had in high school. Squats were first. The more I worked on building my strength, the better I felt. It'd been days since I'd had any real activity other than fighting Barrett. My body burned with satisfaction.

Sweat beaded on my forehead, and I swiped at it before it rolled into my eyes. After I'd run through my circuit training, I made my way to the sink and washed my face, pits, and lady bits the best I could. Satisfaction pumped through my veins. I would work out three times a day. More if I had real food to eat.

A loud creak set my nerves on edge; anxiety hummed beneath my skin.

I leaned against the back wall where I could see better. This time Barrett wouldn't catch me off-guard. I'd been half asleep yesterday morning. My fingers flexed as I imagined slamming my fist into his face and the bones in his nose crunching. I waited, holding my breath, but no one ever appeared. I frowned as the sound of Reid's cell opening reached my ears. My pulse kicked up a notch. What if something awful had happened to him?

I was frozen in place, listening for the retreating footsteps and the clank of the door closing before I rushed to the bars. "Reid?" I whispered.

"River," he responded immediately, relief obvious in his tone. "I've got a surprise for you."

"Wait, are you okay? I didn't think you were here during the day." My voice trembled, images of a bloody and broken body slamming into my mind. Reid had to be all right. He was the only friend I had here.

"I'm fine. Well, considering. My clients cancelled, so I'm here today."

A heavy sigh of relief slipped through my lips. "I thought you were hurt," I confessed.

"No, nothing like that." Confusion clung to his words.

"But?"

"Thank you. It's strange to hear that someone is concerned about me. It feels ... weird."

A lump formed in my throat, and I swallowed several times, pushing the tears down. "I do care about you."

A heavy silence hung in the air before he spoke again. "Reach over here, River. I want to give you something."

Even though we couldn't see each other, I frowned. I shoved my arm through the opening, squishing my body against the iron until I touched warm skin.

"Palm up."

I grinned. "Bossy much?" I teased.

"You have no idea." Reid chuckled as he wrapped my fingers around a small item.

I carefully navigated my hand back into my cell and stared at the package. "Oh, my God." I slapped my free hand over my mouth in a poor attempt to not break down sobbing.

"You don't like it?" Worry clung to Reid's words.

My heart ached for him—for us. "I love it. I wasn't sure I would ever see a bar of soap again." I leaned against the wall. "This is fucked up, Reid. I shouldn't be crying over a hygiene product." I sniffled and wiped the tears from my cheeks with my fingertips.

"I know. Unfortunately, you get used to it. It's funny how the simple things mean so much. Like you thinking about me, wondering if I was okay."

My chest tightened, a slow ache spreading through me. I walked to the sink and placed the treasured item near the faucet. "Do you have some?" I'd share if not. I could easily break it in half and give him a piece.

"Yeah. As I said, I have some benefits for taking care of a few of the guards."

"Is that how you got mine, Reid?" Guilt elbowed me in the side. I wasn't certain I really wanted to hear his answer.

"It's how I get everything I need." His voice trailed off.

"Can ... can I ask you something?" At this point, there probably weren't many topics that were forbidden, but I didn't want to over-step any boundaries either.

"Sure."

I sat on the edge of my bed and chewed on my thumbnail. "Do you prefer men or women?"

"Are you asking if I'm gay?" A hint of surprise weaved through his tone.

"Am I? I hadn't meant for it to come across that way."

"It's okay." Reid sighed. "I don't have a preference. I've been with both since I was ten. It's just sex." Reid sounded exhausted and blasé about the one thing that had hurt me my entire life ... until Holden. I wanted to reach through the stupid-ass bars and hug him. I wondered how much longer he would live. Would he eventually be too old for these fuckers to make money, and they would simply eliminate him? Letting him go wasn't an option. He probably knew way too much about his clients. My body trembled with the sudden knowledge of how disposable we were.

A sharp pang stabbed me in the chest as images of Holden flickered through my mind. I never knew it was possible to miss someone so badly. "This is probably a stupid question, but have you ever been in love?"

A pregnant pause hung in the air.

"I think so."

My face lit up with a smile. "Tell me about her." I scooted across the mattress and leaned my back against the wall, eager to discuss a lighter topic.

"I obviously met her here. Ya know, since I don't get out often." His chuckle filled the cell.

My brows shot up, and I snorted. "You're making jokes about it?" I wasn't judging him at all. I understood that humor and laughter were necessary components of sanity, but I was surprised Reid said it.

"Yeah, and maybe it will help you as well," Reid said.

I relaxed a little. "I don't want to piss you off." I chewed on a hangnail, suddenly missing my fingernail clippers.

"Don't worry about that. I'm just glad you're here. If you ask me something I'm not comfortable with, I'll let you know. But River, I had to get over being shy or offended a long time ago."

"What's her name? Do you still see her? What's she look like?" Grateful for a topic other than the horror we lived in, a smile pulled at the corner of my mouth.

"Nadia. She's a regular client, along with her husband."

I wasn't used to hearing about couples bringing someone into their bedroom, but maybe it wasn't much different than Holden's sex club. One thing that was definitely different, no one here was giving their consent. We were being forced against our will.

"Does she ever come alone?"

"No, it's always with him."

I wiggled in my seat. Reid wasn't offering details unless I asked him, so maybe this conversation was off-limits after all.

He must have sensed the awkwardness. "She's thin, blonde, in her late thirties. She and her husband own a successful technology company. I get the impression they have a ton of money. Well, all the clients do. I mean, we're either bought or hired and the prices aren't cheap. The younger the kid, the more money is charged. Like millions."

I slapped my hand over my mouth and darted to the toilet, dry heaving. Apparently, I didn't have enough food in my stomach to puke up anything of substance.

"Are you okay? Is it the baby?"

"I don't know. The idea of a kid ..." I retched again. "Fuck." I rose slowly and made my way to the sink and rinsed my mouth.

"River, do you have a toothbrush?"

"No." I wiped the droplets of cold water off my face with the back of my arm. "And do not under any circumstances fuck some-body to get me anything else." I crawled into my bed, willing my stomach to stop churning.

"As I mentioned before, the guards will rape you, or you can find some common ground and trade for items. It's just how it goes. You're pregnant, so sleeping with someone ... it was best that I slept with him instead of you."

I pursed my lips, tears burning my eyes. "I don't know how to process what you're telling me, or what we're living through."

"I wish you didn't have to," Reid said softly.

Unwilling to bring up Nadia again, I stretched out and pulled the blanket over me. I was suddenly depleted of any energy. Maybe I'd been foolish to exercise without any food.

As if reading my mind, Reid asked, "Did anyone show up with breakfast for you?"

"No. I guess I really pissed off Barrett."

"I'll see the guard tonight, so I'll get some snacks for us."

My eyelids grew heavy. "Make sure it's for you, too." I stifled a yawn.

"It is. You sound tired. Grab a nap while you can."

"Sounds good."

***

I wasn't sure how long I'd been asleep, but the sun had started to shift to this side of the building, which told me it was late afternoon.

"Reid?" I called out. No answer. How had I slept through him leaving? The cell opening always woke me. I sat up and swallowed, my mouth tasting bitter. I needed food and to brush my teeth. Hell, I'd probably kill someone with my breath. I snorted. At least I had a weapon against Barrett if he returned.

I walked over to the small sink and turned on the faucet. Cupping my hands, I drank the fresh water, then used my finger to brush my teeth the best I could. Cool droplets dripped from my chin down my bare stomach, trickling over my skin. Too fucking bad I didn't have a towel, but the back of my arm would work.

The creak of the door caught my attention, and I turned off the faucet. Footsteps approached, but these sounded different than

Barrett's or Reid's guard's. I sucked in a sharp breath and remained rooted in place.

A small black boot appeared in my line of sight first. My gaze traveled up the slender body, then landed on a familiar face. My mouth hit the floor, then I slammed it closed. No fucking way. I hadn't hallucinated after all. I was staring into the same pair of eyes owned by the person who had tried to drown me ... and failed.

"You look surprised to see me." She offered a malicious grin as she unlocked my cell.

"Are you back to kill me this time?" Anger, fear, and red-hot adrenaline pumped through my veins. Maybe this was my chance to get free.

Chapter Six

The door opened, and I strode forward with one purpose in mind ... To end that bitch. I stood toe-to-toe with her, reminding myself to stay alert and focused. I couldn't afford for my emotions to screw this up.

"*You're* why I'm here?" I held her gaze and refused to back down.

Becky released a cackle.

"Do you have any idea how unattractive that makes you look?" I folded my arms in front of me, then dropped them to my sides, ready for her next move.

Becky's smile faded away, and her hands landed on her hips. A flicker of light bounced off a badge secured to her belt.

"FBI?" I asked in a whisper. "You're here to help me?" Confusion muddled my mind as I tried to sort through the memories. Becky had held a knife to my throat, but warned me that Holden's family wasn't who I thought they were. She was definitely right about that. Next, she tried to fucking drown me. What I didn't understand was the fact she'd just let me walk out of my cell and flashed her credentials. "I don't get it. You tried to kill me. Were you really trying to hurt me, or was it all part of this?" I waved my hand around in exasperation.

Becky raised a blonde eyebrow. "You're full of questions, aren't you?"

"All I need to know is which is it, Becky? Do you want to kill me, or are you helping me?"

Becky grabbed my bicep and gave it a painful squeeze. "Actually, my name is Michelle. I do work for the FBI, but this is my side gig."

I attempted to jerk out of her grasp, but her fingers dug into my flesh. "What do you mean *your side gig?*"

"Let me show you." She dragged me a few steps and stopped abruptly. "Oh, here." She reached into her jacket pocket and produced an apple. "Eat something. I hear you're pregnant."

I took the food, searching for any marks or nicks where Michelle could have laced it with poison. I couldn't trust her. After all, she was an absolute witch.

"Oh, for God's sake!" Michelle snatched the fruit away from me, took a big bite, then handed it back. "It's fine. No one tampered with it. We'd all lose our jobs if we screwed with you right now, and I make way too much money to mess it up."

My mouth watered as the juice streamed down the shiny red skin. *Dammit.* I was fucking starving. I snatched the piece of fruit away from her and chomped down on it, the crunch echoing through the hall.

"Let me get this straight. You're FBI, but work for a sex trafficking ring, too?" I asked while chewing loudly, completely ignoring any manners I'd typically have. Becky ... Michelle didn't deserve my politeness.

"Something like that." She led me to the exit. The harsh sunlight temporarily blinded me, and I squinted in order to shield my eyes. "You were easy prey. The night I warned you away, I really was trying to help you, but you didn't listen, so you became fair game."

"That was a fucked-up way of trying to help me. Are you sure you didn't just want Holden for yourself? Not that it would have happened, but you could have kept dreaming." I gave her a little smirk, trying my best to ruffle her feathers.

She raised her hand to slap me, then caught herself. "I would have had him until you came along." Anger danced across her features, then she masked her emotions. "When the furniture arrived at the club, I had one of the men lock the door to the stairwell when you left to use the bathroom, which forced you to use the elevator. Even though you were excited about the furniture, something was bothering you. I figured it was only a matter of time before my men were able to corner you or find you alone."

My furious gaze narrowed at her. "How did you know where I was, and who I was with?"

"You really are dense, aren't you?" She rolled her eyes. "I was communicating with the men the entire time, and they were giving me a play-by-play. When you arrived at the loading dock alone ... It was too damn easy."

Fucking bitch. If I could have reached her gun, I would've put a bullet in her head and never felt bad about it. "I owe you an apology." I wiped the sweet juice off my chin.

Michelle stopped and glared at me. "For what?"

I released a dramatic sigh. "Because I underestimated how big of a bitch you really are." Tossing her a grin, I ducked the slap headed toward me. Once she was off-balance, I punched her as hard as I could in the nose.

Michelle stumbled backward, and I took advantage of the seconds I'd bought myself. I scanned the area, seeking a safe place to hide, but I was too disoriented. Deciding that standing here any longer wouldn't help me any, I booked ass across the open field.

"Goddammit," Michelle yelled from behind me.

A loud pop sounded, then something whizzed by my head.

"Stop, or I will fucking drop you," Michelle ordered.

No way would I listen to her. I glanced over my shoulder and realized Michelle had pulled her gun and tried to shoot me. *Pop. Pop. Pop.*

I ducked and ran in a zigzag. Her accuracy sucked, but I would have a better chance of getting hit if I ran in a straight line.

A loud siren filled the air, and I peered around nervously. Someone had sounded an alarm, alerting everyone that I was trying to escape. But from what I could tell, I wasn't even close to the edge of the compound. Not to mention, there was a tall, chain-link fence that ran for as far as I could see.

Three men in grey pants with matching shirts ran toward me, carrying weapons.

"On the ground! Now!" one of them yelled.

Fuck. It was either toss the white flag or die. Honestly, I wasn't sure I could live like Reid. If I had my baby here, he or she would grow up in slavery. Maybe death was the better choice. Holden's beautiful face flashed in front of me, and my heart ached. I had to live for him. He had to know what Michelle was capable of. I couldn't give up yet.

Defeated and unwilling to dance with death, I slowed and dropped to my knees. The bright green grass tickled my bare legs.

"Thanks, boys," Michelle said, jogging up to me. She whipped out a pair of cuffs and slapped them on my wrists. "River is on her way to shower and get some clean clothes. You can gawk at her later."

The three men stared at my makeshift top and skirt, their tongues practically hanging out of their mouths.

Michelle jerked me to my feet and jabbed the barrel of her gun into my back. With a hard shove, I stumbled forward.

"Nice try." She smirked as she directed me to a warehouse next to the large white home I'd spotted yesterday. "It's time to get you cleaned up and fed. Then I'll give you some clothes. You'll get the grand tour of the facility after that."

"Sorry if I can't contain my excitement," I grumbled.

"You really are a fucking smartass, aren't you?" Michelle stopped as we reached the door of the building.

"Meh, you just bring it out in me." I winked at her. I'm not sure what I was trying to accomplish other than pissing her off. If I could ruffle her feathers, then I would have a better chance of catching her off-guard and escaping. At least my lame attempt to flee a few minutes ago had helped me understand what I was up against—men with guns and a tall-ass fence around the perimeter.

"We'll see about that." Michelle led the way, and we entered the building.

The heavy scent of sex overwhelmed my senses. It might have looked like an ordinary building from the outside, but it sure as hell wasn't on the inside.

"What the fuck?" My attention swept the rows of glassed-in rooms with small holes for ventilation.

"Take your time and look around, River. Afterward, we'll see if you have anything to say." Michelle remained next to me as horror blossomed to life in my chest. The glass room closest to me contained a bed and chair. A grown, naked, blonde-haired man leaned against the wall as he stroked a young lady's head. She was on her knees, sucking his dick.

"No! I told you no teeth, you little bitch." He raised his hand and slapped the girl, knocking her backward.

She curled into herself as he beat her in front of us. Once his anger subsided, he jerked her off the floor by her brown hair and slammed her face into the glass wall. Two tired, empty eyes stared at me.

"Jesus. She looks like she's barely over puberty," I hissed at Michelle.

The young girl's cries rang out as the guy began to fuck her from behind. I turned away before I hurled apple chunks all over Michelle.

"I don't need to see anymore. I get your point." I wondered if Reid had trained anyone or if he'd been the trainee—beaten and raped like the girl. If he was here, I wouldn't even know. I had no clue what he looked like other than dark hair and muscular. That could be a million different guys.

"Walk." Michelle poked me in the arm with her weapon.

The next glass room held a young woman who appeared to be in her early thirties. Two well-developed girls that appeared to be in their late teens were naked and wore collars. The woman pulled on the long chain, forcing them toward her.

She raised a whip and lowered it on one of the girl's backs, ripping her flesh. Blood bloomed from her wound, and she whimpered as she lifted her arms to defend herself.

"Now. Let's try this again." The woman sat in a chair and spread her legs. "Eat me like your life depends on it. Because it does."

I slammed my eyes closed. This was training camp. *This* was where I would end up. My pulse galloped into a full-on frenzy. Undiluted fear and dark rage snarled in my stomach as the realization seeped deep into my soul. I was trapped, and from the looks of it, there was no way out.

The woman in the glass room looked at me. A spark of lust gleamed in her wicked smile as she scanned me up and down. My pulse pounded so hard in my ears, I felt it in my veins. I swore Michelle could hear its rapid rhythm. I sucked in a deep breath, only smelling blood and sex. Bile swam up my throat, and I gulped, forcing my apple to stay down.

"You get to look forward to all of this. Then you'll either be sold to a wealthy son of a bitch who collects girls and discards them as soon as he's bored, or ..." Michelle's intense gaze locked on mine. "You'll be serving clients just like these are. On occasion, you might be treated well, but not often."

Michelle urged me forward. Room after room was filled with adult men and women abusing people.

"Why me?" My voice cracked with anxiety and fear. "I'm older than everyone here."

"There are plenty of people your age. Don't worry. We won't let you go." Michelle snickered as if she'd told the best joke of the year. "The other part of why you're here ... you'll find out soon enough."

With Michelle now in the picture, I leaned toward Tim and Logan being behind my kidnapping. Hell, Logan's guy holding her at gunpoint could have all been staged. The image of the photo with

Logan and Tim I'd found on Holden's desk flickered to life in my mind, linking possible dots and connections. *Sick fucks.*

"What's your part in all of this?" I had to know.

We passed the last of the rooms, and I mentally released a sigh. I couldn't witness the horror anymore.

Michelle opened a door, and we entered a bathroom. A shower large enough for three people stood in the corner, and a clawfoot bathtub rested beneath a window. The clean, black granite counter offered two sinks, making me think of the one Holden and I had picked out for the penthouse. Pain and longing speared me in the heart, gutting me even more. I should be with Holden instead of in Hell.

"Go on. There's bodywash, shampoo, and conditioner available on the shelf." She tilted her head in that direction. "When you finish, you need to get dressed. Someone will come in to dry and style your hair, take care of your nails, and apply your makeup."

My forehead creased in confusion. "Why?"

"Just fucking do as you're told." Michelle waved her gun around, and I stepped out of my shoes, then into the tan, tiled shower, and turned the handle.

I quickly removed the rags I was wearing, then flicked my fingers beneath the spray to test the temperature. It was scalding hot. I moved the lever to the right a little and allowed it to cool. A groan nearly escaped me as the water trailed down my body. Although I'd managed to stay somewhat washed up in the cell, this was an indulgence I wasn't sure I would ever experience again.

I grabbed the strawberry shampoo and lathered my hair, breathing in the fruity scent and dreaming for a moment that I wasn't living in captivity. Michelle remained quiet and allowed me this luxury. Suddenly overwhelmed with grief, I choked on my tears. "Holden," I whispered behind the noise of the powerful stream. "I love you." I found a second of peace as his name crossed my lips.

Then cruel reality slapped me. I scrubbed the dirt and shame from my skin, hatred for myself consuming me. My hands fisted, and I smacked the wall.

"What was that? Do I need to come in there?" Michelle asked.

"No," I responded through clenched teeth. *Be smart about this River.* "I dropped the soap."

Michelle grunted her response, but she didn't poke her head in and check on me. I lifted my face and rinsed my tears. Searching for anything at my disposal to knock Michelle out with, I realized it was a hard no. I would have to think of something else.

"Time's up."

For just a few more heartbeats, I pretended that I didn't hear her.

"Get out, or I'm coming in after you. Your choice." Michelle's tone was sharp and commanding.

Rolling my eyes since she couldn't see me, I turned the handle off. I squeezed as much water from my hair as possible, then poked my head out. "Is there a towel somewhere?"

Michelle collected a white one from the countertop and handed it to me.

I stepped back in order to have a few more seconds of privacy and dried off. After finishing, I wrapped it around my body and stepped out onto the cold tile floor.

Without a word, Michelle opened a cabinet and removed a plastic bag. "Get dressed."

I took the package from her and looked inside. A pair of black pants, panties, and a light blue top were visible. I removed the underwear and tossed the rest down. Stepping into them, I hurriedly tugged them up my legs and over my hips. Next, I put on the pants. They were a little big, but I wasn't complaining. This was the most clothing I'd worn since arriving at Satan's fortress. I slipped the top on, pulled it down, then dropped the white towel into a heap on the floor. I removed my long hair from the collar of the shirt and straightened my shoulders.

"You'll find socks in the bag along with deodorant, a brush, a toothbrush, and toothpaste." Michelle checked her watch. "Get a move on. We're going to be late."

I located the additional items and worked through my tangles. The fresh mint that lingered in my mouth after I'd brushed my teeth tasted heavenly. Maybe I would be able to keep everything when I returned to my cell. *If you're returned.* Oh, God. What if I wasn't taken back. *Reid.* Shit. I had to return. We were all that each other had. I needed his friendship to help me through this. My body trembled, and I pretended that I was cold.

Michelle waved me forward and opened the bathroom door. "Turn right. We're going to the last room on the left."

My chest tightened as we drew closer. Michelle pointed me in the right direction, and I walked into a full salon. Girls were having their hair done, getting manicures, pedicures, and makeup.

"So, you get everyone looking their best, then what?" I glared at Michelle, waiting for the answer I was terrified to hear.

"Then they meet their trainers."

My throat tightened, threatening to cut off my air. I curled my fingers into a fist behind my back, determined not to let her know she was getting to me.

Michelle shoved me toward the only vacant seat in the room. I stumbled for a moment but managed to catch myself before face-planting.

"Sit," she commanded me like I was nothing more than a misbehaving child. "You, however, will be meeting with someone else," she said, squeezing my shoulder and staring at me in the vanity mirror.

I met and held her gaze. "Who?"

She flashed me a wicked smile. "You'll find out soon enough." Then she turned and walked out, whistling as if she didn't have a care in the world.

Chapter Seven

Once my hair was trimmed and highlighted, I received a French manicure, and my makeup was applied. Afterward, I was taken to a dressing room. It sickened me that I was forced to select a dress to be "presented" in. Struggling to find something ugly and unattractive, I realized that wasn't an option. The clothes offered were stunning. I was pretty sure at least half of them were hanging in Brynn's closet right now.

Brynn. I missed her so much. Her sass, her laugh, her hugs. Would I ever have the opportunity to see her again?

Finally, I selected a deep blue fitted dress that flared at the skirt. I'd hoped to find something not form-fitting. Michelle handed me a pair of black Louboutin's, and I slipped them on, towering over her by a few inches. I contemplated kicking her in the stomach, ditching the high-heeled weapons, then running for my life. It was too risky, though. I had to bide my time carefully.

My shoes smacked against the walkway to the white home with black trim as I eyed the area around me. The grass had recently been mowed, the scent tickling my nose. A large, puffy, white cloud floated across the sun and blotted it out momentarily. I spotted a row of smaller homes on the other side of the property and wondered if other people were trapped beneath them. A shiver shot down my spine at the reminder of my days living in darkness—naked and alone.

Michelle led me to the back as she held my arm firmly, digging her nails into my flesh. Fury boiled to life inside me and I imagined grabbing her weapon and beating the shit out of her with it. I'd decided a bullet to the head would be too good for her. *Soon. Soon that bitch would get what she deserved.*

We reached a door, then stepped into a dark hallway. I craned my neck and peered through the darkness, attempting to see what was in front of me. Michelle flipped a switch, and the bulb in the ceiling illuminated our path with a soft light.

My breath hitched as we passed an elevator. The house appeared to be only two stories, but with every turn, I saw a set of stairs leading down. Nausea swirled in the pit of my stomach. I suspected the elevator went underground, where more human beings were held. Black dots floated in front of me, and I placed my palm against the wall, trying to steady myself.

"Don't pass out on me now." Michelle ushered me into a living area. "You're about to eat. I'm sure it will help you feel a bit better."

I wasn't sure I wanted anything—*my baby*. I fought the urge to place my hand on my belly and reminded myself I needed my strength. If I ate slowly, I might keep some food down. I had to try.

"This is it. Have a seat and eat up." She motioned me forward.

"Holy crap," I whispered, stepping into the room.

Michelle nodded to a table filled with fruit, meats, crackers, and cheese. My stomach growled, unwilling to be ignored any longer.

"Good luck." Michelle gave me an exaggerated wink, then stepped back. She smirked at me before she slammed the door closed. I spun around and turned the handle. The bitch had just locked me in. Although I was thrilled to get rid of her for a while, my fears told me I was about to meet someone much worse than Michelle.

Searching the place, I spotted a crimson red, Victorian couch with two matching chairs. A fire roared in the fireplace, warming the space. Dark bookshelves lined the walls, and a desk was nestled in the corner. If I hadn't known that whoever this belonged to also operated a fucked-up sex ring, I might have enjoyed this area as well as their taste.

My belly rumbled again. I reluctantly headed over to the snacks and spotted the fresh fruit. If I had pockets, I would sneak some back to the cell for Reid, but no such luck. Selecting a cracker resembling a Ritz, I popped it into my mouth. The crisp, buttery disc melted on my tongue, and I released a groan. Definitely better than any Ritz I'd ever had. I selected another one and loaded it with meat and cheese. I nibbled slowly, searching for something to drink.

Spotting the plates and glasses, I poured some water from the crystal pitcher. Someone certainly liked to entertain. I located a chair near the table of food and sat on the edge of it, alert. Within minutes, I'd polished off a few more snacks, then grabbed an orange. I desperately wanted to take some food back with me ... *if I went back.* A part of me had just lost my appetite. The other reminded me to eat as much as I possibly could and take care of the little one I was growing inside me.

I peeled the orange, the juice sticking beneath my freshly manicured fingernails. My mind shifted to Holden, and I wondered if he was close to finding me. Shutting my eyes for a moment, I allowed myself to feel his arms around my waist, his gentle kiss in my hair, his full lips against mine. A lump clogged my throat, and I quickly popped a piece of the sweet fruit into my mouth. I couldn't afford to fall apart at the moment. Not when I was minutes away from possibly learning who was behind my kidnapping and the sick shit show I'd witnessed. I wasn't certain that's why I was here, but in my mind, there were only two reasons. Either I was about to meet the person responsible for snatching me or the person who wanted to buy me.

Finally realizing there might be a weapon to use, I scanned the area. Nothing. No knives, no forks, no fire poker, no pens or pencils. I jumped out of my seat and hurried to the desk, hoping to locate a letter opener or pair of scissors. One shot to the carotid artery in the neck would kill anyone. I searched the tidy area, then tugged on a drawer. Empty. I tried the next and the next. Every fucking one of them.

Since my fingers were sticky with the juice from the orange, I made my way back to the table and dipped a napkin into my water, cleaning my hands. Tired after getting my belly full, I sank into the chair again and patted my stomach. At least I'd eaten, which meant I'd taken care of my baby. For a fleeting second, I allowed myself to consider what I might look like in a few months. Would I have a bump by then? More importantly, would I still be here or with Holden? One thing I was certain of: I couldn't deliver my son or daughter in this shithole. There had to be a way to get out of here.

Shifting in my seat, I realized I could see anyone walking into the room. I rubbed my arms, warding off an imaginary chill and wishing for the nightmare to end.

The creak of the wood floors pulled my attention to the left. I gaped at the person who had entered, seemingly from behind the wall. Had they been watching me the entire time? *Of course, they were!*

I shook violently as my brain scrambled to piece this together, including how I'd gotten here and why I'd been singled out. More importantly, who was running it all? Who was the monster behind the veil?

"Hello, River."

Chapter Eight

U nable to form words, I stared at the beautiful woman in front of me. Dark hair, brown eyes, cream-colored slacks, and a soft green blouse. She was stunning, but I already knew it the first time I met her.

"Hello, Catherine," I ground out between clenched teeth. My fists curled as white-hot fury swirled beneath my skin like a demon possessing me.

She tilted her head to the side and studied my horrified expression, then strolled over to me as though she didn't have a care in the world. "I get that a lot." She offered me a kind smile.

"What do you mean?" I refused to take my attention off of her.

"Come, sit down." She patted the back of the couch. "Let's chat."

Even though she was attempting to be nice, I knew better. Still, I did as I was told. A chill skated up my spine, and I chose the seat nearest the fire. My heart jackhammered against my chest while I waited for her to continue.

She sat across from me and crossed her legs. "My name is Kassandra."

Fuck. Holden's mom had multiple personalities!

My palms grew sweaty, but I still had the presence of mind not to wipe them on the dress or expensive furniture.

"Kassandra," I repeated.

"Yes. I'm Catherine's twin sister."

I didn't fucking believe her. She looked and moved exactly like Catherine. She tucked a lock of hair behind her ear, and I paid attention to the subtle differences. The way she walked, how her upper lip curled at the right side before she smiled, and the beauty mark on her left cheek next to the corner of her eye. Shit. She wasn't lying. I struggled to breathe, the truth crushing my chest.

"It's okay, darling. I realize all of this must be a bit of a shock to your system, a fact I understand very well. You can't imagine my reaction when I was informed that you're pregnant. Not to mention that my nephew is the father. Holden hasn't seen me since he was a toddler. I'm not even sure he remembers me. Regardless, it makes us practically family."

I squirmed in my seat, trying to contain my racing pulse. Kassandra was like a lion waiting to devour its prey—me.

I nodded stupidly. "I took a pregnancy test the day I was kidnapped and brought here," I finally said, finding my words again. A spark of courage ignited inside me, and I straightened my back and shoulders. "Are ... are you the person behind the sex ring?" Apparently, I'd found a pair of balls.

"I am. Along with someone else." Kassandra peeked at her watch. "I'm sure you have so many questions, but I would like to wait for a few minutes."

I frowned, then realized whoever the other person was would most likely join us.

"Would you like anything else to eat?" Kassandra's tone was overly sweet, the spider luring in the fly to her sticky, inescapable web.

"No." I cleared my throat and nervously glanced around the

room. "Thank you for the food earlier." I could match that sweet side of her with my own, but given a chance, I wouldn't hesitate to take her out either. Thoughts of countless people being hurt and raped assaulted my mind. Anger roared to life, and I quickly stuffed it down. *Tread carefully.*

"I'm terribly sorry I'm late." I twisted around in my seat, identifying the new voice.

"Not a problem. River and I were just getting to know each other a little better." Kassandra stood and kissed the older woman on the cheek.

"Ah, yes, River. You're as stunning as Michelle claimed." The woman gave me a smile that matched Kassandra's as she strolled over to me. She searched my face as she tilted my chin up and turned my head to the left, then right.

I blanched. "Michelle told you about me?" My pitch rose with my question.

"She did. We also had an investor in 4 Play scout for us, but then she was exposed and has gone into hiding. When girls are drunk, they're easy to take. As for Michelle, she's an exceptional employee, but I digress. My name is Opal. I'm Kassandra and Catherine's mother."

I stared at the two women, pleading with my stomach to keep the food down. If not for me, for the baby. A sex ring run by women—not men. Twisted, depraved women. These two were what mother-fucking nightmares were made of. Goddammit, Holden needed to know. I had to make it out of here so he could learn the truth.

Opal settled next to Kassandra and tucked a strand of her salt and pepper hair behind her ear. Diamonds sparkled from every manicured finger. She slid her hands down her white blouse and navy slacks.

I gulped, unsure where this conversation was going. Once I was returned to my cell, I would allow myself to process everything, but not yet. I couldn't afford to lose my shit now. I'd been so wrong. I wasn't here because of Dan, Logan, or even Tim. I was here because of Michelle, along with Holden's aunt and grandmother. *Fuck. Fuck. Fuck.*

"How long have you and Holden been together? From what Michelle said, you two were serious," Opal said.

For a second, I looked at her blankly. *Were? More like are, you crazy bitch.* Opal was insane and intelligent, which made her incredibly dangerous.

"Five months."

Opal glanced at Kassandra. "I see." She offered me a tight smile that didn't reach her cold, emotionless eyes.

"Does Catherine know?" I blurted. "That her sister and mother sell children?" I slammed my mouth closed, chiding myself for not being careful with what I said.

Kassandra laughed. A beautiful melodic sound that made me want to punch her in the throat. She was a twisted, sick fuck and didn't deserve to have a nice laugh.

"Catherine and I are . . . estranged. We haven't spoken in nineteen years."

"Opal, what about you?" I figured if I'd been blunt already, there was no harm in asking more questions.

"Catherine thinks I'm dead." She ran her palm over her thigh, her sharp gaze assessing me.

"That makes sense why Holden never mentioned either of you." My attention bounced between them as I attempted to assess their intentions.

"Barrett says you're pregnant. I'm assuming it's Holden's?" Kassandra said nonchalantly.

"Of course it is." I placed my hand protectively over my lower abdomen.

"Have you had an appointment with a medical professional to confirm?" Opal asked.

"No. As I told Kassandra, I took the test only minutes before a needle was jabbed into my skin, a bag was pulled over my head, and I was thrown into the back of a delivery truck. It made it a smidge difficult to schedule an appointment." Apparently, my hormones were playing with me. Normally, I knew when to shut my mouth, but this time I didn't seem to have control over what spilled out.

"Well, we're about to do just that. I've called a doctor to examine you and verify that you're, in fact, pregnant," Opal said.

Instincts did their best to protect me, sending my heart hiccupping before catapulting into an all-out sprint.

"For your sake, let's hope you are. I hate liars. Liars are severely punished here." Kassandra flashed a pearly white smile at me.

I nodded, terror pulsing through my veins at what that might mean.

"Why?" I asked softly. "Why would two women run a sex trafficking ring?" I was struggling for something to make sense.

Opal and Kassandra looked at each other before they broke into laughter. "Money, darling. I know you're young and in love, but one thing that's been available through the years is sex. Men and women will pay handsomely to feed their illegal fetishes. Luring young girls in is incredibly easy. Girls don't trust men. They're warned against them. Stranger danger." Kassandra added air quotes to her last words. "But society doesn't warn against women, so girls blindly talk to us, befriend us."

My nostrils flared, and I wondered if I could aim the rising puke in my gut to land on Kassandra. "Michelle. That's her job, isn't it?" I fidgeted in my seat, squelching the overwhelming desire to run for my life.

Kassandra's expression gleamed with dark thoughts and deadly secrets. She was lethal, sneaky, and made Tim and Logan appear angelic.

"She's one of our best," Opal confided. "After all, she brought us you."

I shot off my chair, unable to pretend any longer. "Fuck you. You both disgust me. Innocent boys and girls are being beaten and raped, and you're proud of your business? How do you sleep at night?" My chest heaved with anger and fear.

"Like a baby," Kassandra crooned.

"I like this one," Opal said to Kassandra. "I have the perfect man in mind for her. He'll pay millions for a feisty fighter."

Kassandra's dark eyebrow rose. "Hmm ... it would probably be best to sell her to someone overseas. I don't trust that Holden will ever stop searching for her." Kassandra's attention returned to me. "The answer to your question, River: I sleep very well, thank you. With millions and millions of dollars at my disposal, I can afford the best beds and security." A cold, calculating expression twisted Kassandra's features.

"Well said, daughter." Opal chuckled. "Now, let's find out if you're actually pregnant with my great-grandchild, shall we?"

Fisting my hands at my sides, I stared at them, not giving a response. They weren't asking me anyway.

"You will comply, or I'll have a few of my men drag you to the doctor and strap you down. Either way is fine with me." Opal rose from her seat, an air of hostility swirling around us.

My mind whirled with options, but I was at an impasse.

"This way," Opal ordered, sensing my cooperation.

I obediently fell in behind Opal, and Kassandra after me. We walked to the back wall, and Opal paused in front of a keypad near the door. She blocked my view, then punched in a code. A soft click reached my ears, then Opal pulled on the handle and led us down a hallway. Once we reached the end, she turned right and into a room filled with light.

A medical office. I glanced around, eyeing the table with stirrups, cabinets, and several medical machines.

"Hello, River. I'll be with you in a moment." A blonde in her late forties sat at a desk, scribbling notes. When she was finished, she rose from the chair and offered me a cheery smile. "I'm Doctor Austin." She held her hand out to me and my gaze cut to Kassandra and Opal.

I didn't want to touch this woman. She worked for monsters.

Kassandra cleared her throat and tilted her head toward the doctor, indicating that I needed to mind my manners. I shook the doctor's hand, her slender fingers cold to the touch.

"Have a seat." She waved to a chair with a small table that rested on the arm while she snapped on a pair of white latex gloves. "This won't take long. I'm just going to do a bit of blood work."

I eased into the seat and propped my arm up, my attention landing on a tray of tubes. The doctor was definitely prepared for me.

She touched the inside of my arm. "You have nice veins," the doctor assured me as she tied a red-colored rubber band around my bicep.

I stared at the floor as she inserted the needle and withdrew a few tubes worth of blood. When she was done, she folded a gauze pad, placed it over the pinprick, then applied the medical tape.

"That's it. I'll run the pregnancy test first. If it's positive, I'll test for any deficiencies or concerns. We'll give you a full workup."

I couldn't stop my frown. "You're going to be my doctor until I have the baby?"

"We'll discuss a plan once we have a firm answer. Don't worry about anything. After all, we're practically family," Opal explained. "For now, we'll wait a few hours."

"Until then?" I stood, my legs wobbling with fear.

"Let's eat. I'm famished." Opal slipped her arm around my shoulders as if I were her best friend.

I fell into step next to her while Kassandra followed. As soon as I thought I understood these women, they changed their approach. I didn't have a fucking clue why I was with them, though. If the test confirmed the pregnancy, would they keep me locked in the cell until delivery? If so, I wondered if the baby and I would be trapped in this hell for the rest of our lives.

Bile crept up my throat, and I choked it down. For now, I had to play the game and figure a way out of this mess. And when I was face-to-face with Holden again, safe in his arms, I would beg his forgiveness for ever ditching Zayne when all they both wanted to do was protect me ... from situations like this.

***

When we returned to the same room as earlier, I noticed that the table had been cleaned, the snacks replaced with three covered plates.

After a hot meal of meatloaf, mashed potatoes and gravy, green beans, and fresh rolls, I was stuffed. Opal and Kassandra had even allowed me to have a Dr. Pepper. Since I was pregnant, they didn't want the baby to have too much caffeine. At this point, I didn't mind. I was mentally and physically exhausted.

"Thank you for the food." I wiped my mouth with the cloth napkin and wadded it into my lap, secretly hating myself for thanking them for anything.

"You're welcome. It's important that you eat healthy right now." Opal's phone vibrated and she retrieved the cell from her lap. She quickly checked the message, then set it down again.

I stifled a yawn as the food settled in my stomach.

"Do you want a boy or girl?" Kassandra asked.

"I don't care. As long as the little one is healthy and happy. That's all that matters." I clenched my teeth in an attempt to not yawn again.

"Nothing like a good, hot meal to make you sleepy." Opal reached out and patted my hand.

I nodded, suddenly feeling lethargic and dizzy. My gaze narrowed as I stared at my empty plate of food I'd gobbled up. Unsure of when I would eat again, I hadn't given it a second thought.

The room spun, and I clutched the edge of the table. My ears rang as I attempted to bring my vision into focus. I tried to lift my arm, but it refused to cooperate.

"You drugged me." My tongue felt dry and thick in my mouth. I should have been in a full-blown fucking panic, but my brain was too foggy to fully register the situation.

Kassandra's mouth was moving, but I wasn't able to make out what she was saying. My chair jerked back, then someone scooped me into their arms. My head lolled backward as I tried to make sense of what was happening, but the harder I tried, the worse I felt. I blinked rapidly, trying to decipher what I was looking at—who.

"Holden, help me," I whispered as my world faded to black.

Chapter Nine

Holden wrapped his arms around me as I snuggled my back against his chest. This man was my entire world. He'd opened his heart to me, his life, and invited me in. The more his secrets were revealed, the more I realized we were both survivors. He'd lost his sister, Hannah. I'd lost my brother, Alan.

"I love you so much, River." Holden smoothed my dark hair, then placed a kiss on my temple.

"I love you more, baby." I wiggled my ass against him, his erection pushing against my butt. I rolled over on my back and peered into his deep brown eyes. "Before I met you, I never knew life could be so good." I raised up and kissed him.

"It's crazy how you walked into my life, and everything made sense again. It was dark and full of pain before you ... slept in my recycling bin." He offered me a beautiful smile.

I slapped my hand over my face. "Yeah, I'm pretty sure I didn't choose a trash container and think that it would lead me to love."

Our laughter filled the air.

"Never in my wildest dreams did I think I would find my future wife sleeping outside, either."

My brows shot up while I sifted through his words, ensuring I was hearing him right. My tongue darted across my lower lip. "What?"

Holden brought my knuckles to his lips and kissed them softly. "I love you, River. My world is so much better with you in it. Stay with me forever."

I searched his passionate gaze, looking for a hint that he was joking. There was none. Nothing but love and adoration.

"I'm not proposing, but I plan to at some point. When I do, I want to do it right. I want it to be something we cherish for the rest of our lives."

"Me, too."

Holden turned onto his back and opened the drawer in his night-stand. He rolled back to his side, facing me, and propped up on his arm, then flipped open a velvet ring box. "Until we're engaged, I'd be honored if you wore this ring. Each time you look at it, know that you're mine and I'm yours."

Holden slid the half-carat diamond ring on my finger. Tears welled in my eyes as I traced my finger around the circle of sapphires that surrounded the diamond.

"Do you like it?"

"I love it." I giggled and looked at the ring. "For the record, I wouldn't care if you gave me a ring from a gumball machine or a Ring Pop. As long as it had the same meaning ... all I want is you, Holden." I slid my arms around his neck.

He pinned me down on the bed and dotted my face with kisses, his hand sliding between my breasts. I laughed as Holden trailed his fingertips down my stomach. He glanced up at me as he pressed his soft lips against my lower abdomen. "I'm ready to start the rest of my life with you ... and our baby."

I stroked his hair and swallowed hard. "I'm scared."

"You're going to be an amazing mother, River. Don't ever question that."

Holden flickered in and out like a lousy hologram of Princess Leia in Star Wars.

"Holden? What's happening?"

I sat up in our bed, the sheet falling to my waist. His bedroom began to dissolve, crumbling away from me. "Holden!" I screamed.

"I'm coming for you, River. Hang on," he whispered before he disappeared.

***

I attempted to peel my eyelids open. My head pounded, and my throat was ungodly dry.

"There she is," Dr. Austin said with a gentle smile.

I stared at her, trying to figure out what the hell had happened. "I ... where am I?"

Dizziness swept over me as I attempted to look around. After a minute, I realized I was in Dr. Austin's medical room.

"Here's an ice chip." Dr. Austin held one between her gloved hands, then placed it on my lips.

I allowed it to melt and trickle over my tongue and down my throat.

"You're still groggy, so I'll repeat this again later. No sex for two weeks. Your body has to recover from the procedure. Although I was careful, sometimes there are complications."

I frowned. Hard. "Procedure. What procedure? I don't understand." Glancing down, I realized I was in a dark green-and-white-checked hospital gown.

Dr. Austin pursed her lips. "When I told Opal that the blood test indicated you were indeed pregnant, she said that you'd opted to terminate the pregnancy. She instructed me to prepare immediately for the abortion."

Anxiety slithered into every part of me, and I shook my head, my eyes filling with tears. "No, there's been a mistake. Don't do it. She ... she never told me the test came in. I would never say that I wanted a ... a ... *I want my baby!*" I sank my teeth into my bottom lip, using the pain to break through the muddy waters of my brain. Suddenly, the details came rushing back. Opal, Kassandra, and I had eaten dinner, then I started feeling dizzy and tired. I jackknifed up in the bed and looked around, my breathing ragged as a shiver danced over my skin.

"Wait. It's over?" Tears streamed down my cheeks. "You took my baby?" I hiccupped through my cries. "You fucking bitch! You had no right to take my baby!" A sharp cramp in my lower abdomen doubled me over. "What the hell?" My fingers gripped the mattress as the pain subsided.

The doctor adjusted a bag on the IV pole, wearing a detached expression. "You're going to need to rest for a few days since you've been under so much stress. You're also dehydrated and undernourished. We'll need to make sure your health is back on track before you start training. While you were under, I gave you fluids in your IV." She pointed to the needle in my arm—the thin, clear line connected to a few bags hanging on an IV pole. "Right now, I've given you a bit of pain medication. I'll be back to check on you in a few hours."

A scream tore from my throat, drowned by my tears. My shoulders uncontrollably shook as I turned away from her. The second the door closed, and the lock clicked, my wails echoed off the white, sterile medical room walls. Opal's face flickered through my mind. *If it's my last fucking breath, I'm coming for you, bitch. That includes your demented daughter and doctor as well.*

***

Broken and exhausted, I mentally checked out over the next few days. My strength was returning, and according to the doctor, I had color in my cheeks again. I spent hour after hour either zoned-out on the drugs the doctor was giving me or trying to plan my revenge. Opal, Kassandra, and that doctor took my child from me without a second thought. My sorry excuse of a mother abandoned Alan and me and obviously didn't give two shits about us, but me? I was shattered. Once again, my choice had been stripped away and replaced with pain.

When my brain was clearer, I was determined to plan exactly how I would expose Opal and her crimes. When the right time presented itself, I would destroy her, Kassandra, and Doctor Austin. As soon as I started to contemplate how to accomplish my goal, defeat and depression pumped through me with every beat of my broken heart.

The only light I could see in this darkness was that my body had bought me two weeks before I would be raped, beaten, and trained to serve. I had to use my time wisely.

The dream I'd had about Holden returned front and center to my groggy brain. I wondered if my subconscious was dealing with the forced abortion, giving me hope that I would be in Holden's arms again. But I wasn't sure I'd make it out of this hellhole alive. Plus, Opal and Kassandra had talked about selling me overseas to a monster that loved a girl with a fighting spirit. I wasn't stupid. Men like that wanted to strip a female of her power and will to live. Break her slowly and draw off the pain to feed their sickness.

One thing was for certain: I had to figure a way out and fast.

Chapter Ten

The next thing I knew, early morning sunlight filtered into my room, waking me. I rubbed the sleep from my bleary eyes, then scanned the area. I was still at the medical clinic, but my mind was clear, alert.

I sat up slowly. This time, things didn't tilt and spin. Glancing at my arm, I realized my IV had been removed. I was free of the drugs the doctor had fed me for the last few days. I carefully swung my legs over the edge of the bed and eased off the mattress. Noting the blue socks with white grips on the bottom, I wiggled my toes. I used to love these in the past. Not anymore.

I clutched the bedrail and took a few steps, then a few more. Other than some occasional cramps, I felt better, stronger.

The door swung open, and the doctor entered. There wasn't even a trace of remorse in her expression. Hell, I suspected she was a soulless bitch exactly like her bosses. "Good morning. It's nice to see you up and around. How are you feeling?" Her body language was stiff and professional, lacking any emotion at all.

"I feel better." I cautiously walked to the bed but remained standing.

"Excellent." She approached a computer and entered a password. "I'll update your information." Dr. Austin focused on her task while I waited.

When she finished, she headed to the cabinet, slipped in a key, and unlocked it. "Here are some clean clothes. I'll send you with some feminine protection as well. You'll bleed for a bit. There will be some clotting, too. Don't be alarmed, it's normal."

The doctor placed a grey sweatshirt and jeans on the bed. "You're in luck. I just happen to have your size." She nodded at the garments before she returned to the drawers and cabinets. "Once you get changed, you'll be all ready to go."

"Go where exactly?" I searched her for any sign of genuine kindness. If she had a weak spot, maybe I could convince her to help me run ... but I came up empty-handed.

"I'm not at liberty to say." She placed a light green and blue box next to my shirt. "I'll see you again in a few days for a checkup. If you need more Maxi Pads, let me know when I see you."

As far as I was concerned, this lady wasn't even allowed to touch me again, but it wasn't my choice any longer. Barrett and Reid had clearly explained that to me. *Reid.* Would I talk to him soon? He was probably worried sick since I hadn't been in my cell the last three days.

"Okay." I refused to tell this bitch thank you.

"See you soon." She gave me a tight smile, then she left.

I scrambled to change clothes, then spotted my shoes in the corner of the room. Slipping them on, I walked around the small space for a minute. It felt good to stretch my legs.

When the door opened again, a tall, lanky, but muscular guard entered. "Ready?" He tugged on his brown beard.

"I guess so. I just have no idea where you're taking me." I didn't expect him to answer, but I could still ask.

"Back to your cell."

I had to stifle my excitement, which had nothing to do with the living conditions, but I could talk to Reid. Right now, I desperately needed a friend.

Twenty minutes later, I was locked in my cage again. I tossed the box of pads beneath my bed and sat down on the edge of the mattress while I waited for the sound of the guard's footsteps to disappear.

"Reid?" I called softly.

Only silence responded.

I didn't really anticipate he would answer because it was daytime, but I looked forward to our conversation later.

Since I'd slept and eaten the last few days, nervous energy hummed through me. My two-week countdown to training had already started, and fear bloomed to life in my chest.

Within days, I'd been stripped, assaulted, and now ... I placed my hand on my lower abdomen where my baby should have been growing. Safe, warm, secure, and trusting that I would take care of him or her. A stifled wail escaped me, my body shaking uncontrollably as the emotional pain crushed my soul. I clutched the side of the bed as tight as I could, desperately needing something to ground me because I was floundering. A silent scream built in the pit of my stomach, and I suppressed it, allowing it to simmer since I needed the anger to fuel me, drive me, and keep me alive and sane.

I gasped for air, giving in to the emotions and berating myself for being so fucking stupid when I'd ditched Zayne. It wasn't anyone else's fault that I was here except mine. When my tears finally ran dry, I wiped my face and promised myself that I wouldn't spend any more time-wasting energy on a pity party.

The clang of Reid's cell opening and closing pulled me out of a deep sleep. Peeling my swollen eyelids open, I gathered my bearings and sat up. When the footsteps faded, I waited to see if I could hear anyone moving.

"Reid?"

"River? Oh, my God! You're back. Where the hell have you been?" His words dripped with panic and worry.

I hurried to the bars and wrapped my fingers around the cool-to-the-touch iron.

"I'm here. Stretch your arm out." I smooshed myself against the door and reached for him. We latched onto each other, and I smiled. For a few minutes, my broken world was okay.

"I was scared you were either gone or ..." He squeezed my hand. "I'm just glad you're here."

"Me, too. I thought about you. Wondered how you were doing and wanted desperately to get word to you that ... I wasn't all right, but it's over now." I ground my molars together and swallowed my devastation. "I have a lot to tell you, but first, how are you doing? Have you seen Nadia?"

Reid's thumb stroked the back of my hand. I wished like hell it was Holden. The second I thought it, guilt jabbed me in the side. I was grateful for Reid, but I wanted Holden so bad it was fucking gutting me.

"No, she hasn't been here in a while. It happens." His tone sounded sad and lost.

"I'd give you a hug if I could."

"At least we can touch. The fact it has nothing to do with sex is nice," Reid said. "Nothing really new to report, honestly. Same thing every day."

"Where do you go when you leave here?" I'd only seen a section of the house and compound.

"This place is a lot bigger than it looks. There's another big-ass house about a mile up the road where the clients can be entertained in luxury. That's where I ... work."

"I didn't realize there were more homes up the road." A beat of silence hung in the air. "Reid, we have to get out of here. How close are you with the guard you ... you're with?"

"I don't know how to answer that. He's been visiting several times a week for a few years, I think. I've not really kept track."

"Does he ... is there a possibility he might be in love with you?" My pulse pounded with anticipation.

"He has said as much, but I don't reply. I don't feel the same. He's only a means to an end, and I know how horrible that sounds, but it's true."

I readjusted my grip on him. "It's survival, there's no shame in that. But what if you did pretend to have feelings for him? Do you think he might help us escape? I mean, think about it. He knows the area and how to leave. What if he's our ticket out of here? What if we can get free, Reid?"

I tried to imagine a puzzled expression on his face.

"It might work. I'll try. Especially if it means you can have your baby safely."

A few tears escaped, dripping down my cheeks, but I angrily swiped at them. I had to stay focused.

"I met the women who run everything. They drugged me and gave me an abortion without my consent." My voice cracked with the confession. It was the first time I'd verbalized what had happened, and saying the truth out loud made it so real I could taste it on the tip of my tongue, which gutted me even deeper.

"What? Goddammit, I'll find them, River, I swear I will. When I do ..." Reid's fingers threaded through mine. "Who's behind it all? Tell me everything."

I swallowed excessively, attempting to clear the lump in my throat. "My boyfriend's aunt and grandmother."

"What the actual fuck? Is that how you ended up here? Because you dated the wrong guy?" Reid dropped his hand.

"It's not his fault." I allowed my arm to relax and leaned my forehead against the fucking cage. "He has no idea they're alive."

"I'm not sure what to do with this. Two *women*?" His shoes smacked the concrete floor, and I assumed he was walking around his cell.

"Evil doesn't even begin to explain what they are. Plus, they have an FBI agent working for them. Michelle befriends the kids, then lures them into this hell. She can't be the only one working for them, either. From what you said, there are too many children here. The FBI would have busted her by now."

"What's an FBI agent?" Reid asked.

Shit, I'd forgotten he'd lived most of his life here. He wouldn't know what that was unless he'd overheard it, or someone had told him. It wasn't as though he lived a life of luxury.

"FBI stands for Federal Bureau of Investigation. They're more powerful than a cop. A cop has more authority than a security guard."

"That's fucking disgusting! So Michelle pretends to be someone who protects people, then ..."

"Yeah," I said softly. "I actually know her. We met and didn't exactly get along because she wanted Holden. She's the reason I'm here, but I had no idea it was a fucking family affair on Holden's side."

Reid remained silent, and I sat down and allowed him to have some space. It was a shit-ton to digest. Hell, I hadn't even processed it yet.

"River, I'm in. What do I need to do with Anthony? That's the guard's name."

My heart skidded to a stop, and I stopped breathing for a moment. "Before we talk about it, I have one concern. I mean I have a lot more than one, but ... you mentioned that normally no one was in the cells here with you. Why do you think I'm here? I mean, now that you know my boyfriend is related to the sick fucks running this place, aren't you curious if this is on purpose?"

"Yeah, it's crossed my mind. I heard one of the clients discussing how many people they could choose from, and that they were running out of room to keep all of them. It sounds like the cells are filling up."

My nostrils flared in disgust. "I guarantee you this isn't the only location, though. They most likely have them all over the world." I chewed my bottom lip. My vision blurred, and my stomach churned. "We have to get the kids help, Reid. Once we're out of here, we'll be able to hide and stay safe while we tell the authorities."

"I like the sound of that. I'll talk to Anthony when he shows up tonight."

"Are you a good actor?" I hoped like hell he was because his ability to pretend would determine if we were freed or not.

"I've had years of roleplay experience." Reid chuckled. "I know that's not funny, but it's true."

"I'm sorry. I wish I could undo all the awful things that you've lived through." I chewed on my thumbnail, devising a plan. "I hate to ask you this, but do you think he would be open to spending time with you each night? I mean, tell him you've fallen in love with him, and you need to see him more—make love, feel his arms around you, kiss you."

"Guess we'll find out, won't we?"

"Guess so. And Reid?"

"Yeah?"

"I have a week and a half until I start training. The clock is ticking."

"Shit. Okay, I'll turn on the charm. If it's too much for you, plug your ears."

I couldn't help but smile. "I'll be cheering you on, quietly."

Chapter Eleven

I paced my cell with my hands on my hips, then ducked out of sight when I heard the door open. Minutes later, the guard left Reid locked up for the night like a wild animal. Our evenings were filled with planning and chatting before Anthony arrived to see Reid. From what I could tell, he'd easily fallen for Reid's lies. Which was good because I was only two days away from training. I would have one more doctor appointment, then I would be released for duty. At least I'd been fed three meals a day, which allowed me to exercise after the first week and build my strength. If Anthony agreed to our plan, I would be running for my life by this time tomorrow.

So far, Anthony had proved helpful, and I honestly believed he loved Reid. Why he hadn't tried to free him before, I didn't know. I wasn't sure Reid had realized he had some leverage in asking for help, either.

Reid had started digging for information, and Anthony quickly confided that there weren't cameras on this building. One guard was on duty, but that was all. Apparently, Kassandra and Opal felt the compound was safe with the fence and guards. Personally, I thought they'd made a big mistake. They'd made another one when they'd abducted me and aborted my baby. They just didn't know it yet.

"Are you nervous?" I asked while I reached through the bars for Reid. We'd fallen into a routine after he returned from work. We held hands for a few minutes, relishing in the fact that we had each other in this storm of insanity.

"Yeah. What if Anthony says no and reports me?" Reid's voice trembled slightly.

I squeezed my eyes closed, unwilling to entertain the idea of what would happen if his conversation wasn't what we hoped for. That's what scared me the most. By the time this was over, I would end up even more damaged than when I met Holden. It would be easier to shove the pain and abuse down, bury it in a dark corner of my soul, and never revisit it. If Holden and I were reunited, I would have to fight the darkness, but even strong people had a breaking point.

If Anthony did agree, we wouldn't know if he was for real until he showed up and snuck us past the fence. It was a gamble all the way around. I wouldn't admit it to Reid because I didn't want to freak him out any more than he already was, but I was fucking terrified. I couldn't lose the only friend I had here.

"He won't. I can't hear everything he says, but it's clear this man really loves you. I almost wish you loved him back." I released a soft giggle, my nerves getting the best of me.

We remained silent for a minute, then Reid spoke. "Do you know what keeps me on track with the plan?"

"What?" I knew a lot of things propelled me forward and kept me focused. Holden, Brynn, Jace, Chance, and Reid. Not to mention all the kids we would be setting free from a cruel and abusive life.

"I'll be able to see your face and hug you."

My heart beat frantically behind my rib cage. "You, too." I gave his hand a gentle squeeze. "Reid, when we're out of here, you'll stay with Holden and me. We have plenty of bedrooms and we'll move you in. I don't want you to be worried about a place to live or a job.

The adjustment to living in the world and not ... in captivity is going to be hard enough. I've got your back ... always."

Nervous silence stretched between us. I scrambled to fill the gap. "If you want, I mean."

"River." Reid's voice was deep and husky. Apparently, I'd upset him. "It never occurred to me that, for the first time in my twenty-three years, I would have to find a place to live. I don't have any skills to work ... I ..."

Dammit. I'd spooked him. "Do you want the chance to see what a good life is about?" My tone was soft and gentle. I couldn't even begin to wrap my head around what this change looked like for him. I would return to Holden and my friends. Reid had nothing—no one. At least he had me, but I needed him, too. He was the only person on this earth that understood what the compound was all about.

"Yeah. I do. I just never figured freedom would look so scary. Shit, I haven't ever entertained the idea that I would leave here unless I was dead."

I slapped my free hand over my mouth, stifling my cry. "That's changing now."

"Thank you," Reid whispered. "I need a few minutes to think about what I'm going to say to Anthony tonight. Is that okay?"

"Of course it is." I desperately wished there was something else I could do for Reid, but our future lay in his and Anthony's hands.

It wasn't much longer before Anthony arrived. Forcing myself to breathe, I blew out a quiet sigh. Anxiety pulled and twisted my insides into a million knots. I closed my eyes and imagined I was with Holden when Anthony and Reid got busy. Hearing them didn't bother me anymore, but I tried to pretend they had some privacy.

A while later, the moans of pleasure settled into a soft hush of whispers. As much as I wanted to, I couldn't pace my cell. I didn't want to break Reid's train of thought.

"We can run away together," Reid said softly.

Come on, Anthony. Say yes. Please.

I struggled to hear more of their conversation, only catching words here and there. I couldn't tell if Anthony was on board or not. Most nights, I didn't care how long Anthony stayed, as long as Reid was content. But not knowing what was going on was fucking torture. I reminded myself that if Anthony didn't agree or backed out, torture would have an entirely new meaning for me in two days. Raped, beaten, forced to have sex with men and women. I swallowed over the panic.

Finally, Reid's cell opened and closed, then footsteps and the click of the door. It was amazing how I'd learned to listen to what was going on around me when I couldn't see.

"River?"

I hurried to the bars. "I'm shaking, I'm so nervous."

"Give me your hand, River."

I extended my arm until our fingers connected. "What happened? Are you all right?"

"I told him if he helped us that I would run away with him. We could start a life together free from this place."

An invisible band squeezed tighter and tighter around my chest. "Were you being honest with him, or telling him what you needed to?" My voice squeaked. "Reid, did he say yes or no? I need to know that first. Please."

"He said yes. Anthony will help us, and we'll leave tomorrow night. It will give him time to put together a plan on his end."

I sank to my knees, Reid slipping away from me. Placing my palms against the cold concrete floor, I struggled to filter through the onslaught of emotions. Fear, gratitude, hope, then reality bitch-slapped me in the face.

"We need a plan to keep you safe in case Anthony betrays us." I rose and leaned against the wall.

"I don't think he will, but you're right." Reid blew out a heavy sigh. "If I deny it, who will believe me?"

"But if he said something, wouldn't he be putting himself in jeop-ardy?" I began pacing, my mind clamoring to make sure Reid wasn't hurt. We could lose everything, and we barely had anything to start with.

"I'll figure out what to do," Reid assured me.

"No, *we* will come up with a plan together. I was the one that brought this up. It would be my fault if anything happened to you." I smacked my forehead with my palm. "I should have already figured this out. I was too scared to play with the idea that he might consider helping us."

"He said something that really makes me think he's serious."

"What?" I tapped my foot, fidgeting with anxiety.

"He said he wanted kids with me, but after the awful shit he'd seen here, he wasn't sure he could."

I frowned. "Then why does he stay?"

"Because he knows too much. They'll kill him." His voice was rough like he'd choked on sandpaper.

"Shit. I hate to say it, but that's good. It means he's got skin in the game as well." I bit my lip, holding the swell of feelings inside. "You didn't answer me about running away with him. Were you feeding him a line or serious?"

"I won't be your burden, River. Anthony loves me, and if he follows through, he'll have proved it. I would want to make him happy."

My nostrils flared. "You're lucky I can't get my hands on you right now," I seethed. "I would slap some sense into you. Listen up, Reid whatever your last name is. You don't owe anyone your happiness. Not anymore. The only person you need to make happy is you. I realize this will be a brand-new concept, and it was for me not too long ago, but if you don't come with me, then ..." I balled up my fingers and released a frustrated groan. "Then I'll kidnap you my damned self."

It started with a soft chuckle, then a full-on laugh.

"What is so funny right now?" I gripped the stupid bars until my knuckles turned white.

"You're adorable when you're pissed."

"You're infuriating when you're stubborn. For fuck's sake, give yourself a chance to find out what you want, who you love, what makes your soul sing." I shook the bars, attempting to release some of my frustration.

"You're really serious about not letting me go?"

I closed my eyes, the insecurity in his tone piercing my soul. "You have no idea how serious." My words were soft and genuine.

"All right. Once we're out of here, I'll tell him I need to get you to a safe place, then I'll meet up with him. It will buy us some time," he explained.

My mind began screwing with me, images of Reid staying in the car with Anthony and waving goodbye to me.

"Don't break my heart, Reid. Just don't fucking do it." I licked my chapped lips and wondered if this was my last night here or if the plan would fail, and we would end up separated for the rest of our lives. Tears blurred my vision, and I blinked them away. "If anything goes wrong, and I never see you again ..." I choked on my words. "Please know I love you, and I'll be thinking about you every day."

Reid sucked in a breath, followed by sniffles and a muffled cry. "I love you, River. You're the only real friend I've ever had."

"Give me your hand." I stretched and waited for his to join mine.

The warmth of his skin comforted me immediately. Hopefully, I helped him the way he had me. "Guess we'd better make sure nothing bad happens, then huh?" I asked.

"Yeah." Reid blew out a heavy sigh.

We stood, clinging to each other the only way we could as tears streamed down my face. Tomorrow would be hell waiting for Reid to return to his cell, not to mention another eternity of waiting for Anthony to show up. Although Anthony said he'd lose his life if he helped, I wasn't convinced that he wasn't playing Reid as much as Reid was playing him. Only time would tell.

Chapter Twelve

The next morning, Reid and I whispered goodbye before a guard showed up to take him to his clients. My stomach dropped to my toes as I realized that if everything went south, this might be the last moment I ever heard his voice.

I suspected Reid and I were both thinking about Anthony and our planned escape. Fear and anxiety danced on my already frayed nerves. It would only take seconds for our entire world to be turned upside down ... again. It wasn't as though we were living a good life, but enduring torture or being beaten to death wasn't on my agenda.

For just a minute, I permitted myself to pretend that Anthony would follow through and that I would be in Holden's arms soon. I closed my eyes, allowing my imagination to soar so that I could smell his clean citrus scent. My fingers twitched as I imagined running them along his slightly stubbled jaw, then kissing his full lips. I loved the way his chest and ab muscles flexed beneath my touch. Desire stirred to life inside me, taking me by surprise. I hadn't allowed myself to miss him sexually. *But what if I never see him again?* Dark thoughts rolled into my head like a storm cloud, and I quickly shut them down.

Rubbing my stomach, I took a deep breath. Emptiness settled over me, and emotions clogged my throat. It was strange how I already missed the baby. According to Dr. Austin, I'd only been six weeks along, but apparently, it was enough for my heart to shatter into a million pieces.

Suddenly, my gut lurched, and I jumped out of bed. I ran to the toilet, reaching it right before I heaved. Gathering my long hair from my face, I remained on my knees as another bubble of nausea forced its way up. There was no way I was sick. It had to be nerves. The only person I'd gotten close to was Dr. Austin. The guard dropped off my tray, then disappeared. Other than food delivery three times a day, I never saw anyone else.

An idea took shape in my mind, and I groaned. Reid and I held hands every night, and he was with people all the time. "Fuck." I stood on wobbly legs and gripped the side of the sink until I could turn the water on. I couldn't be sick. I couldn't. How would I make it out of here if I was puking and weak?

After brushing my teeth, I crawled back in bed and dozed off again until the guard dropped off my breakfast. The smell of eggs turned my tummy, and I lay still as tiny beads of sweat dotted my upper lip and forehead. I snuggled beneath the blanket, refusing to give in to the idea I had the stomach flu. It didn't matter if I did. If Anthony followed through, I would have to run anyway. It would be best to rest and save my energy.

A painful reminder wormed its way into my mind. The last time I'd been sick, I was pregnant. It wasn't possible now, though. The loss stabbed me in the chest. Mental images of Holden kissing and holding me soothed me a little. If our plan worked, I would see him soon, but I was too scared to allow myself to entertain the idea for long.

Finally, my eyelids grew heavy, and I drifted off into a fitful sleep.

Footsteps pulled me from my tormented dreams, and I struggled to sit up. From the sun's position, it appeared to be late afternoon.

Scuffed, black dress shoes appeared, then I glanced up at a man in a black suit with a white shirt. His dark hair was thin, and I guessed he was in his forties. He must have been a client, but why would he come to my cell?

"River Collins?"

I nodded, assessing him in hopes of figuring out why he was here. *Fuck. Anthony sold us out. This is it!*

I climbed out of bed and stood, ready to scratch his fucking eyes out, kick, and scream—anything to protect myself.

"What do you want?" My words were harsh and clipped.

"I'm Brian Donovan with the FBI." He raised his badge with his left hand and unlocked my cell with his other.

"Wow, two dirty FBI agents working for this shit show." I massaged the back of my neck, willing my stomach to settle down. Maybe if I puked all over him, I could run past him. He wasn't in great shape, but probably not bad either.

Mr. Donovan rubbed his chin. "I'm the good guy. I can prove it." He removed a phone from the inside of his jacket and made a call.

"I found her." Brian paused, then gave me the cell.

I shook my head. If I got too close to him, he could grab me.

"I'll put it on speaker." Brian tapped the screen then held it in my direction. "Go ahead."

"River? Baby, is it you?"

I narrowed my gaze at Brian, my brows furrowing and my brain not comprehending what was happening for a minute. "Holden?"

"It's me, River. I'm outside waiting for you. Please, come out. Brian Donovan is a good guy. You can trust him."

"Y-you're here?" My legs trembled violently as the pieces began to fall into place. "Holden? You're here?"

Disbelief taunted me as I scrambled to understand. "This isn't a trick? It's really you?"

"It's me, baby. I swear. I'm outside. The FBI wouldn't let me come in."

A cry escaped me, and I looked at Brian. Kindness filled his expression as he stepped away from the door. This had to be real. It had to be. Even if it wasn't, I had to take the chance. Holden had never lied to me. Ever. It wasn't him I was worried about, though. I'd been puking earlier, and maybe I was dehydrated and hallucinating. I had to choose, and I trusted Holden. Now, I had to trust myself. "Can you take me to him, please?"

"You bet. It's over, River. You're going home." Brian gave me a friendly smile and stepped back, allowing me the room to leave this cage.

I slapped my palm over my mouth, tears flowing freely down my cheeks. My hand shook as I reached for the phone. "Can I talk to him while you're walking me out?"

"You bet." Brian delivered the cell, and I took it off the speaker. "Holden?"

"I'm here, baby. It's so good to hear your beautiful voice. I've missed you so much."

"I can't believe this is real. I'm dreaming. I have to be. I've had so many while I've been ... here." I gulped, terrified to wake up and realize I was still trapped in my cell, waiting for Reid to come back.

"I'm real and I'm outside. I can see the building Brian walked into. Just keep talking to me, okay? I don't want to hang up until I can see you. Are you coming out?" Holden asked with fear and excitement in his tone.

"Yeah, I'm going to keep you on the phone." I eyed the FBI agent, who had fallen in step next to me as I walked down the aisle, glancing at the rows of cells on both sides of us. "How? How did you find me?"

"The second we realized you were missing, I called Pierce and Sutton, Zayne's bosses. They work with Brian. I promise you he's a good guy." Holden sniffled. "Fuck. I can't wait to see you. I've been so goddamned scared. I just need to hold you."

"I love you, babe," I whispered as Brian opened the door, and I stepped outside for the first time in days. My only activity had been a visit to the doctor's office. "It's bright out here." The fragrant, delicious, untainted air tickled my nose, and I sucked in a deep breath.

The compound was flooded with agents and dogs. Men and women were running in and out of all the houses. I assumed they were searching for more victims, as well as Opal and Kassandra if they hadn't found them yet.

I shielded my eyes as I looked around, attempting to find Holden in all the activity. Even with the SWAT members running around, I had to make sure this was real. That everything happening was actual reality and not a messed-up trick my mind was playing on me. I'd been sick all morning, then fallen asleep. I contemplated pinching myself, but then Brian's voice broke through my mind.

"This way, River." Brian pointed and headed to the left of the building.

The soft green grass crunched beneath my shoes as I followed him.

"I'm in the crowd of people, and I see you and Brian. Look up, I'm waving."

I blinked rapidly, clearing my vision from the tears and golden rays of blinding sunlight. Off in the distance, I made out a hand waving in the air, but I couldn't see him very well. "I think I see you. You're kind of far away."

"Can you walk faster?" Holden asked, excitement in his tone.

I laughed. "I'm going to hang up. I'll see you in a minute." I was shocked that I had the clarity of mind to make any decisions.

"Brian, here's your phone. Is it okay to go ahead of you?" I gave him the cell.

"You bet. We have SWAT and FBI everywhere, so you're safe."

I hesitated, then threw my arms around him. "Thank you." With that, I took off in a sprint across the wide-open field I'd first seen when I had arrived. As I grew closer to the crowd, I noticed that the section was taped off, but it didn't seem to matter to Holden. He ducked beneath it and ran toward me at full speed.

Once I could see him, I would know if this was a dream.

We slowed as we neared each other, our intense gazes locking. His dark hair was messy on top, a few strands resting against his forehead. His brown eyes were filled with so many emotions. Love, hope, fear. He looked beautiful in his basic black T-shirt, and jeans that hung off his hips, caressing his sculpted legs. I wanted this image of him imprinted on my mind forever.

"River." Holden closed the gap between us, tears streaming down his face as he cupped my cheeks. "River, River, River." He chanted my name over and over, kissing my forehead. "My, God. I was so worried—terrified ... but you're here now."

"Baby." I hiccupped through my cries as he wrapped me in his arms, and we clung to each other as though our lives depended on it. I sobbed against his shoulder, digging my fingers into his back while I prayed that he was real. My body trembled against his as he kissed the top of my head, cradling me as if I was the most precious and vital person in the world to him.

"Hi." I grabbed his hands. "Are you really here, Holden? Please tell me I'm not dreaming."

Holden tipped my chin up and gently brushed his lips against mine. "We're going home, River. You're safe."

His words hit me like a ton of bricks, and I collapsed against him. "I've been sick all day, so you probably shouldn't kiss me anymore." I peered up at him beneath my damp eyelashes.

"Fuck that." He laughed and pressed his lips to mine tenderly. "Let's get you checked out."

He was here, in front of me. I was free. I was fucking free. We walked slowly to the crowd, our arms around each other's waists. "Holden, how long have I been gone?"

He gently rubbed my back. "Three weeks."

I tugged on my lower lip with my teeth. "I guess I marked time pretty well." I couldn't tell him about the abortion yet. It had taken me two weeks to heal, and tomorrow I would've started training.

Grief twisted my stomach into knots. None of this should have happened, and we should be at the penthouse planning our future with our baby. I stared at the ground, wincing from the emotional stab to my heart. Glancing at him again, I asked, "How did you find me?"

"Pierce and Sutton are amazing. Zayne, too. But actually, it was Tim who helped us. He finally cracked and gave up the location."

My mouth gaped. "Wait, what?" I massaged my forehead, trying to understand. Tim wasn't involved ... unless he also worked with Kassandra and Opal. What I did know was that this family was fucked up beyond belief. Not everyone, but enough to make me want to hide for the rest of my life.

"I'll tell you everything later. The paramedics are waiting for you." Holden's arm tightened around me.

Terror shot through me, and I stopped in my tracks. "No." I shook my head. "No one can touch me. Only you."

A brief flicker of panic danced across Holden's features, then it slipped away. "I'll stay with you, I swear. They want to ask you a few questions, and make sure you're not hurt." He smoothed my hair. "If you say no, then that's it, River. I won't make you."

"You'll stay with me the whole time?" I grabbed his forearms, steadying myself.

"Yeah. Right next to you, I swear. I'll get Zayne, too. You'll have both of us. How does that sound?"

More tears streamed down my cheeks. "Zayne is here?" I vaguely remembered the mention of his name, but my head was still trying to register that this was actually happening.

"Yeah. He insisted he be here." A lopsided grin tugged at the corner of Holden's mouth. "He's a really good guy, babe."

"I know he is." My breath stuttered in my throat. "If you're both with me, then I'll go."

We walked in silence as we reached the tape and ducked beneath it. My head spun with the scene in front of me. Boys, girls, and people my age made up the majority of the crowd. "There's so many of us, Holden." I nearly gagged on my words, then I sank to my knees, overcome with horror.

"Hey, it's okay." Holden scooped me up in his strong arms and began to carry me. "You're free, babe. They're all free, River. Every one of them."

I sobbed into his shirt, my tears soaking through the soft material.

"I love you, River. I've got you." He kissed the side of my head as my cries slowed. "You're safe—everyone is safe."

Shit. My head popped off his chest as my cloudy thoughts cleared. "Holden, put me down for a minute."

He gently set me on my feet, and I frantically searched the multitude of people. I inhaled deeply, then yelled, "Reid! Reid!" No response. I tugged on Holden's arm. "I have to find him."

"Find who?" Concern clouded his features.

"My friend Reid," I said slowly so he could understand me. It was definitely a unique name, but I loved it.

Holden cupped his hands around his mouth, his deep voice rippling through the air as he called for him. As Holden continued to yell, I searched all of the people. Then I heard it.

"River!"

"Reid!" I yelled. Raising my arm, I realized I was too short for him to see me over everyone.

"River!" He was closer.

I glanced around. "I'm in the front by the water coolers!"

"I'm coming!"

Holden dropped his arms, searching for the male that I had so insistently asked for help finding.

"Do you see him anywhere?" Holden asked, his gaze sweeping the crowd.

"Uh ... that's the thing. I have no idea what he looks like. We've never seen each other. He was in the cell next to mine."

A tormented expression twisted Holden's face, and he gulped. Almost as quickly as the pain showed, it disappeared, and he pulled himself together. "Okay." He yelled a few more times to help Reid pinpoint our location.

After what seemed like an eternity, the crowd parted. A tall, gorgeous, muscular guy stood in front of me. "River?"

I knew that voice, but as I looked at him, I lost mine. Speechless, I nodded and cocked my head to the side. I was freaking the hell out. "Holy shit," I finally managed to say. "Holy, fucking shit."

Reid smiled, but he hadn't seen who was standing next to me yet. "No kidding. You're beautiful." He squeezed my shoulder before wrapping his arms around me. We clung to each other as the tears fell fast and hard.

"Reid, you're safe now," I murmured in his ear. "We're going home."

I stepped back and peeked at Holden, who had gone utterly still behind me. I tugged on his hand, leading him to stand beside me.

"Reid, this is Holden, my boyfriend. Holden, this is my friend Reid. He kept me sane while I was here."

The two stared at each other, unmoving. The air between us became thick and charged, questions demanding to be answered.

My attention bounced between them—same color hair, same brown eyes, same chiseled jawline. The cold hard truth stole my breath.

Holden squeezed my fingers, then spoke in a whisper. "Jesus, I think you might be my brother."

Chapter Thirteen

Reid blinked a few times, still quiet. He cleared his throat and shoved his hand through his shoulder-length hair. "I think you might be right. How old are you?"

"Twenty-two."

"Twenty-three ... I think," Reid said.

"Reid has been here the majority of his life." I looked up at Holden. "I promised he could stay with us. He ... he saved my life and kept me sane. He's important to me."

From the expression on Holden's face, I didn't need to explain anything. He was all in. "Absolutely." I didn't miss the hitch in his voice. Something was off, but I was pretty fucking certain he'd just found a brother he had no clue about.

"I'll pay for the DNA test if you want to find out for sure," Holden said to Reid.

"I have no idea what that is, but if it tells us if we're related, then I'm all in." Reid looked at Holden quizzically. "This is some freaky shit," Reid said quietly. "I feel like I'm looking into a mirror."

"Yeah, man. I agree." Holden's thumb stroked the back of my hand as he looked at Reid.

I quickly hugged Reid. "We should get checked out and answer any questions."

"Let me call Zayne and tell him where to meet us." Holden fished his phone out of his back pocket.

While Holden made the call, I talked to Reid. "When the FBI came to get me, I assumed Anthony had turned on us. I was scared shitless."

"Me, too. I think they raided the properties farther out first so no one would have the opportunity to run."

Pressing my lips together, I realized I had a ton of questions. We all did.

"River," a warm, deep voice said from behind me.

I spun around, identifying Zayne as he walked toward me. He flashed me a huge grin, his green eyes sparkling. As usual, he wore dark pants and a polo shirt with the Westbrook Security logo on it. Zayne had been Holden's bodyguard first, then, after Tim tried to assault me and we learned about his secret life as an illegal weapons dealer, Zayne had been reassigned to protect me. It was so good to see him.

"Hey, Zayne." A huge smile eased across my face, and I closed the gap between us. I threw myself at him, hugging him tightly while blurting apologies. "I'm sorry, Zayne. I'm so, so sorry ... I'm glad you're here."

Zayne returned my embrace, then took a step back and assessed me. "Are you all right? Are you hurt?"

"I'm a lot better now." I reached over and squeezed Holden's bicep. "I'm ready to get all of this over with and go home."

"Let's do it," Zayne said, gawking as he glanced behind me.

He didn't have to say a word. I knew who was standing there. "I would like to introduce you to someone." I led him in front of the two men.

"Wow." Zayne didn't bother masking his surprise as he stared at Holden's almost-twin.

"This is Reid. He was in the cell next to mine." The casualness in my tone scared me. It was like I'd introduced a classmate or the next-door neighbor in a residential neighborhood. I had to be in shock.

Zayne and Reid shook hands.

"Brothers?" Zayne asked, his attention bouncing between them.

"We think so. I suppose we could be doppelgangers," Holden said, his long fingers rubbing his stubbled chin.

"Shit, you're practically identical. Who's older?" Zayne crossed his arms over his massive chest, the corded muscles rippling beneath his shirt sleeves.

"I think I am," Reid said. "But I'm not sure when my birthday is, so I'm not sure."

I snuggled up to Holden's side, never wanting to let him go. "Reid is going to stay with us for ... as long as he needs." I peeked up at Holden. The man who hadn't given up on me. The love of my life.

He tucked my hair behind my ear, then pressed a kiss to my forehead. "We have the space, so it's no problem."

I followed Holden's gaze as Zayne's brow lifted ever so slightly. Something felt off. I didn't have the mental capacity to absorb any more information at the moment, but I asked anyway.

"Holden, what is it? What's wrong?"

"Nothing for you to be concerned about right now. I'll fill you in later, I promise. First, let's have you two checked out and debrief with Brian. I'm ready to get the hell out of here." Holden's gaze locked with mine, and I allowed myself to get lost in his deep brown eyes.

"Holden, there you are." A tall, muscular guy broke through the crowd of people and beelined straight to us. A gorgeous blonde was beside him, wearing a huge grin.

She approached me, then said, "You must be River. I'm Sutton, Pierce's wife."

"They're my bosses and best friends," Zayne added.

"You two are the ones that helped Holden find me? Find us?" I asked, my attention cutting over to Reid.

"The second you went missing, we started the search. You have a lot of people who love you. You're a lucky girl." Sutton squeezed my hand.

Once again, I threw my arms around a stranger and hugged her. "Thank you." I choked on my gratitude. Opal and Kassandra's words haunted my mind. They were right. Women did trust other women more easily than we did men. Disgust bubbled to life, and I shoved their words to the side.

"We'll talk more. Once you're settled, I have a few ladies I'd like you to meet. My sister Claire, for one. Each of them has gone through hell and back, including kidnapping. I think they'll be good for you. I just want you to know that you're not alone in this." A genuine smile spread across her pretty features.

I released her and wiped the moisture from my cheeks. "Thank you." Turning to Pierce, I stuck my hand out.

Sutton laughed. "It's fine, you can hug him."

That was all I needed. I pushed up on my tiptoes and quickly embraced him. "Thank you." I glanced at Holden, then back to Pierce. "Thank you for helping us."

"Holden's a good one, River. He really loves you," Pierce said.

A blush crept up my neck and across my face. "I really love him, too."

Sutton gently squeezed Pierce's arm. "Hon, you embarrassed her." She winked at me.

"Let's get you taken care of so we can head to the airport," Pierce said.

"You had to fly here?" I looked at Holden quizzically. In all the hustle and bustle, it hadn't occurred to me to ask where we were.

"We're in California, babe. Pierce flew us down in his plane," Holden explained.

I froze, reality shaking me to my core. I was *states* away. They might have never found me. *But he did.* The little voice in my head reminded me.

"Do you have room for one more?" I looked around, spotting Zayne and Reid chatting a few feet away from us. I pointed at Reid.

Pierce and Sutton followed my finger. I watched them as their shock registered, then slipped away.

"Who the hell would have thought you had a relative in this hell-hole," Pierce said to Holden, massaging the back of his neck.

"No fucking idea. I had a lot of nightmares where a kid kept calling out to me, but I hadn't expected to find my doppelganger. Well, possibly a brother I don't remember."

Sutton pulled herself together. "We have plenty of room. Is there anyone else we need to help?" she asked me.

I liked this lady. She had to be pretty awesome if she owned a security company and was close to Zayne and Vaughn. I suspected she could hold her own with the guys.

"I never met anyone else. Reid was in the cell next to me. We never saw each other until today," I explained softly. "He kept me sane while trying to prepare me for training. I don't think I would have made it through without him."

"If he did that for you, then he'll have whatever he needs," Pierce said.

I hoped that the support would ease Reid's mind about starting a new life. I knew first-hand how scary it was.

The afternoon turned into nightfall, and I shivered from the chill in the air. The EMTs were super nice and talked me through the checkup. Once they'd asked me questions and taken my vitals, they released me. Holden wrapped his arms around me as soon as I was finished.

The stars lit the black sky, and a full moon cast a golden glow over the field where I was questioned by Brian and another FBI agent over the next several hours. I'd shared how I'd been kidnapped, the hole I'd lived in for days beneath Barrett's home, and the kids I witnessed being abused. I also mentioned Becky-Michelle was involved. Before I had the opportunity to share about Kassandra and Opal, the agents were called away to another area of the compound. That piece of information would have to wait. Plus, I had to figure out how to tell Holden his family was behind the sex ring. In this case, it might be best to rip off the Band-Aid. He would have a million questions, and I needed some sleep before we tackled that conversation. The rest of our meeting would happen at Pierce and Sutton's place the following day.

Although Holden stuck by my side and listened intently, the recap of some of the details had shaken him up. Verbalizing what I'd lived through had ripped me to shreds. I wasn't sure how I made it through other than dreaming about Holden and having Reid's friendship.

When I was finished sharing my account for the day, Holden sent a group text to let Jace, Chance, and Brynn know the FBI had found me. His phone immediately blew up with responses. My chest swelled with love for my friends. I couldn't wait to see everyone and introduce Reid.

From what Brian had said, they had rescued hundreds of sex slaves. A cry escaped me as I witnessed an agent carrying a little girl. She rested her head on his shoulder. Her blonde hair was tangled, and her blue eyes held a blank expression. She couldn't have been more than nine years old. I hoped Kassandra and Opal burned for fucking eternity for what they'd done.

The more reality sank in, the more my heart hurt. I wasn't sure I could tell Holden or anyone about Barrett's assault. It broke me to know that I was one of the lucky few here. I'd only endured Barrett and the abortion. I hadn't been beaten and raped over and over. Anxiety skated down my spine at the thought of Barrett. Maybe tomorrow I could ask Brian where he, Opal, and Kassandra were being held.

A little after eleven that evening, we climbed into the Westbrook Security Mercedes. Holden and I took the backseat while Reid hopped into the front passenger seat. It was nice to have Zayne with us again.

Once we were on the road, I stared out the window, seeing trees and the landscape for the first time. My ride here, I'd been unconscious, then I woke up in the hole beneath Barrett's house. The only thing I'd seen was the large field and homes on the property when Michelle dragged me to one of the buildings with the trainers.

Holden reached over and released my seatbelt, pulling me into his lap.

"Zayne isn't going to let us ride like this. It isn't safe." I slipped my hand around the back of his neck and kissed him gently. "Plus, I stink. I desperately need a shower."

"I don't care about any of that. I fell in love with you the moment I found you in the recycling bin. You were dirty and needed a shower then, too."

I leaned my forehead against his, turning my head toward Zayne when he spoke.

"Holden, stretch your legs out on the seat, then let her sit between them. It will be safer that way," Zayne said, his green eyes connecting with mine from the rearview mirror.

I slid onto the leather while Holden unbuckled and settled in. I rested my back against his muscular chest, and he wrapped his arms around me.

"I'm never going to let you go again," he whispered.

"I'm so sorry, babe. I'm so sorry I put everyone through hell." I peered up at him. The love in his expression was deep and unconditional. I melted into him, allowing his feelings to penetrate my soul and begin to heal the pain.

"I refused to give up. I love you, River. I would have torn the world apart to find you." He smoothed a stray hair from my face and pressed a kiss to my temple. He gently placed his hand on my lower abdomen. "By the way, I found the pregnancy test in your purse."

Tears streamed down my cheeks, and I buried my head in his neck. "Holden," I whispered, my body trembling against him as I began to release the agony of losing the baby. I hadn't allowed myself to think about it in the cell. I had to stay sharp and calm, and the realization of what those monsters had done to me ...

He rubbed my back, allowing me to process a bit of the chaos that was running amok in my mind. I raised my head and placed my lips against his ear. "I realize we have a lot to talk about, and I promise I'll tell you everything later. But for now, all you need to know is that I lost our baby." I wanted to apologize to him again, but I already had multiple times. There was nothing else to do other than grieve together.

Holden leaned to the side, cupping my chin. His jaw clenched, and I suspected that he was trying to remain calm.

"You can tell me later, but I love you, and regardless of if we have a baby now, in five years, or never if that's what you want, the fact that you're in my arms again is good enough for me. Don't apologize for something that was out of your control, babe. There's no need to."

I nodded, then he kissed me tenderly. Resting against him again, I allowed myself a deep breath. Peeking into the front of the vehicle, I realized that Reid and Zayne were also talking. I was glad that Zayne was taking to Reid so quickly. I hoped Brynn, Jace, and Chance would too.

My eyelids grew heavy as the gentle rise and fall of Holden's chest eased my mind. Then, it hit me.

"Wait, back up. Five years from now?" He had his future planned out already? *Our* future?

A chuckle rumbled through him. "We have the rest of our lives to figure out if and when we want a family."

I snuggled into him again, a smile on my face. "I like the sound of that." After he learned what had happened, I hoped like hell he would still feel the same about me and that future he'd planned.

Chapter Fourteen

The flight home was quiet. Everyone was exhausted and slept on the way back to Washington. I sat between Holden and Reid, holding onto Holden's hand. I kept looking at him, hoping he wouldn't suddenly fade away like he had in my dream during the abortion.

Reid continued to run his fingertips along the buttery, cream-colored leather seats. I was in awe of the gorgeous plane as well, but my brain wasn't soaking in the details like Reid's was. We dipped and bounced with some turbulence, and Reid's knee began to bounce. He calmed down after Holden explained to him what was happening. A part of me wondered if it would be fun witnessing Reid explore his new surroundings, or if it would continue to break my heart. I had to figure out a way to cope with the situation and with my guilt. Even though I'd lived through hell, I hadn't lived through the same hell he had.

We landed at the Spokane airport a little after two in the morning. Sutton and Pierce had offered for us to stay at their house, but Holden and I had politely declined. We needed to help Reid settle in and have some privacy. Brian wouldn't meet us at Pierce's place until the following day in the late afternoon, so we might be able to grab a few hours of sleep. I wasn't sure I would be able to, but I'd try.

Once again, we climbed into a Westbrook Security-owned Mercedes and buckled in for the last leg of the trip. Holden's club was only twenty minutes away. My head throbbed with the idea of walking back into the same place from where I'd been abducted. Anxiety hummed beneath my skin, and my grip on Holden's hand tightened.

I glanced up at him.

"Hey, it's okay." He stroked my cheek with the pad of his thumb. "Now that we're in Spokane, I need to tell you something."

I shifted in my seat, facing him. "What is it?"

Holden massaged the back of his neck and sighed. "While you were gone, the club ... it caught on fire. Everything is gone, babe."

"What?" I screeched a little too loudly. I shook my head in disbelief. "We ... you lost everything?" This wasn't what I'd wanted to happen. I wanted to move forward, return to work, and live in the penthouse. Just not yet. A sudden and unexpected relief washed over me. My expression must have given me away.

"River?"

I slumped in the seat, my fingers fidgeting in my lap. "I wasn't sure I could go back, and I was scared to tell you."

Holden's jaw clenched, the muscle in his face popping. "You can't do that. River, you have to be a hundred percent honest with me. I was already worried about that. If it were me, I'm not sure I could return to the scene of the crime. I had to see the place you were kidnapped from every single day, and it was fucking torture. Maybe 4 Play burning to the ground was a blessing in disguise."

I sniffled and wiped my nose with the back of my arm and stared at my dirty jeans. I hadn't had a fresh change of clothes since my last visit to Dr. Austin a few days ago. "Returning to the club hadn't crossed my mind until now. I've stayed in a cell or ... in a hole beneath a guard's house. Every fucked-up minute, I was in survival mode." My fingers balled into fists. "I can't do this right now," I whispered and turned away from him, the images assaulting my brain, stealing my breath away. How the hell would I deal with everything now that I was safe again? I never thought this day would happen, so I'd shoved all the pain and anger down, using it for protection and to keep myself alive.

I peeked at Holden. Tears glistened on his cheeks. "I never meant to put you in danger."

Sadness tingled in my stomach, and I took his hand in mine. "I know. You're going to have to forgive yourself."

"So are you. Ditching Zayne ... it was a normal reaction after the pregnancy test."

A part of me realized that he was right, but my poor decision had landed me in a training compound, ready to be sold to some sick asshole overseas. Bile swam up to my throat. I swallowed, forcing my stomach to behave. "Maybe, but it was a reaction that cost me dearly. It cost all of us so much, Holden."

We sat in silence for a few minutes. "Where are we going to stay?" I nodded to Reid in the front seat.

"Chance's place. You and I will take Chance's room and Reid can have one of the guest rooms. We'll get things worked out."

I frowned, my mind spinning faster than a weathervane in a tornado. "Where's Chance? For that matter, can I see everyone tomorrow? And how in the hell did our home and club catch on fire?"

"I'll tell you about the club later. Chance and Brynn are in Portland on business for a while."

"Business?" What the fuck had happened while I was gone?

"Yeah, hopefully they'll be back soon. Jace is at Chance's waiting for us." His attention fell to his lap, then back to me. "River, you have my word, I'll tell you everything tomorrow, but for tonight, I need to just hold you. Is that okay?"

"Yeah," I whispered, grateful I didn't have to blow his world wide-open with the truth about his family yet.

***

Half an hour later, Zayne pulled into the driveway of a tan house with black trim. I hadn't ever seen Chance's place before. Even through the darkness, I could see the abundance of leafy trees. The home was nestled toward the back of the property, allowing for privacy.

We all climbed out of the car. My muscles were screaming at me. The cell had been cramped, and the trip home had been long. I was definitely ready to walk around and try to eat something.

I rounded the vehicle, slid my arm through Holden's, and took Reid's hand, giving it a gentle squeeze.

Holden glanced at Reid, his gaze traveling down to our interlocked fingers. He gave Reid a tight-lipped smile. "This is where my friend Chance lives. We're going to stay here for a few days. Make yourself at home. If you want to shower, then I'll give you shorts and a T-shirt to change into. Hell, I probably have some boxer briefs that are still in the package that you can have. After the fire, Brynn went shopping for me." Holden cringed, then quickly masked his expression.

"I guess I hadn't considered clothes. The ... work always supplied mine." Reid fidgeted, obviously feeling awkward with the conversation.

Holden patted him on the back. "Not anymore."

I loved Holden's big heart. Even if he and Reid weren't related, I suspected he would help him get on his feet. But I had so many questions. If they were brothers, how? How could Catherine not tell Holden? Had she given up Reid when she was young? Was Tim not his dad? I realized all of this would come up in conversation after the DNA test, but I was as stunned as Holden. Not to mention it was a little bit unnerving with how similar they looked.

The front door of Chance's house flew open. Jace stared directly at me, then barreled down the stairs. He practically knocked Holden out of the way and wrapped me up in a warm embrace.

"River," he whispered. He clung to me, and I hugged him hard.

"Hey, it's really, really good to see you again," I said, basking in the sweet welcome.

He pulled away and wiped the moisture from his cheeks. "Are you hungry? I can make a mean grilled cheese." He grinned, eyeing Holden for a moment. Jace's smile faltered as his attention landed on Reid.

"Son of a fucking bitch." Jace's brows shot up to his hairline, and he rubbed the corner of his mouth with his thumb.

"Uh, Jace ... this is Reid. He was with me ... at the, uh, place we were held," I finally said.

Jace shook Reid's hand. "I'm sure you've heard you and Holden look like twins, right?"

"Yeah, a few times. I'm starting to get used to everyone's reaction." Reid skeptically assessed Jace.

"Jace, Chance, Brynn, and I are all best friends," Holden explained. "Let's get inside and we can talk more there."

Holden slid his arm around my waist as we climbed the steps to the porch. The setup was adorable, with white furniture and red cushions. I could definitely sit out here and drink my coffee in the morning. It would be nice to walk around and remind my brain that I wasn't at the compound anymore.

Chance's entryway and open floor plan reminded me a little of the penthouse. I'd loved helping Holden with the layout and interior design, but I hadn't seen our new home fully furnished. I hadn't had time to get attached to it, so I wasn't sure if I would miss it or not.

A mocha-colored loveseat and couch occupied the living room, and a black rug covered the floor between them. A whitewashed brick fireplace was the focal point on the far wall. A large Samsung flat-screen television was mounted to the left. Tan, full-length blackout curtains hung over the windows. I immediately felt comfortable. I hoped Reid did, too.

Reid stopped walking once the door was closed. "The only reason I know that's a flat screen television is because of the house I worked at. It was decked out with expensive furniture, televisions, bars, and all of the amenities. But this ... this looks like ..." He glanced at me. "Like it's safe."

I released Holden's hand and grabbed Reid in a huge hug. "It's going to take us a while to realize it, but yeah, we're safe here. We also have Zayne outside. He'll take care of us. He's an excellent body-guard." I dropped my arms and looked over at Holden. "Will you give us a tour?" I didn't miss the pain in Holden's features. I assumed he was recalling the day I was taken, but I wasn't sure.

"Of course." He pressed a gentle kiss to my forehead, then showed us around. It wasn't large, but it was perfect for a single guy and his friends.

Jace was in the kitchen, unloading ingredients from the stainless-steel fridge onto the black and white marble countertop. "Breakfast anyone? I mean, granted, it's almost three a.m. but it's still morning."

"I could eat," Reid said behind me.

"I'll try. I might keep it light, though. I haven't felt well today," I explained.

"Do you want to take a shower while he's cooking?" Holden asked me.

I looked at my dirty clothes. "I don't have anything to wear. Can I borrow a T-shirt?"

"You don't have to ask, babe. We'll get you both some clothes tomorrow. Let's see what we have here for tonight." Holden rubbed my back, and I leaned into his soothing touch.

I reached out and placed my palm on Reid's arm. "Are you okay while I shower?"

He gave me a lopsided grin exactly like Holden's. It was unnerving as hell. "I think I can take Jace if he messes with me."

"Dude, you have no idea who you're dealing with." Jace puffed up his chest and stuck his ass out, strutting around the kitchen.

We all laughed at how ridiculous he looked, but we all needed his humor right now.

"I'm good, I promise. Go get cleaned up," Reid said.

"Okay. See you in a bit." I walked to the master bedroom, Holden right behind me.

He shut the door and locked it. We were finally alone. In two long strides, Holden closed the gap between us and pulled me to him. We stood there, embracing in silence as his body began to shake. An anguished cry reached my ears, the pain evident in Holden's strangled sobs. How was I supposed to give him comfort and support when I was a total fucking mess myself?

"I'm so glad you're here," he said against my hair.

"Me, too." We clung to each other as a mix of relief and fear swirled around us. If we'd survived for this long, we could find a way to get through this as well.

"Shit. I'm sorry, baby." Holden released me.

I reached up and wiped his tears. "Don't apologize. I can't imagine how terrified you were."

"Every time I thought I wouldn't see you again, I swore to myself I would. There was no way I would ever give up on you." He tucked my hair behind my ear, then pressed his lips against mine.

I sighed, content with his touch. I broke our kiss and offered him a weary smile. "I need to get cleaned up. I might feel slightly human afterward."

"Of course. I'll look for something you can wear while you're getting washed up." He ran his fingers through his hair, then crossed the room to the closet. "Maybe Brynn left a few things here. She did that if we were out late. Then she didn't have to worry about packing a bag every night. She had some of her clothes at Jace's and my mom's place as well."

Catherine. Shit. I was concerned about Holden dealing with his family secrets, but Catherine knew about her other son, if Reid was his brother. I wanted to know why she hadn't told Holden, though.

"That would be great. We're the same size, so anything should work." I made my way to the ensuite bathroom, noting the counters and cabinets matched the kitchen.

A large square shower big enough for two was in the corner of the room. I seriously contemplated inviting Holden in, but I desperately needed to clean up. Plus, as much as I wanted to, I wasn't ready to be with him yet, and when we showered together, it always led to sex. I noted the jetted tub and wondered if Holden would want one in the new house.

Leaving the door cracked, I removed my clothes and turned on the water, allowing it to warm while I relieved myself. My fingers lingered on the soft toilet paper, a luxury I hadn't had in the cell. Soft and gentle weren't words I would ever connect to the compound.

Once I finished and flushed the toilet, I stuck my hand beneath the spray, testing it. The temperature was perfect. Realizing I needed a towel, I rummaged through the cabinet and grabbed a plush white one. After placing it on the countertop, I stepped in and pulled the glass door closed. I hadn't had a real shower since the one Becky-Michelle had accompanied me to.

The mere idea of her kicked my pulse into high gear. Had the FBI found her? Had they found Kassandra and Opal? Barrett? At this point I had no information at all.

Attempting to control my fear, I moved beneath the hot water and allowed it to stream over my body. Then, tilting my face up, I closed my eyes and inhaled the steam. I was home. I was safe. Holden was in the next room, waiting for me. Anxiety coursed through me as flashes of the last several weeks bombarded me. Images of the hole, living in complete darkness for days at a time, squatting in the corner to pee ... I shook my head as though it might clear the fog from my overwhelmed brain.

Opening my eyes, I stared at my feet, but I didn't see the tan tiles in the shower. It was dark, with only a tiny crack of light peeking through above me. I smelled fresh soil. The dirt walls started to close in on me, and I held my arms out, attempting to make them stop. *Oh, God. Oh, God.* I'd been dreaming this entire time. Had someone drugged me? I was still in the fucking hole. My head buzzed with my churning emotions as terror ripped through me. Memories swirled faster, blacker, thicker. They clawed at me until I bled.

"No! No!" I banged on the dirt walls, screaming for someone to let me out as I choked on my sobs. I wasn't free at all. Anthony had turned on us, and now Reid and I were separated. The idea that I was locked underground again sent a scream tearing through me. I knew I couldn't make it through that twice.

Chapter Fifteen

"River!"

I jerked away as the door opened above, and light spilled into the hole. Barrett descended the ladder into the pit and leered at me. "Don't!" I shrieked. "Don't you dare fucking touch me, Barrett!" My legs wobbled as I attempted to steady myself. I would have to fight off this motherfucker again.

"Babe, it's Holden. River, listen to my voice. You're home with me. We're at Chance's. Reid is in the kitchen with Jace." Holden reached out to me, then hesitated.

I grabbed the sides of my head, my body trembling uncontrollably. "Don't touch me." I backed away as much as I could, but the space beneath his house was small, and there wasn't anywhere I could go.

"Look at me. River, you need to look at me. It's Holden."

My mind was playing horrible tricks on me. Barrett's face blurred, then Holden was in front of me, then Barrett again. Once Anthony had turned on us, they must have drugged me because I swore that I heard Holden talking to me. The image of the shower flickered in and out of my vision. The tiles came into view, as did Holden. But I still didn't trust what I was seeing.

"Holden?" I raised my head, my tears mixing with the water.

"It's me." He reached out. "I swear, it's me, baby."

I glanced around, once again in Chance's shower. The love of my life had jumped in with his clothes on, horror written all over his features.

My body trembled as I reached out to him, images of Reid and I holding hands flickering through my exhausted brain. I hesitated, still unclear where I really was, and which one was a horrible flashback.

"Can I touch you?" Holden remained rooted in place.

Our eyes locked, and I nodded.

He took my hands, and we stood motionless, staring at each other. The slurp of the water circling down the drain confirmed where I was. "Can I—I want to stay with you if you need me to. I'll keep my clothes on ... we don't need to do anything. That's not why I'm here. Let me help, babe." Holden's chest heaved with his words. "Maybe I can wash your hair and just talk to you?"

Could I trust my own mind to understand that I was really with Holden? Or had I split inside myself, unable to manage what had happened at the compound?

Tentatively, I stepped out of the spray and moved a cautious inch toward him. "Okay," I said softly. I fought the urge to cover myself, but Holden had seen me naked plenty of times. He also wasn't leering or trying to hurt me.

Holden's wet shirt molded to his skin, revealing his muscular chest and washboard abs. I wanted to reach out and touch him, but I was too afraid that he would disappear like he had in my dreams. I desperately needed him to be real right now.

Holden reached for the blue bottle of shampoo and gently smiled at me. "Do you want to know what happened with the club?"

"Yeah." I turned around so he could lather my long strands. My nerves had settled down some.

Holden worked the shampoo into my hair and massaged my scalp as he talked. "I met Tim for breakfast to see if he had any information about you. He didn't, but he offered to ask around to see if he could learn anything. While I was talking to Tim, Zayne put a tracker and a recording device in his car. Later, we heard Tim trying to negotiate with your kidnapper. He's a piece of shit, but he honestly tried to bring you home."

"What? Do you know why?" My voice cracked, rising in pitch. *What the fuck?* Tim was the last person on earth I thought would fight for me.

"My best guess is that he knew I would never stop looking for you. Plus, once I found out who took you, I think it would be obvious that he was connected to those monsters somehow. He didn't want to take the fall along with them."

"It's always about him. Tim doesn't care about anyone else. Not even his kids." Sadness clouded Holden's features. "I'm sorry, Holden. I shouldn't have said that."

"Why not? It's the truth."

I tilted my head back, the sensation of Holden's hands in my hair comforting me. "Zayne's fucking smart. I probably wouldn't have thought to do that."

"I agree. We've gotten to know each other pretty well." Holden ran his sudsy fingers through my strands, then touched the back of my neck. An uncontrollable shiver coursed through my body. The fact that Holden was fully clothed helped. It was clear he was here because he loved me, not to hurt me.

"Can I rub your shoulders?" he asked.

"Yeah." I gathered my long brown hair and draped it over the front of my shoulder, allowing him better access. I needed Holden to touch me. I needed him to replace the horrible experiences with Barrett. How far we could go was the question. Apparently, I had more triggers than with Dan.

"Tim actually provided a video of him boarding his flight from Monte Carlo. And we were right, he and Logan are business partners. Have been for a long time. We suspect that Logan stays at the trailer park in Montana as his cover. It most likely keeps the FBI from breathing down his neck, because the man definitely has money."

"They're both such pieces of shit." Fresh hatred pumped through my veins for Logan and Tim.

"They're pretty tight from what I gathered. So, Tim was able to prove he wasn't in Spokane when everything went down. In my mind, it didn't absolve him, though. But it gets better." He continued to massage my shoulders, the stress easing a bit. "Tim offered me a job to work with him. He said I would have more money and power than I'd ever dreamed of."

I squeezed Holden's hands and turned to him, unable to mask my shock. "Shit. Seriously? What did you say?" I tipped my head back and rinsed the shampoo from my long strands, focusing on Holden.

"I told him no. At first, I thought he didn't take it hard, but ..." Holden blew out a sigh. "He continues to surprise me. When Zayne and I were on the way to the club, Chance called. 4 Play was on fire. I could see the black smoke billowing up in the air from the highway. It wasn't long after I arrived on the scene that Tim called me and admitted to having his men start the fire. He told me to deal with the insurance and let him know if I reconsidered his offer."

My mouth gaped, and I quickly slammed it closed as the bitter taste of shampoo trickled over my tongue. "What was the point of Tim destroying your club?"

"A power play. It was a reminder that he could get away with it and force me to work with him."

"That's so fucked up. He's your father, for God's sake." I turned, rinsed my face, and looked at him again. "Where's the soap?"

"Tim isn't normal, that's for sure." Holden reached behind him, then gave me a bottle of lilac body wash. I cracked a grin as I sniffed it. "I would have never taken Chance as the floral type."

Holden chuckled. "There's a lot that would surprise you about Chance."

I gave him a curious smile. After spending a little time with Chance, I gathered there was a lot more to him. "What happened next?" I squeezed a healthy amount of soap into my palm after realizing I'd forgotten a washcloth. Holden kept his eyes on mine as I lathered up. I wondered if it was too difficult for him to look at me because he wanted to be with me or because I was damaged goods.

"I accepted Tim's offer, but only under the condition that he brought you back. You were pregnant and if he could return you safe and sound, he would own me. I would do anything he asked me to."

"Holden Alastair," I whispered, my arms slowly lowering to my sides and my chest aching from his confession. "Don't you *ever* sell your soul to save anyone, least of all me."

"It wasn't like that, baby. I was working with the FBI, plus the recording device picked up some of his phone calls. They weren't on Bluetooth though, so we weren't able to know who he was talking to. But he knew who had you. My plan was to string him along until he gave us the information we needed. There's no way I would ever actually work with that fucker." He raised his hand, cupping my cheek. "There's nothing I wouldn't do for you, River."

Deep down inside, I knew this. He was proving it right now. Not once had he touched me in a sexual way. My heart and logic warred against each other, tugging me in opposite directions. I wanted Holden. My body needed him inside of me. I needed to reconnect with him, but I was afraid I would freak out, and it terrified me. *Being scared never stopped you before,* my mind said.

I rinsed my skin, grateful I no longer reeked of the compound. "I'm sorry Tim burned the club." I squeezed the excess water from my hair. "I know how much it meant to you."

"Maybe it's for the best. We can talk about it later, but in order to stay sane and hold onto the fact that we would have a future together, I looked at some lakefront property." Holden stepped out of the shower and onto the white, fluffy floor mat. He leaned over, collected the towel off the counter, and gave it to me. I wrapped it around my body, then followed him.

"I was thinking about building a log home for us to live in. There's acreage, so we would be outside of the city, but the lake view is incredible." He rubbed his chin. "I thought it might be nice to have a fresh start now that the penthouse is gone."

"Really?" I gazed up at him. "I would love to see the property."

"Yeah?" Holden grinned at me. "You'll see Pierce and Sutton's place tomorrow, then maybe we can talk about what we want in a home." He took my hand and kissed my knuckles. "It might give us something to think about while we're settling back in."

"I think it will help a lot. I'm not sure what our new normal will look like." A beat of silence hung in the air as my mind raced. "I'm definitely curious to see the DNA results with Reid. I do think he's family, I'm just not sure if you two are first cousins, or how all of this fits together." I searched for another towel but didn't spot one. Opening the cabinet, I grabbed him one. "Were you able to find some clothes for me?"

"Yeah, on the bed. They're Brynn's, but she tends to buy new underwear and pajamas to leave at all of our houses. They still have the tags on them." Holden appeared a little sheepish.

"I know you all are close, Holden. Don't worry, it doesn't bother me. I'll be glad when she and Chance get back. It's too early to call her, but maybe later. Do I still have a phone?" I opened the bathroom door, the steam flowing into the adjoining room.

"Sutton has it unless she turned it over to the FBI. Which, now that I think about it, she was supposed to give it to Brian. I'll have Jace get you and Reid new ones tomorrow. Until then, you can use mine."

"Thanks. I just want to hear my best friend's voice." I walked into the bedroom, then poked my head into the bathroom in time to watch Holden peel off his wet shirt. His six-pack rippled as he moved. My core clenched, longing for him to touch me, but I couldn't. Not yet. When Holden and I were together, it was special, electric. I wanted to make sure I could handle being with him on every level. Hope-fully, he would be patient with me again.

"I can get you some dry clothes," I offered. "Where are they?"

"The guestroom. I haven't had time to move anything over."

"I'll get dressed, then I'll grab some for you." I left him in the bathroom as I spotted a black lace thong, pink Victoria's Secret shorts, and a matching tank. Changing quickly, I realized that my nipples pushed through the soft, thin fabric of the top. My lips pursed. I couldn't run around in front of Jace and Reid like this. I didn't want to encourage any unwanted attention.

I joined Holden in the bathroom again. "Um, babe? We've got a problem ..." I pointed at my nips. "I don't want anyone to ... ya know."

Holden's focus remained on my chest, his gaze darkening. His tongue darted across his bottom lip as he became transfixed. He looked at the wall and scrubbed his face with his hands. "When you're in my room, find an extra T-shirt for yourself."

"Are you marking me as yours?" I smiled, then it melted away as I touched my neck. "The necklace with the H. It's gone isn't it?"

Holden nodded. "Everything, babe. I've already filed the insurance claim, so we'll have money to start all over with. We can rebuild our home and the club if that's what we decide to do." He tugged the towel around his shoulders. "For now, we need rest. We have time to figure everything out."

"I know, and it's not about the material things. I don't care about that. It's the memories we made together." I sank my teeth into my lower lip, my mind skipping down memory lane—the first time he took me to the club and introduced me to the basement floor. How he insisted we wait to make love until I was sure of my feelings for him. This man was the exact opposite of his grandmother, aunt, and father. Holden was genuine, good, and mine.

"I get it. I guess we'll have to make new ones, right?" He watched me while he waited for my reply.

"I want that." I closed the gap between us, pushed up on my tiptoes, and pressed my mouth against his. "I love you, Holden Alastair." With that, I spun around and left him standing there.

At some point, I knew I would have to push through the assault and physically be with Holden again. I refused to allow what happened to paralyze me. I reminded myself that Dan had raped me for years, but it hadn't ever been as brutal and horrible as what I'd recently experienced. Holden had provided me the space and love to grow and heal so much after I wound up in his recycling bin. If I'd done it before, then there was no doubt that I could do it again. Anxiety coursed through me. Seeing those kids being raped and tortured, beaten ... I swallowed hard. I definitely needed something positive to look forward to, so I was happy that Holden had looked at the property. The lake sounded peaceful. A place to heal. I hoped it helped because even the strong shattered into pieces, and although I was trying my best to be brave, I could feel my mind teetering on the edge of sanity.

Chapter Sixteen

The early morning rays of sunshine peeked around the blackout curtains, and I opened my eyes, expecting to wake up in my cell. My sleep-deprived brain was foggy as I attempted to sit up and recognize my surroundings. I struggled to move but realized I was pinned against the mattress. A sudden panic struck me in the temples, causing me to wince. Why couldn't I get up?

"Babe?" Holden's groggy voice broke through my fear. He jerked his arm off me and propped up on his elbow. "Are you okay? I didn't mean to scare you."

I peeked up at him and tried to hide the turmoil of emotions bubbling to life inside me. "Morning." I offered him a smile.

"You didn't know where you were, did you?" Holden's cool fingertips stroked up and down my shoulder.

I looked away from him. I hated being this weak. Shattered.

"I thought I was in my cell." *My cell.* The horror of my words churned in my gut, and I rolled over on my back. Once I'd fallen asleep, I hadn't woken up again. Somewhere in my heart, I must have realized I was in Holden's arms, safe.

"You're here with me." Holden kissed the tip of my nose. "I've missed this. You cuddled up next to me and seeing your beautiful face first thing every day. Let's stay here forever and hide from the rest of the world. What do you think?" A sweet, lopsided grin eased across his features.

"I love the sound of that, babe. Maybe breakfast in bed, then we could binge on Netflix and snuggle." Everything I had ever cared about had been snatched from me, but not Holden. He was here.

I sat up, the blankets dropping to my waist. Holden's gaze traveled to my breasts, then quickly back to my eyes. Sadness enveloped me. I knew he was trying to give me space, and I loved and appreciated that, but it didn't change the fact that I wanted to be with him. Reaching up, I placed my palm against his warm cheek. "I want you, Holden. Don't doubt that. I'm still attracted to you. My body wants you ... I ... I don't know if or when I would ... if it would ..."

"Hey, hey, shh ..." Holden ducked his head and lifted my chin. "There's no pressure. I'll never push you into anything you're not ready for." He took my hand and brushed his lips across my knuckles.

"For when I am ready, I need to go ahead and start a new prescription for my birth control pills."

"I'll call the doctor and have her write a new one. She'll want to see you soon, but it will take care of things for a little while. At least, buy you some time."

"Thanks. I just want to be prepared." I nervously pulled at the corner of the sheet. "You were so patient with me when we first got together."

"And I will be again. You're steering the ship, babe."

I leaned over and kissed him as I placed my palm against his bare chest. "I've missed you so much."

He swallowed, multiple emotions flickering in his expression. "I've never been so terrified in my entire life, River."

"Me, either."

We sat in silence, reveling in each other's company. Sometimes words weren't necessary.

"Do you want some coffee?" Holden tucked my hair behind my ear.

Excitement pumped through me. *Coffee. Nectar of the Gods.* I hadn't had any since the morning of my kidnapping. "I would love some." I swung my legs around, and my bare feet grazed the soft rug. Last night, I hadn't noticed the polished wood floors and black and tan carpet. I was too exhausted, struggling to remain connected to reality.

"I like Chance's house. I'm glad he's letting us stay." I grabbed Holden's T-shirt off the nightstand and slipped it on.

"Yeah, he's a good guy." Holden stepped into his basketball shorts, then slipped on a Seahawks jersey.

I crawled over to his side of the bed. My nerves were standing on edge as I realized I needed to have a difficult conversation with Holden. "I'm not sure what time it is, but I need to talk to you before we go to Pierce and Sutton's to meet Brian. There are things you should be the first to know." I peeked up at him, afraid to share the truth. "Maybe we can get some coffee before we talk, though?"

He stood, then slid his arms beneath mine and lifted me off the mattress. Without a second thought, I wrapped my legs around his waist. Threading my fingers through his hair, I pulled his head back, then brushed my lips softly against his. Our mouths lingered, tasting and taking from each other. His tongue danced with mine, and heat licked beneath my skin like fire.

Holden's erection pushed against my center, and a gasp escaped me.

He immediately broke our kiss and set me down. "We should get some coffee." He placed his finger under my chin and tipped my face up. "Don't take that as rejection, River. You have no idea how much I want you, but I won't risk losing you emotionally and mentally. We're going to take it slow."

I loved it when he took control, protected me even from myself. Wrapping my arms around him, I rested my head against his chest and listened to the steady beat of his heart. "I love you. Not just because you're sexy as hell, but because you're so good to me. You make me feel as though I'm worthy to be loved even when I've done some shitty things." *Like orgasm with a monster.* I shuddered at the memory, then pulled away.

Holden must have sensed not to ask me about the shiver because he opened the bedroom door and led me to the kitchen. I hopped up on the counter, the black and white marble countertop cool against the backs of my thighs. The light wood floors complemented the space. His stainless-steel appliances were top of the line like the ones we'd selected for the penthouse. He obviously owned a nice coffee pot with an alarm option, which was amazing. "I guess Reid is still asleep," I said quietly.

"That's good. I'm sure he needs it." Holden rummaged around in the cabinet and removed two mugs, filling them almost to the top. He glanced over his shoulder at me. "Creamer?"

"Mm, yeah." My eyes widened. It was funny how creamer had been available most of my life, but now it was a luxury. So was a comfortable bed and a bathroom without bars.

He topped it off with white chocolate creamy goodness and handed it to me. I sipped it slowly, basking in the glory as the warm liquid coated my tongue and ran down my throat. "Heaven." I peered at Holden over the rim of my cup.

He flashed me a beautiful grin, and my soul lit up. "When ... when I was first taken," I held up my finger, taking another drink. My arms lowered, and I shook my head, attempting to clear my thoughts.

"Take your time, babe." Holden leaned against the opposite counter.

"Becky—well, Michelle—tried to drown me."

Red-hot fury crawled up Holden's neck and cheeks. I had never seen him so angry. "She did *what?*!" His tone curled with venom.

"I'm obviously fine, but she was in on it. She's why I was taken." I set my cup down and rubbed my arms, suddenly chilled.

Holden stared at his feet, then his furious gaze connected with mine again. The muscle in his jaw ticked as he clenched his teeth. "Did you know that she's FBI?"

I nodded. "I found out when she gave me a tour of the training compound." Hopping off the island, I paced the small space in front of him. "Is there a possibility that we can go outside while we talk? There's so much to tell you. Plus, it would be amazing to enjoy the fresh air. Just knowing that I can walk in and out of the house a hundred times if I wanted to ... it helps me remember that I'm not living in a cage any longer."

A look of pain and worry etched into Holden's features. In two quick strides, he closed the gap between us and gently kissed my forehead. "If it helps you, I'll pitch a tent outside and we can sleep there every night."

I giggled and slid my arms around his waist. "I prefer a real bed and bathroom, but I'll let you know if that changes." I released a sigh of contentment. Even if it didn't last long, I'd learned to take those moments when I could. "I'm sure the guys will be up soon, so we should take advantage of the time to ourselves."

Before we left, I glanced at the clock on the oven. It was a little after ten. I hadn't slept long, and exhaustion tugged at me. I yawned, then plunked into one of the oversized white wicker chairs on the porch and inhaled the warm spring air of the new day. The chair creaked beneath Holden as he settled in the seat next to me.

"It's pretty here." I waved at Zayne as he appeared from the backyard. "Morning." I smiled at him.

He stopped and grinned at us. "It's good to see you both together."

Holden raised his cup to him while he reached for my hand and gave it a gentle squeeze. "Thanks for all your help, man."

Zayne nodded. "I'll let you two catch up." He strolled off, then continued to keep his focus on the property.

I nestled into my seat, my attention drifting to all the different trees. "Wherever we live, can we have maples and oaks like Chance?"

"We can have anything you want."

I sighed, wishing I didn't have to have this next conversation, but I had to tell Holden. It wouldn't be fair to him if he learned the truth at the same time his friends and FBI did. Besides, it wasn't about their families. It was about Holden's.

Shifting in my seat, I tucked a leg beneath me and studied him. "I'm going to tell you what happened. I'll probably skip parts, but eventually I'll be able to tell you everything." I nervously drummed my fingers against the white ceramic mug. My French manicure looked like shit since my nails had grown out over the last few weeks, and I'd bitten them down. "I know you're going to have questions, and I'll help with as much as I can."

"As I said before, take your time." He slid his palm over his thigh. I suspected Holden was trying to be strong for me, but we'd been together long enough for me to realize he was nervous.

I pursed my lips and gathered up all the courage I could muster. "When I was first taken, I wasn't even sure where I was. I'd been drugged, and I woke up underwater. Becky ... Michelle was behind it. I finally got free, but she hit my head and knocked me out again. The next time I woke up ..." My throat tightened, the memories of the hole beneath Barrett's house bombarding me. I covered my mouth with my hand, attempting to control the onslaught of fear that threatened to destroy me. *I can do this. I refuse to let those fuckers win.*

I sucked in a shaky breath as I looked out over Chance's property. The birds sang and chirped at the tops of the branches, relaxing me a little. "I woke up in a hole. Underground with no light, no food, and no water. I don't know how long I was there, but I suspect it was at least a few days. On occasion, a thin stream of light would come through a crack over my head. It was one of the guard's homes, and there was a door in his floor. I was naked and dirty, and I'd lost my voice from screaming for help." A nervous knot of hysteria formed in my throat as I willed myself not to fall apart. I was here with Holden. Safe. Images of the hole plagued me, and I shot out of my seat, sloshing coffee all over my shirt and down my legs. My body trembled as I tried to set the cup down.

"I've got it, babe. It's okay." Holden ran inside, then returned with a kitchen towel. He knelt, patted my thighs dry, then dabbed at my shirt. He rose slowly. "Are you okay? It didn't seem like it burned you."

"It wasn't very hot," I mumbled. Instead of returning to my seat, I paced the length of the porch. "This is hard," I choked. "It's hard to say it out loud, but I know I have to this afternoon, and you need to know the truth." I chewed on my broken thumbnail, refusing to look at him. If I saw the agony in his expression, I wasn't sure I would be able to force the words out.

"I'm not going anywhere." He settled into his chair again and placed his ankle on the opposite knee.

"After I was allowed out of the hole, Barrett, the guard, moved me to a building with a long row of cells on both sides. He shoved me into one, but the rest were empty. Later that first night Reid was returned to his. He was to the right of me, so we couldn't see each other, but we became friends fast. He gave me some advice and shared with me how to get the things I needed like soap and extra clothes." I gulped, my stomach flip-flopping at an uncomfortable speed. "Reid said the guards would either rape me, or I could offer sex in trade for items." I dared a glance at my boyfriend. "I didn't do it. I fought with everything I had." Tears pricked my eyes. "I fought, Holden." I turned away, unwilling to witness the pity or disgust on his face. Chewing on my bottom lip, I struggled to contain the over-powering shame and guilt that threatened to consume me.

The creak of his chair indicated that he'd stood. "I'm behind you. I want to touch you. Is that okay?"

I nodded but didn't turn around. His muscular arms encircled me, and I nestled my back against his chest. "You're the strongest person I know." He rubbed my arms. "Can you tell me one thing?"

"I'll try."

"Were you ... were you raped?" His voice hovered above a whisper, and fear rolled off of him.

I turned in his arms, tears streaming down my cheeks, and shook my head. "Assaulted, but not raped. I told the guard I was pregnant in hopes of stopping him." My shoulders shook with my sobs, the pain eating me alive. "It's why I lost the baby. The fact that I told them about it. I should have never said anything."

Holden's hold tightened, and he kissed the top of my head. "Oh, babe. I'm so sorry. It wasn't your fault. You did the right thing."

"I tried to protect our child." I fisted his shirt, giving in to the heartbreak. "I mean ... I probably would have miscarried under the circumstances anyway, but I fucking tried to keep our baby safe."

"I believe you, River. I do. You're a fighter, I have no doubt in my mind that you did everything in your power."

I ground my teeth together and screamed. "They fucking took it. *Our* baby, Holden." I pushed him away, needing to walk, unable to handle the confines of his arms. Running my fingers through my hair, I turned from him. "They drugged me and gave me an abortion against my will." My anguished cries ripped through the air as I sank to my knees. "It was *our* child. *Our* choice. No one should ever be forced to give up *or* have a baby, but this ... I swear to God, Holden, if I ever see any of them again, I'll fucking end them or die trying." I placed my hands on the porch rail, sobbing.

With a quick move, Holden pulled me into his lap and sat down on the porch. I wrapped my arms around his neck, allowing him to rock me the way I'd imagined someone doing when I was a little girl.

I sniffled and steadied my breathing. "One of these days, I'm going to hunt them down and make them pay for what they did to me, to Reid, and all the children and other victims."

Holden remained silent but rubbed my back as the memories tumbled out of my mouth. I couldn't imagine how hard it was for him to hear. It would fucking gut me if he'd lived through all of this. I wanted to spare him the pain, but I was barely dealing with my own. I wasn't sure I could manage to protect him from the darkness that threatened to devour me.

Once my tears had subsided, I lifted my head. Holden had kicked out his muscular legs on the steps.

I glanced up at him from beneath my damp eyelashes.

A crease formed between his brows. "Who?" He wiped the moisture from my cheeks. "Who did that to you?" He snarled, frustration thick in his throat.

"Baby," I whispered. "I don't want to tell you."

"You have to. Whatever, whoever it was, we'll deal with it. You and me. Together. Nothing can stop us, River."

I tore my attention away and gathered up some courage. He didn't know what he was saying. Something—some*one* had the power to stop us.

Chapter Seventeen

I nodded, dread consuming me. My tongue felt thick and dry, but I forced the next words out of my mouth.

Before I could speak, Holden placed his fingers against my lips. "Babe, you don't have to say it. I know who is behind it all."

My brows knitted together while I looked at him. "You do? How?"

"Hypnosis. While you were gone, Jace and I revisited an experimental technique. I was desperate to find you, and we'd messed around with it in high school, so I figured it would work. Almost immediately after you were taken, I'd started having nightmares again where everyone was faceless, and a little kid kept begging me not to let them take him."

"Reid?" I whispered.

Pain and desperation flashed across Holden's features. "I didn't know it was a young boy until Jace took me under a few times. When I did see him ..." Holden hung his head, then his gaze met mine again. "It was me. *My* face. The second I saw Reid, I knew in my gut it was him. I'd lost a block of memories from three to five years old, but I didn't realize it was all connected until you were gone."

I frowned, shaking my head. "You never told me that."

"I know. A part of me was so relieved the dreams had stopped ... I was afraid that if I ever talked about them, they would come back. They did, worse than before. I kept telling Jace that my subconscious was trying to tell me where you were. I could feel it deep in my bones."

"Was it telling you where I was?"

Holden threaded his fingers through his hair, his shoulders slumping. "Yeah, but I wasn't connecting all the pieces until after Tim described the property to me, and Jace hypnotized me again. I saw an open field with a big white house. I don't know if it was one of the compounds or not, but it was familiar to me. At the end of the last session, a lady grabbed little me, then she turned and stared right at me. For a second, she was faceless like everyone else, but then it cleared up. That's when I finally saw who she was."

I tipped his chin up, forcing him to look me in the eyes. "Who did you see?"

Holden swallowed, his Adam's apple bobbing in his throat as the color drained from his cheeks. His tongue darted over his lower lip, and he looked away from me, then back again. "It was Mom."

Fuck. I shook my head. "I can't imagine how horrible all of that was, but baby ... it's not your mom."

Holden held his hand up, his palm facing me. "I understand that a lot of people don't believe in hypnosis, but this isn't your normal kind. I knew the second I saw her face that it was her."

I cupped his chin, forcing him to look at me. "Holden Alastair, I love you, but you need to listen to me. I suspect that you really did see who took Reid, but it's not your mom."

Confusion clouded his expression. "I don't understand."

"I thought it was Catherine, too. I was face to face with both women, but it wasn't Catherine." I nervously tucked a strand of hair behind my ear. "Holden, it was your grandmother and aunt."

Holden's forehead creased. "Babe, my grandma passed away

123

years ago, and Mom doesn't have a sister. Not once has she ever mentioned a sibling."

Hell, if I had a sister that insane, I wouldn't mention her either, but I couldn't say that to Holden. Dryness seized my throat and I attempted to swallow, then I continued.

"Your mom has a twin named Kassandra, and your grandmother is very much alive. She faked her death, and now they run the sex ring together. Michelle is FBI, but she also works for them. She's a dirty agent and I'm sure she's not the only one. Her job is to befriend young boys and girls, then take them to the training compound drugged and unconscious. They're stripped, raped, beaten, and starved into submission. I personally saw all of that." I choked on my last words, shoving the agony down again so I could explain more. "I was in the middle of being sold to some wealthy monster overseas so you could never find me. The people who took me know who you are. They know Tim, too," I blurted before I could stop myself.

He blinked excessively, staring at me in shock. I could see the ache and betrayal in his stunned gaze. It saturated him.

"Say something," I whispered.

He rubbed his chin, his frown deepening. "I ... I. Kassandra?"

"Yeah." I touched the area near my eye. "She has a small beauty mark here. Kassandra walks a little bit differently, too. It took me a minute to realize the differences myself. Also, she has a very soft lilt in her accent. Catherine doesn't."

Holden scrubbed his face with his hands. "Does Mom know? Or has she lied to me all of these years?" His voice was strained, tight.

I couldn't miss the alarm in his question. Fire burned up my throat, and I bit my lip, holding the swell of feelings inside. "I don't think she does. If Reid is your brother, then obviously she realized she had another pregnancy. But maybe she was forced to give him up? I'm not sure." I shrugged. "We won't find out until we talk to her."

After meeting Opal and Kassandra, I could understand if Catherine had decided not to have anything to do with her sister. As far as Catherine knew, Opal had died years ago. Even if Catherine didn't have a clue about the sex ring, they were fucking crazy, and she was smart to keep her distance.

I rested my forehead against his. With the new information, I understood the anxiety about asking Catherine if she knew. He was looking for an answer to who he saw. "It sounds like you witnessed something horrible, and your brain blocked it out to protect you." Slipping my hand around his neck, I gave him a gentle squeeze. "It wasn't your mom, though, I promise. It was her twin." For some reason, I felt it necessary to repeat that to him. He had to be in shock. I was when I first saw her.

Holden softly sighed. "When I saw her face, it fucking terrified me. I'd led you straight to her. You'd been taken at my club, lived in my house ... I never, ever meant to put you in danger, River. I swear I didn't know." Tears welled up in his eyes, and my stomach twisted into knots.

I kissed him gently. "Baby, it wasn't your fault. Neither of us had a fucking clue. I sure as hell don't blame you, so you can't blame yourself."

He wiped away the moisture, and his breath stuttered. "As soon as I came out of the hypnosis, I called Pierce immediately. He said after we found you, then we could investigate Catherine, but hypnosis wouldn't hold up in court so they couldn't arrest her unless they discovered evidence during the raid."

Dread bundled inside me, twisting my stomach into knots. "Do you know if the FBI found anything that connected Catherine to all of this?" Even though I hadn't ever seen her at the compound, it didn't mean she was innocent. She could still be involved. Opal said Catherine thought she was dead, but Opal lied as easily as Satan himself. If Catherine was tied to the sex ring, Holden would lose both of his parents. I clutched my chest while I wrestled with the possibilities.

"I don't know. I was hoping to find out today when we talked to Brian. Reid and I should get a DNA test before we meet with everyone, though. I'm not saying shit to mom until we have as many pieces to the puzzle as possible. At this point, we can't trust her."

A heavy silence descended over us. Holden's grip tightened on me, then he stood, taking great care not to drop me. "I need a minute." He set me down, and the moment my feet touched the porch, he gave me a clipped nod, but a storm brewed in his eyes. "I'll be back." He took off down the steps.

I smashed my lips together in order to keep myself from calling after him. I knew this would be hard for him to wrap his brain around, but it fucking broke me to see him this way. His whole world had been a lie. And somehow, Tim was involved as well. I had no idea how, though. Holden's entire fucking family wasn't who he thought they were. My heart shattered into pieces for him. At least I'd known from a young age that my piece of shit mother had betrayed my brother and me. Dan hadn't hidden his true self from me for long, either. I was clear on who they were. But this ... the secrecy and lies ... it had to be devastating for him.

The door creaked open behind me, and I turned to see Reid take a hesitant step out. Worry twisted his handsome features, so closely resembling Holden's that it was eerie. "What happened?"

"I told Holden about Opal and Kassandra. He didn't take things well and took off down the road." I pointed in the direction I last saw him.

Reid gave me a quick kiss on top of the head, then darted down the steps, looked both ways, then turned right and disappeared behind the row of tall bushes that lined Chance's front yard.

Zayne strolled over to me as I grabbed my coffee, my hands trembling. "I can't go after him, River. He ordered me to not leave your side."

"I understand. Maybe Reid can help."

Zayne massaged the back of his neck. "That was a big blow. He's going to take this hard. He already felt like it was his fault you were taken."

"It wasn't. He can't carry that burden."

"But he is. It was his club. He introduced Michelle to you, brought her into his house, and now this. His family was behind it all. It will take him a while to process everything. Not to take anything away from your experience, I don't want to come across as an asshole. I'm just trying to help."

I studied Zayne. He seemed to really care about Holden, and I was glad he was here. "I appreciate it. I'm floundering around, grasping for things to make sense." I took a sip of what was left of my coffee. "Sutton said she wanted me to meet her sister."

Zayne flashed me a sweet smile. "Claire's pretty amazing. She and Vaughn are engaged."

"He seems like a good guy. While Brynn and I were out shopping, he was very kind to us. Took us to a great spot for lunch, too."

Zayne chuckled. "He's a great guy. He and Sutton are super tight, but she freaked on him when Claire admitted she and Vaughn were together. Vaughn—well, all of us—played around, but Vaughn played around a lot more. Sutton wasn't convinced he was what Claire needed. She was so furious with Vaughn, she punched him." A huge smile split Zayne's face, and he laughed. "I watched the whole thing go down. It was epic."

My mouth gaped. "Holy shit. I figured she could hold her own with you guys." I grinned at him, grateful to have something else to talk about.

"Anyway, Vaughn and Claire are good for each other. They have that deep connection like you and Holden do. Claire was a fucking wreck when she moved in with Pierce and Sutton, though. She'd been held in a shipping container for days with a hundred other women. They were about to transport them overseas to be sold when Brian and the FBI found them."

"Wow." Sutton was right. Claire would understand what I'd gone through.

"She's tough but had flashbacks, and it took her a while to recover. Gemma and Mackenzie were super good for her. They're all sexual assault survivors, and they immediately bonded. You will too. Trust Sutton. She's in your corner."

"Gemma and Mackenzie?" I quirked a brow at him.

Zayne's attention traveled across the front of the property, remaining alert while we talked. "Yeah, Gemma is the female lead in August Clover along with her husband, Hendrix Harrington. Mackenzie, Mac for short, is Cade's fiancée. He's the guitarist."

"Wait, wait, wait ... You know Gemma?" I squeaked, completely caught off-guard.

"Yeah, I know all of them. Super good people. They all have stories to share, but that's their place, so I should shut my mouth." Guilt flickered in Zayne's green eyes.

I sank into my seat, a bit perplexed by the revelation. "Sutton said she wanted to introduce me to a few girls who had been through hell and back. I wonder if it's them?"

"I have no idea. Sutton loves helping people. She's an amazing human being." Zayne placed his hand over his chest. "We've all been in each other's lives since high school. They're my family."

"Just like Holden with the guys and Brynn."

Zayne glanced away, but I didn't miss a flicker of pain in his features before he did. Before I could ask him what he was hiding, the guys returned. I stood, wanting to run to Holden, but I held myself back.

He looked at me, pain etched into his features. What if the new information about Holden's family ripped us apart? What if we couldn't move forward and heal? I waited for him to approach, my pulse pounding in my head so hard I thought I might pass out. I set my coffee down on the table between the chairs as he climbed the steps. Then, taking me off-guard, he grabbed the sides of my face and kissed me possessively. "We'll talk more later. I love you."

I melted into him as relief washed over me. "Okay." My answer was muffled against his chest, but I knew he heard me when he rubbed my back.

The door flung open, and Jace appeared. His brown hair was still damp. He tugged on the hem of his black T-shirt. "Man, it sure is good to see you here, River." He stood there looking at each of us, grinning. In a few steps, he gathered me into a bear hug, then he smacked a noisy kiss on my cheek.

I laughed. "You, too."

"Who's hungry?" Jace asked. He pointed at Reid. "I know he is. This dude can eat."

Reid blushed and smiled sheepishly. "It's nice to not have to beg for food."

Even though Reid was trying to make light of it, I knew everyone well enough to recognize that all of our hearts broke a little more for him.

"I could eat." We kept the conversation fun as we filed into Chance's house. Since Holden knew about Opal and Kassandra, I was itching to talk to my bestie. I tugged on his arm. "Can I borrow your phone to call Brynn? I'm missing her something awful. I just need to hear her voice."

The room quieted, and my attention bounced from Jace to Holden. "What is it?" That fucking annoying feeling in my gut returned. I'd known something was off, but I dismissed it after Holden told me about the fire and Tim. "What aren't you telling me?"

Holden rubbed my arm. "Babe, you should sit down."

Jace pulled a bar stool out for me and patted the black cushion. Reid sat on the one next to me. Holden stepped between my legs and took my hands in his. "I know we have a lot to work through, and I was hoping you could get some rest first ..."

"Spit it out, please. You're scaring me." I glanced at Jace for help, but his head was bowed. "Holden?"

Chapter Eighteen

He nodded, tears in his eyes. "She's sick, River. Brynn is sick." He threaded his fingers behind his neck and looked up at the ceiling briefly.

"What?" I gently shoved him backward and jumped off the barstool. "What do you mean, Brynn is sick?" I tossed my hands up in the air and began to pace. "And why haven't you told me? Where is she? Sick how? I had better get some answers before I tear this place to pieces!"

"She's at the Knight's Center in Portland. She ... she has cancer. It's B-Cell Lymphoma and in her stomach right now, babe." Holden lowered his arms, reaching out to me. "I didn't know how to tell you, yet. We got home late last night, and you needed some sleep."

I jabbed my finger into his chest. He winced as I looked up at him. I was furious that he'd waited to talk to me. "You had no fucking right to keep that from me. Brynn is my best friend. The only other one I've had except for Addison, who has barely talked to me since I left Montana." I poked him a few more times. "If you ever pull that shit with me again, I'll—"

"River," Reid said softly, interrupting me from telling my boyfriend off.

I spun around to face him, my fingers clenching and unclenching into tight balls, daggers shooting from my eyes. "What?"

"He did the best he could in a fucked-up situation. Holden was trying to protect you as long as he could." Reid eliminated the space between us and rubbed my arms. "Take a deep breath."

"No," I seethed. "I need to talk to her right *now*." I resisted the urge to stomp my foot like a little girl.

"Not until you calm down. Your friend can't see you like this. It won't help her any." Reid brought me in for a sweet hug.

My shoulders sagged, the anger easing a bit. He was right, and I knew it, but I was still mad at Holden for not telling me immediately. "Okay." I broke our embrace and turned to my boyfriend.

An odd expression, one I couldn't quite place, flickered across his features as he stared at Reid.

"I'm sorry." I placed my palm on Holden's shoulder and gave it a gentle squeeze. "I shouldn't have treated you like that. All you've done is take care of me since I've been back ... since we met, actually."

Holden smoothed my hair. "I didn't expect you to react any differently. It's been really fucking hard. Why don't we FaceTime her?"

"Can we? I really need to see her." Anxiety hummed in my ears. Brynn couldn't have cancer. This wasn't happening.

Holden looked at Reid. "I'm not going to mention you until after we have the DNA results. No offense, but I can't overload Brynn right now."

Reid raised his hands. "I totally understand. I would do the same." Reid's attention shifted to me. "You know where I am if you need anything."

Finally, Jace chimed in. "How about I take Reid to buy some clothes and toiletries while you two talk to Brynn? Tell her I love her." Jace kissed me on the cheek, then disappeared into the other guest bedroom.

131

"It will be good for you to get out, to see Spokane a little." I gave Reid an encouraging glance.

Jace returned, shoving his wallet into the back pocket of his jeans. "Let me know if anything changes," he said to Holden.

"Of course. Thanks for helping Reid." Holden flashed a wistful smile at them.

"Later." Reid kissed me on the top of my head.

"Bye."

"Let's sit on the couch so we can prop the phone up." Holden slipped an arm around my waist and led us across the room.

Wearily, I sank into the seat in the middle. Holden propped his cell up with the stand on his iPhone case, then he tapped the app for FaceTime.

My knee bounced uncontrollably, fear, grief, and anxiety somersaulting inside of me, leaving me a bit dizzy.

Chance's face filled the screen, a huge smile easing across his handsome features as tears welled in his eyes. "You have no idea how happy I am to see you, River." He ran a hand through his blonde hair.

I pursed my lips and cleared my throat. "You, too. I missed all of you more than you'll ever know." I swallowed the lump of emotion down, willing myself not to burst into tears as the hospital room came into view.

"Same here. You're family now," Chance choked out.

"I feel that way about you guys, too." I placed my palm on Holden's knee, my anger dissipating.

"Do you want to see her? She's doing better, but ... I wanted to try to prepare you." Chance blew out a sigh, clearly stressed.

"Please." I bounced my leg up and down, unsure of what to expect.

Chance tapped the screen and flipped the phone's camera, Brynn's pale face showing in the background. "She's sleeping right now. Her parents and Catherine have been with her off and on the last few days. It's good for her, but it wears her out." Chance reversed the image, focusing on him again.

Even though Chance tried to warn me, nothing could have prepared me for the drastic difference—pale skin, prominent cheekbones, and obvious weight loss. My stomach dipped, and an anxious, fluttery feeling descended on me. She didn't look like the beautiful, sunny Brynn I knew. How could everything have taken such a radical turn so damned fast? Trying to mask my disappointment, I chewed on my thumbnail. "She knows I'm back, right?"

"Oh yeah. I woke her up to tell her that. I would have lost my balls if I hadn't." Chance's low chuckle filled the phone line.

I snickered and glanced at Holden. "Yeah, this one almost lost his a few minutes ago when he finally decided to tell me about Brynn."

Chance grimaced. "I told you, man. It wasn't a good idea to wait." Chance shook his head as Holden narrowed his gaze on him, most likely irritated that Chance threw him under the bus.

"What?" I playfully smacked Holden on the arm.

Holden winced and rubbed the spot as though I'd actually hurt him. Suddenly, I had an overwhelming desire to kiss him.

"When can I see her?" I asked the guys.

"Get your fucking ass down here as soon as you can," Brynn said, her voice sleepy and groggy.

Chance moved to the side of her bed and held the phone up, flipping the camera forward-facing.

"Hey, bestie." I sat on my hands to hide the fact that I was trembling. Now that we were up close, I could see how bad the cancer was treating her. Her cheeks were sunken, skin pale, and her coloring was off. She needed a facial and her nails done to help her feel a little more human.

"I'll be there as soon as I can." My chin shook, a rush of grief and shock hitting me all at once. I placed my fingers against my chest, rubbing at the pain gouging my heart.

"Listen, babe. No crying. You're home, and that alone makes me feel so much better. I've got an amazing team, and we're going to kick cancer's ass." She gave me an exhausted smile. "I can't wait to hug you."

I nodded, big fat tears slipping down my face. "What do you need? How can I help?"

"Stop crying, for one." Brynn winked at me.

A laugh escaped me, and I dried my cheeks. "Okay, consider it done. What else?"

"If everything looks good on my next set of scans, then I'll get to bust out of here. I'll be free for a week before I have to come back. The only downside is that I need to stay in Portland just in case. But it wouldn't suck to have my bestie with me. I've missed you so much."

Hope rose inside me, and I looked up at Holden, who had remained quiet. "Babe, can we go down? Please?" It wasn't necessary, but I gave him the best puppy dog eyes I could muster.

Holden leaned in a little. "Chance, should we see if we can get the penthouse again?"

"I thought about it, but I don't want her to get too worn out. With everyone around ..."

The picture shook, then only Brynn's face appeared. "Ignore him. I'm making the decisions here." She grinned. "The penthouse sounds great because you're not prying River and me apart. If I'm tired, I'll sleep. End of discussion." Her attention cut to the side. "Got it, mister?"

I stifled a giggle. Our Brynn was still in there.

Holden chuckled. "I'll call and book everything. If the penthouse isn't available, I'll get three rooms."

Brynn scrunched up her freckled nose. "Bribe them if you have to. Otherwise, all five of us will be sharing a room."

"Six," I said without thinking.

Brynn tilted her head, her attention bouncing between Holden and me. "Oh?"

"Yeah, um, Reid. He was in the cell next to mine. We became really close," I explained quickly.

Her blue eyes flashed with concern, but she wasn't looking at me. She was studying Holden. Brynn recovered quickly. "I can't wait to meet him. I can't imagine what you went through, but if you found someone to help you, then I'm eager to see what he's all about."

I hesitated, waiting for Holden to mention that he and Reid might be related, but he didn't say a word. Honestly, I wouldn't either. At least not until the test results were back.

A nurse popped into view briefly, and Brynn nodded. "I gotta go, but I'll see you soon. Text me all you want." Brynn blew me a kiss. "Love you, babe."

I blew a kiss to her. "Love you, beautiful."

Chance reappeared on the screen. "Let me know when you guys will be here and what the room situation looks like."

"You bet. With us there, you can take a break and get some rest, man. No offense, but you look like shit," Holden said.

Chance frowned. "I know. Her parents are here, but I don't like leaving her alone with them. Catherine has given me some breaks, but I can't make myself leave Brynn for too long. I don't trust her parents."

I squeezed Holden's knee. It was clear that all the guys loved Brynn, but this was different. Chance had it bad for my bestie.

"We won't be able to peel the girls apart, so take advantage of the help."

"I will. Can't wait to see you guys. And River?"

"Yeah?"

"Thanks for making Brynn's day. She's been a fucking wreck without you. We all have, actually." His cheeks flamed red from the admission as he scratched the back of his neck. "You know we all love you, right? Not just that asshole beside you."

I clutched the hem of my coffee-stained T-shirt and nodded.

"Don't ever doubt that, okay?" Chance gave me a sweet smile.

I opened my mouth and tried to speak, but the words wouldn't come out. I blinked rapidly to keep the tears away and cleared my throat. "I love you all, too."

"I hate to cut it short, but I need to see what's going on with our girl. I'll catch you guys later."

135

After Chance ended the call, I sat in silence, my wheels turning a million miles an hour. Slowly, I looked at Holden. "Is she going to die?" I pinched the bridge of my nose, holding back the onslaught of tears that were trying to escape.

Holden shook his head adamantly. "No. Not again."

"Again?" *What the fuck?*

A tight line cut across his forehead as he observed me. "The first time Brynn had chemo ... she had a bad reaction. Turns out she was allergic to the treatment. She flatlined." Pain flashed across his features, and his jaw clenched as he obviously struggled to hold it together.

Fear dug its claws into me. I blinked several times, breathing in, hoping to fill my lungs with much-needed air. Brynn wasn't allowed to die.

Slowly, I rose from my seat and knelt in front of Holden. I laid my head on his lap and wrapped my arms around his waist, giving into the heartbreak. I muffled my cries against his stomach. Holden smoothed my hair as we grieved over Brynn's diagnosis together.

"I love you, River."

I sat up, our gazes locking. His eyes were rimmed red, and mine burned. "I love you, too."

He leaned forward, pressing a gentle kiss against my mouth. "I need to ask you something, and please be honest with me."

Frowning, I nodded. From his tense posture, this wasn't going to be good. "Yeah, of course. What is it?"

He looked away, then back again, his expression blazing with determination. "Are you in love with Reid?"

Chapter Nineteen

I stared at him in disbelief, attempting to articulate my response, but I was too stunned. Licking my lips, I shook my head. "No, Holden. You're the only guy I'm in love with."

Holden's shoulders visibly relaxed. "I needed to make sure."

Still puzzled, I needed to understand where this was coming from. "Why would you ask me that?"

Holden collapsed back on the couch. "The way you two look at each other, and you're comfortable in his arms."

"I am comfortable with him."

A flush crept across my cheeks. This wasn't good. At all. Reid and I had been in cells and assaulted. He kept me sane, and I gave him hope. But I wasn't *in* love with him.

Holden rubbed his face, and I suspected our conversation spiked his insecurity.

"I'll try to explain it to you, but I'm not sure I can. Reid and I went through a trauma together. No one else was with us the nights we talked until the sun came up. The secrets he shared with me, how he'd been beaten and raped over and over again. I promised that, if we managed to escape, he would have a family here. Reid is *my* family, and I'm his. He was a light when I was in a horribly dark place. All of this was said before I ever saw him. We had no idea what the other one looked like." I rose, needing to pace and work out my anxiety. "When he found out I was pregnant, he fucked a guard to get me a blueberry muffin because I hadn't eaten for a few days. That was our life there. That was *his* life, Holden. Since he was a little kid. Giving sex in exchange for basic shit we take for granted."

Holden blanched, and he rubbed his clean-shaven jaw. "That's screwed up."

"I was lucky. Even though I lost the baby, he or she saved me in more ways than I even understand. I was never raped like Reid or the hundred other victims. And ... and when I was assaulted, I fought like hell until I was held down, then the only person I thought of was you." My pulse thumped wildly against my wrist with my omission. If Holden was concerned about us, I couldn't fuel the worry with my confession about Barrett.

Holden stood, anger evident in his expression. "When I meet that motherfucker, he *will* pay for touching you." His tone was laced with venom, and I wondered if he would kill someone for me. I had no doubt in my mind that I would end a life to protect him.

Heat coursed through me with his possessiveness. I pushed up on my tiptoes and kissed him. "I call dibs. I have plans for the son of a bitch."

Holden brushed the hair off my forehead. "I didn't mean to upset you concerning Reid. Guys just know this shit. Babe, I think he's in love with you."

"I can't right now, Holden. If he is, he's going to have to deal with it. I'm at maximum capacity, and unable to give anyone any more than I already am. You're my first and only love. I would die for you. I'll go through hell for you. Only *you*." Standing so close to my boyfriend sparked a flame in my lower belly. Inside, I shook with anticipation, and my body hummed with longing. I wanted Holden's skin against mine, his mouth all over me, replacing the stench of the memories with Barrett.

His lips shadowed mine, inhaling my desperation and desire.

"Can I touch you?"

He didn't need to ask. I moved his hand beneath the T-shirt and my pajama tank. He gently cupped my breast. "I need you." I arched into him. "Please."

Holden released me, then scooped me into his powerful arms and carried me to the bedroom. He placed me on the bed, then closed and locked the door. His erection tented his basketball shorts.

"I don't want to trigger you, babe. Tell me to stop anytime."

I sat up and tugged off his shirt, then my tank. The cool air brushed across my nipples. I shed my shorts and thong, tossing them on the floor.

His gaze raked up and down my body, love and lust evident in his expression.

"Take off your clothes," I said, parting my legs for him. I'd be damned if Holden thought he was losing me, and the fastest way to prove it was to show him how much I wanted him. Needed him.

Holden stepped out of his shorts and boxer briefs, his thick cock pressing against his stomach. As he pulled his shirt over his head, I moaned at his perfection. A dark smattering of hair covered his chest and trailed down his abs. He wrapped his long fingers around his shaft, a bead of precum leaking from the tip. My tongue darted across my lip.

Holden crawled onto the bed next to me. He rolled to his side and propped up on his elbow. "You're so beautiful."

I touched his jaw, his skin warm and smooth beneath my fingertips. "You don't have to ask, just touch me. I'm all yours." Mentally, I promised to focus on him in hopes it would stop any flashbacks.

"Okay, but if—"

I placed my fingers against his mouth. "Stop talking." I leaned up and kissed him, then directed his hand between my thighs. A gasp escaped me as he gently spread me apart. His thumb grazed my clit, massaging it in slow circles.

"Get comfortable, babe, and let me take care of you."

I sank into the pillows, then Holden took my nipple between his teeth. I fisted his dark hair and my back arched off the bed.

Barrett's ugly mug flickered in and out of my vision, and I mentally punched him in the nose. That bastard wouldn't come between Holden and me. Focusing on Holden, I attempted to relax as he eased a finger inside me. I froze as flashes of Barrett's assault rippled through me.

He gently kissed me, then peered deep into my eyes, his expression determined and sincere. "We're moving too fast, babe." He removed his hand from my core, and I clenched my teeth.

"Don't stop. I need to push through this. Please." I gripped his arm, my plea sounding desperate, needy. I was. I wanted Holden to wash away the memories that haunted me.

"I can't rush you. I love you. If you fell apart because we were together too soon after everything you've gone through, I wouldn't be able to live with myself. We can take our time. You're more important to me than the sex."

"I don't deserve you," I whispered, struggling to breathe above the panic running rampant inside me. If Holden knew that Barret had made me come, he wouldn't want me anymore. I'd betrayed him. I'd betrayed myself. He would never forgive me. Intense pressure settled on my chest, and I swallowed painfully over the anguished lump in my throat.

"Whatever happened, River, you don't ever have to talk about it. We'll be okay. I promise."

I curled into a ball and hid my face. Agony ripped through me, threatening to shatter me beyond repair. Holden held me as I shook. Dan, my asshole guardian, had been child's play compared to Barrett and the compound. I'd used my anger to protect me, shield me from losing my mind. I'd built steel walls around my heart, but Holden held the key to breaking through them. If the floodgates opened, I wasn't sure I could survive the pain.

***

Once Holden booked the penthouse and our flight to Portland for that evening, we made sandwiches for lunch. Jace and Reid returned shortly after, carrying bags from Nordstrom and Target. I couldn't help but smile at the contrast between the stores.

Jace had also picked up a few things for me, which was super sweet. Holden must have called the doctor because there was a Walgreens bag with my new birth control pills. Excusing myself, I hightailed it out of the kitchen and into the master bathroom. As soon as I was behind closed doors, I popped the first pill immediately. I loved Holden, but another pregnancy couldn't be on the table at the moment. Within minutes, I'd brushed my teeth, applied deodorant, and brushed my hair. Jace had also chosen a package of thongs, a few T-shirts, polo shirts, three pairs of designer jeans, socks, and a new pair of Nikes. Brynn had shopping competition. He was amazing.

Feeling human, I waltzed out of the bedroom with purpose. Holden released a low whistle, making me giggle. The soft turquoise top and light wash skinny jeans fit perfectly. Reid had changed clothes as well, now sporting a navy polo shirt and jean shorts. I swallowed hard. He would never know how much it startled me when I looked at him. It was like Holden was standing in front of a mirror.

Jace and Reid turned, and Jace's face lit up. "Damn, I'm good." He attempted to high-five Reid, but Reid stared at him with a blank expression, confused about what he was supposed to do.

"It's all good, man. Just leave me hanging like that." Jace folded his arms across his chest, feigning hurt feelings.

Our laughter filled the air, then I explained to Reid how a high five worked. If I pretended hard enough, I could imagine that he was an exchange student who didn't know much about our culture. It was easier to teach him and not sink into a dark mood. After years of being a sex slave, Reid might be a master in the bedroom, but he was naïve about how the rest of the world worked.

"Oh, one more thing." Jace slid an iPhone box to me. "Brand new and all yours."

I clutched it to my chest. "Thank you for picking it up for me."

"I got one, too." Reid held his cell, frowning at it. "I've seen these, but I have no idea what to do with it."

"I'll help set both of them up," Holden offered.

"Thanks, babe." I pushed up on my tiptoes and kissed him.

I snuggled up to Holden, finding comfort in the warmth of his body. Peeking up at him, I gave him a soft smile as my heart pitter-pattered against my chest. I loved Holden more than anything or anyone. Even though I was disappointed that he'd stopped in the bedroom, the images of Barrett had hammered my brain almost immediately. I probably would have full-on freaked out if we'd continued. Normally, my style was to push through the problem, but my decisions also affected Holden, and I couldn't put him through that. It wasn't fair to him.

Once Jace and Reid grabbed a bite to eat, we piled into Zayne's Mercedes and headed downtown for the DNA test. It was over in a few minutes, and I was grateful that Holden paid a rush fee for the results. Hopefully, we would know if Holden and Reid were brothers in a few hours.

Jace climbed into the front passenger seat, and Reid, Holden, and I sat in the back. I sat between the guys and nudged Reid in the side with my elbow. He gave me a lopsided grin in return. Sometimes I startled a little when I looked at him, the similarities between him and Holden were eerie. If Holden didn't have a few inches on Reid in height, I was pretty sure I would get them confused more than I already did. I couldn't wait to see Brynn's reaction. I could almost hear her now. *"Oh, double the trouble. I'll take the middle please. Twice the pleasure."* I snickered out loud.

"What are you laughing about?" Holden asked, curiosity flickering in his eyes.

"I was wondering what Brynn will say when she sees you and Reid." I arched a brow, implying something steamy.

Holden chuckled. "Guess we'll find out soon." He kissed my

cheek, then shot a quizzical look at Reid. I wondered if he was marking his territory, so to speak. I touched my neck, remembering the diamond necklace that I'd worn at the club. It was Holden's warning to all the men that I was untouchable. I cringed as I recalled Opal and Kassandra's words about how women trusted women. I doubted it had crossed Holden's mind ... that he'd protected me from Tim and other men, but not the women.

I glanced at Reid. "We should have some fun and make a bet on the DNA results."

Reid's forehead creased. "I don't have any money."

"And what are we going to bet against?" Jace asked. "I mean, I'm almost certain they're related. But the big question is how. Is he a brother or cousin?"

"So, Kassandra would be his mom if they were cousins." I grimaced. "Shit. No. If she's his mother, we're going to ignore it and claim you're brothers."

"No kidding," Holden muttered. "Tim, my father, is a piece of shit, but I don't think he's anything like Kassandra," he said to Reid.

Reid's expression morphed from happy to disgusted. "I hope we get some answers soon. I never cared before, but if we are ..." Reid leaned forward, his intense gaze connecting with Holden's. "But if you're my brother, it means that I have family. That's all I'm interested in."

"You have family anyway." I reached for Reid's hand and gave it a gentle squeeze. He looked at me, his dark eyes filling with adoration.

"I know," he whispered, his voice gruff and haunted.

Butterflies fluttered in the pit of my stomach. The warmth of Reid's palm spread up my arm, sending tingles through my body. I pulled away and smiled before I gave Holden my attention. *What the hell had just happened? Why had I liked his touch?* Oh, God. I was confused as hell. I hadn't considered Reid more than a friend, but something had transpired between us—in front of Holden. I chewed on my bottom lip, worry blossoming in my chest. I needed Brynn. Badly. Maybe she could explain things to me.

Chapter Twenty

Twenty minutes later, Zayne stopped at an iron gate. I looked around the property as he pulled into the driveway and parked the car.

"I know today will be intense, but if you think about it, take a look at the details of the house. I would love to build a log home for us." Hope flickered across his handsome face.

My brows shot up. "Really?" He had no idea how much I loved the idea. In Montana, there were a lot of log homes, but not many in Spokane.

"Yeah. If you want, I'll take you to the lake property after we visit Brynn."

"Yes! I would love to see it."

I filed out of the car behind Holden, then threw my arms around his neck. "I love you. We could live in a tent for all I care. The important thing is having you next to me."

Holden brought me closer, then gave me a sweet kiss. "Love you, too." He smoothed my hair and sighed. "Are you ready to talk to Brian?"

"No, but I don't have a choice. Plus, I need to know if Kassandra and Opal are in custody. I've only been home twenty-four hours, but in some ways it seems longer."

"I don't want to overload you. Regardless of how you feel, your emotions and brain are still processing. It's going to take time. One minute you'll think you're okay, the next ..." Holden massaged the back of his neck with his free hand. "As far as Opal and Kassandra, they had better be in custody. If so, I'd like to pay them a visit," Holden said between clenched teeth. He slid his arm around my waist as we followed Zayne up the sidewalk and to the front door.

Zayne waltzed in as though he owned the place, and I grinned. It felt good to laugh. The last three weeks had been full of pain and sheer terror. At times I wondered if I would ever experience happiness again. But here I was.

Nearly tripping over my feet, I gasped as we entered the living room. The floors were stunning, with red and blonde woven into the wood. The matching ceiling accentuated the dark rafters. Normally I didn't like the red, but it was softer with the mix. I gripped Holden's muscular bicep and beamed up at him. "It's beautiful."

Holden rubbed my back as we entered the living room. "So are you. I love seeing your face light up. It makes me happy." Pierce, Sutton, and Brian stood in the middle of the space, talking quietly.

"Boss," Zayne said as we neared the small group.

"Hey, everyone. It's good to see you all." Pierce nodded at us.

Sutton didn't hesitate as she gave me a big hug. "How are you doing?" Concern danced across her beautiful features. "Were you able to get any sleep?"

"A little bit."

"Hi, Reid." Sutton patted him on his arm. "It's nice to see you as well."

"Likewise." Reid shoved his hands into his pockets, suddenly appearing shy.

Jace greeted everyone, then we all sat next to each other on the black couch, the soft leather dipping beneath our weight. Zayne stood behind Sutton, who sat in the matching recliner across from us. Brian sat in the additional wingback chair with Pierce behind him. Pierce crossed his arms over his massive chest and rocked back and forth on his heels. I hadn't spent much time with Pierce, but I was pretty sure something was up—something big.

Brian leaned forward and looked at Reid and me. "How are you two holding up? I can't imagine what this has been like for you."

"I'm just grateful we're home." I glanced at Reid, and he nodded in agreement.

"Thank you for all the help," Reid added.

"I'm glad it turned out the way it did, and everyone can start to adjust to their life of freedom." Brian looked at Holden. "Have you had time to tell her about your hypnosis and mom, yet?"

Holden cleared his throat. "We talked about it this morning. Apparently, it wasn't my mom I saw, it was her twin."

Brian nodded. "Your aunt's name is Kassandra Winfield. It took some digging, but we were finally able to verify her identity."

"She's not my aunt. I won't ever claim to be related to a monster." Holden's fury was almost tangible as it seeped from his pores.

I dug my nails into Holden's muscular leg, terrified to ask the next question, but I needed answers. We all did. "Does this mean she's in custody?"

Brian leaned back in his seat, his expression morphing from business to compassion. As I scanned left, right, then did another sweep, I lost my breath. Everyone was on edge. This wasn't good. At all.

"Kassandra and Opal fled and have basically disappeared. We're searching for them, but it's best if you and Reid lay low until we are able to locate and arrest them. We think we have a lead on Michelle, so hopefully we will be closing in on her soon."

Tears prickled my eyes. My knees quaked, and nausea bubbled in my belly. "They know about Holden. Where he lives, his job ... Becky-Michelle, too." I slapped my hand over my mouth, muffling the cry that fought to be released. "Michelle is crazy. She fed the FBI information to keep you off her trail. She hated me before, but now ..." Wide-eyed, my focus landed on my boyfriend.

Holden slipped his arm around my shoulders. "Babe, we're keeping security. Also, we can still see Brynn in Portland. We'll stay tucked away at the hotel."

I nodded, tears streaming down my cheeks. My pulse kicked up a notch as I glanced at Reid. He was stone-still. If I hadn't focused, I'm not sure if I would have realized he was even breathing. I squeezed his arm. "We're safe."

Reid's attention bounced from Holden to me, and I hoped I wouldn't burn in Hell for lying to him. Nothing about this seemed safe.

"I think since Reid is also involved, two bodyguards would work better," Pierce said. "Especially while you're in Portland."

"Yes, please," I blurted before Holden had a chance to respond.

"Is Vaughn available? River and Brynn already know him. I want them to be as comfortable as possible," Holden explained.

"I need to check the schedule, but I want to say yes," Sutton added. She retrieved her phone from the end table and tapped the screen. "He just finished an assignment. When are you going to Portland?" she asked Holden.

"Our flight is booked for seven tonight."

"Cancel the flights and keep your money. I'll fly you all down," Pierce said. "You don't want to share a small space with a bunch of strangers when Brynn's immune system is already compromised. If you even have a cold, you won't be able to see her."

Fuck. I hadn't thought of that.

"Let me pay you, then," Holden said to Pierce.

Pierce waved him off. "I don't want or need your money, keep it. This is a friend helping friends."

"Thank you," I said, my voice cracking with emotion. "I haven't been able to see Brynn yet, and ..."

Jace leaned forward and peered around Reid at me. "She's ready to see you, too."

I rubbed my arms, fighting off a chill caused by my nerves and not the temperature. "Have you found any evidence concerning Catherine? What about Tim?"

"We haven't found anything connecting Catherine to Opal, Kassandra, or the sex ring. As far as Tim, from the tracker and recording device that was planted in his car, we learned that he tried to negotiate to bring you home. He knows the kidnapper, which makes sense now that we understand that Opal and Kassandra are related to Catherine. What we don't know is which one he was speaking with. We never heard the other person during his phone calls."

"Do you have enough evidence to arrest him? I realize the recordings aren't admissible, but what about connecting him to burning my club to the ground?" Holden asked.

Brian's intense gaze rested on us. "We haven't heard anything from Tim at all. The tracker showed that he was in Portland and at the Knight Center where your friend Brynn is being treated. Do you happen to know anything about that? Did he see her?"

Holden didn't miss a beat, but his body stiffened ever so slightly against mine. "I left a voicemail for him and mentioned that she was sick. He's known her since she was a little girl, so I figured someone should tell him. He visited her."

Brian's attention held steady as he continued. "Did Brynn mention how the visit went, or did you see him when he was there? I know you and your friends have been flying back and forth between Spokane and Portland."

"Yeah, I saw him. He told me where the property was located, then I contacted Pierce about the information." Holden's forehead creased in confusion. "I don't understand what you're getting at. You already know I saw and talked to him. Pierce updated you."

Brian shifted in his seat and propped his elbow up on the arm of the chair. "You were the last one to see him."

I gawked at Brian. "Are you implying that Holden did something to his own father?"

"No, I'm not. All I'm saying is that we can't find Tim anywhere.

He hasn't used his car, made any calls, or checked into hotels. He's disappeared," Brian explained.

"That was the last time I saw him ... at the hospital after he visited Brynn. I've been with Pierce or a bodyguard ever since, so they can verify my whereabouts. I'm not particularly happy with your line of questioning, but I have nothing to hide. I've been up front about everything, including Michelle."

"I agree. You've been fantastic. If you hear anything from him, would you let me know?" Brian asked. "We're simply trying to track him down."

What in the hell was going on? Had something happened to Tim, and if so, was Holden involved?

Conversation and questions continued over the next few hours as I shared my experience with Brian. I nearly cheered when he explained that Barrett and several other guards had been arrested. Holden's arm tightened around me with the mention of the guards. I wondered if he was recalling our chat about Reid trading sex for essentials. Several of the victims at the compound were willing to testify against them, which was great news. It should have made me happy to know that at least Barrett couldn't touch me again, but I needed more. I needed Opal and Kassandra. I needed blood, and I was okay having it on my hands.

Surprisingly, I was relieved when Brian said they hadn't found any evidence that connected Catherine with the sex ring. I hoped they were right. Holden deserved at least one good parent.

Once we were finished at Pierce and Sutton's, Zayne drove us back to Chance's place to pack. I didn't have many belongings, so it was easy to toss things into a duffle with Holden's items. I couldn't wait to see Brynn—to hug her. Hopefully, the guys would give us some time alone over the next week, so we could talk. If she was up for it, I desperately needed her help.

***

Pierce's plane touched down a little after four in the afternoon. It had been much faster than going through TSA and trying to find a seat next to Holden on the puddle jumper. At least I was able to sit near Reid and Holden, like on the flight to Washington from California. Reid seemed calmer this time as well.

A guy named Jeffrey, who worked for Pierce, met us with two company Mercedes. Vaughn would drive one, and Zayne would drive the other. I followed Holden and Zayne while Jace and Reid climbed into Vaughn's car. I bet Brynn would be tickled silly to have so much eye candy. Hell, I wasn't sad about it either. Between Holden, Reid, Jace, Chance, Zayne, and Vaughn, my hormones were returning to normal at times. Even with the hell I'd gone through, I was still curious what it would be like to have them in the playroom. Holden's cell rang, interrupting my fantasy.

"This is Holden." Holden was silent, then impatience etched his mouth. "What exactly does that mean?" Holden glanced at me and mouthed 'test is in.' "I see. Thank you very much for rushing the results. I appreciate it." Holden slowly lowered the phone to his lap. He stared at me, waves of dense fury rolling off him and filling the small space of the car.

"Babe?" I wanted to touch him, but I hadn't ever seen Holden so furious.

"Reid ... the test ..." He shook his head and rubbed his clean-shaven chin.

I held my breath, willing myself to allow Holden to finish in his own time, even though I mentally pleaded for him to hurry up.

"Reid is my brother." Holden clenched his jaw, then looked out the window. "Mom better have a damned good explanation for keeping this secret from me." He ground his teeth together. "But it's deeper than that." His attention landed on me again. "Mallory and Hannah had to have known, which means they lied to me my entire life as well."

Fuck. I'd forgotten about his sisters. How had all of this happened? "Are you sure they knew?"

"Yeah. Reid is younger than both of them, so it's not like Mom could have gotten pregnant, then disappeared for nine months. Tim would have gotten suspicious, and from what I remember, Tim and Mom were close back then, but I was little, so I'm not sure."

"We should hear what Catherine has to say, Holden. It could explain so much. Can you try to keep an open mind until we have time to ask her?"

"I'll try. She's in Portland with Brynn, so the minute she sees Reid ... my brother. Goddammit." He rubbed his temples and released a heavy sigh. "I have a *brother*, River."

Everything inside of me wanted to unbuckle my seatbelt and slide over to Holden, but I didn't want to risk getting pulled over. I would feel bad if Zayne got a ticket. "When are you going to tell Reid?"

"I'll wait until we're face-to-face. I know we all suspected it, but it's different now that it's confirmed."

"I get it. We can't talk ourselves out of it now that there's proof that he's your sibling."

Holden looked out the window, remaining silent for a few minutes. "Zayne, I think we should all go to the hotel first. You can take River to see Brynn. That way if my mom is at the hospital, she won't see Reid before we're ready to talk to her."

"You got it," Zayne replied.

✳✳✳

An hour later, Zayne escorted me down the hall to Brynn's room. He knocked on the door, and Chance opened it, grinning at us. "River!" Chance snatched me off the ground and swung me around. He planted a kiss on the side of my head, then set me down.

"He's such a flirt," Brynn said, laughing.

I laughed and patted Chance on the chest. "It's so good to see you." Tears pricked my eyes, and Chance warmly embraced me.

"You're back. I never doubted that you would be," he said softly.

I nodded against him, unable to talk around the lump in my throat. There were times I thought I would never see my friends again, much less hug them.

Chance released me and smiled. "I'll be outside if you need anything." He winked at me before he slipped out of the room and closed the door behind him.

I glanced at Brynn. My breath halted in my lungs. My vision blurred and my pulse pounded in my ears. She wasn't allowed to die. I'd fucking lost enough, and I refused to lose her, too.

"Hey." I hadn't ever been in a hospital other than when I broke my leg and certainly not to spend time with someone I loved. Even though she was my best friend, my awkwardness suffocated me. What should I say? Did I pretend that nothing was wrong? Thank God, I'd seen her on FaceTime yesterday or I would have been shocked by her appearance. Although her coloring was better today, and she had the familiar sparkle in her green eyes, I could tell she wasn't feeling well after the chemo. She still looked pale, and the ugly white and blue hospital gown didn't help matters either.

"Hey yourself." She patted the side of the bed, all smiles.

I stood rooted to my spot while I stared at my best friend. "Zayne is parked in the hall." I approached her slowly. I blinked back tears as I peered into her concerned gaze. As hard as I was trying to be strong for her, I suspected I was about to lose my shit. Brynn was the only person I'd ever known with cancer. I was out of my element.

Moisture welled in Brynn's eyes. "Good." She sniffled. "I wasn't sure I would ever see you again." Her voice cracked with emotion, and I struggled to hold my relief at seeing her in person in check.

I hadn't visited with the intention of turning on the waterworks, but I wasn't sure I could control it, either. Finally breaking out of my daze, I sat on the edge of the bed. Before I was even settled, Brynn threw her arms around me.

"Don't you ever leave me again." Brynn tightly squeezed me. "You scared the shit out of me. Thank God for Pierce and Sutton. Zayne reached out to them within minutes of realizing something awful had happened." Brynn's shoulders shook, her fingers digging into my back, clinging to me.

"I've missed you so fucking bad," I whispered against her red hair. "Thoughts of you and Holden encouraged me to hang on, gave me hope. I knew deep down that you guys wouldn't ever stop searching for me." Swallowing painfully over the anguished lump in my throat, I blew out a soft sigh.

After a few minutes, we released each other, then Brynn scooted over and rolled onto her side. "Come on."

"Will I fit?" I asked, assessing the small space on the bed next to her.

"Of course you will. We wear each other's clothes, remember?"

I crawled in and leaned my head against my arm. I offered her a shaky smile. "I don't like seeing you here." A sharp ache pierced my chest. "You can't die on me, Brynn," I whispered.

"Babe, I'm not going anywhere. I cheated death once, and I'll do it again. You're stuck with me. Besides, I kissed your boyfriend while you were gone." Brynn gave me her best puppy dog eyes.

"You what?" Jealousy reared its ugly head before I had time to process that she was toying with me. I hoped.

"I asked Holden if you would mind. We thought ... it was right before I died. I could feel something was off. I kissed all of our guys goodbye."

My forehead creased in confusion. "Why are you telling me this?" I didn't understand what the point was.

Brynn placed her hand on my shoulder. "Because nothing about the kiss was what it used to be. He loves me, they all do, and I know that. But Holden was different. It was a potential goodbye, no attraction, no confusion. He was crystal clear. River: you own him. He loves you so much. If I had any doubts about his feelings for you, I don't anymore."

I averted my attention, considering what she said. "Under the circumstances, I won't beat your ass, but don't let it happen again. Since you're not going to die, there's no reason to kiss my boyfriend."

Brynn erupted into a fit of giggles. "I love you, River Collins. You're a badass bitch, and I'm so fucking happy you're back."

I cracked a grin. "I'm not really mad at you. If I'd been in your position, I would have done the same." My pulse slowed, realizing that what I said was true. I'd been kidnapped, assaulted, and returned. I didn't have time to be angry when Brynn was fighting for her life, and I was fighting for my sanity.

"If you'd been here, I would have kissed you as well." Brynn winked at me, then her expression faltered. She placed her warm palm against my cheek.

"Maybe I would have kissed you back, but I guess you'll never know, huh?" I laughed softly. I was comfortable enough with Brynn to tease her. She'd made it clear that she had feelings for me the same day she told me about her father and Tim's affair. As flattered as I was, I think Brynn's heart was misdirected.

"It's stupid." Brynn smoothed a stray hair from my face. "I just want to look at you for a little while. Maybe my brain will accept that you're home and ... safe." The last word fell off her lips, and I winced. "You are safe, right?"

I lifted my shoulder in a half shrug. "I don't think so, but I won't ever ditch a bodyguard again. Do you know how much I hated myself for running from Zayne? That one decision changed my entire life, Brynn." I slammed my eyes closed for a moment.

"Babe, you can't do that. It would have simply been a different time or day from what we learned about Laura, the investor at Holden's club. She scouted 4 Play for victims. When Holden learned that, he was fucking beside himself. It's been hard on him, but when he saw the pregnancy test ..." She searched me for a reaction.

Grief consumed me as tears streamed down my face. "I'm not pregnant any longer."

"Oh, babe. I'm so sorry. Do you need to talk about it?" She leaned over and kissed my forehead, then took my hand in hers.

"They drugged me, then forced me to have an abortion. I had no idea until I woke up after the procedure." I hiccupped, then my shoulders shook with my sobs.

Brynn wrapped her arms around me and held me while I fell apart again. She patiently waited for me to calm down, then she reached behind her for a few tissues. "Here." She gave one to me, then dabbed her own eyes.

"Thanks." I wiped my cheeks, then laid my head back down. "Even though I'm here with you, I feel like I'm still trapped in the cell."

Agony twisted Brynn's features, and I rubbed her arm, attempting to soothe her. It was bad enough she was fighting cancer, but to hear my horror on top of it was enough to send anyone running. "The cell wasn't that bad compared to everything else."

Brynn ground her molars together, but she remained quiet.

"I ... I need to tell you something, but I'm scared."

Brynn's brows knitted together. "There's never any judgement, River. If you need to tell me something, you're safe with me. I won't even tell Holden if you don't want me to."

I furiously shook my head. "You can't say anything to him or anyone else." I gulped, realizing that I would eventually tell Holden, but not right now. Brynn and Holden had grown up together, fucked, and shared secrets for years. She couldn't tell him before I did. "Promise me. Swear to me you won't tell another soul no matter what."

Chapter Twenty-One

"River, I realize how tight the guys and I are, but you're my best friend, and I would never, ever betray your trust. I promise."

I focused on the white wall behind her, attempting to find enough courage to tell her. "First, you should know I wasn't raped. I told the guard I was pregnant, and he stopped."

Brynn's gaze filled with compassion and understanding. "That's how they found out about the baby?"

"Yeah." I wiped the moisture from my eyelashes. "But ..." I blew out a big breath, my shoulders tensing.

"Take your time." Brynn rubbed my arm.

If I was going to tell her, I needed to tell her quickly, so I didn't back out. "Barrett assaulted me, but he made me ..."

I bit my lip, shame washing over me as I prepared my next words. "He made me come. I hate myself for it, and I can't tell Holden. I'm afraid he'll leave me." I slapped a hand over my mouth, muffling my cry, finally releasing the pain I'd shoved into a dark corner of my soul.

Brynn pulled me to her and smoothed my hair. "He wouldn't ever hold that against you, River. Never."

I peered up at her. "How do you know?"

"First, you have to forgive yourself. It was a normal bodily response to stimulation. That's all. It didn't mean you cheated on Holden or liked being assaulted. That's not what happened. You were terrified and forced against your will. I'm guessing that this son of a bitch knew exactly what he was doing." She paused. "He was fucking with your head. It's common between an abuser and their victim."

Reid's reminder returned to me. "Someone told me it was their way of manipulating and controlling us."

"Yeah, it's a sick, psychological game. Don't buy into it. You did *nothing* wrong."

"How do you know?" I shifted on the bed, not breaking eye contact with her. I might be fucked up right now, but there was something deeper going on with Brynn. I could sense it.

Brynn tucked her hair behind her ear. "We'll save that for another day. All you need to think about is healing. Holden loves you so much, River. I've never seen him so crazy about anyone—ever. If you decide to tell him what happened, he'll scour the earth looking for that man."

"He won't have to. Barrett is in custody."

Brynn's gaze narrowed. "That could be good and bad. Holden has the means to bribe people when necessary. I don't think Barrett's safe." She shrugged. "Meh, you win some you lose some." Her tone was nonchalant as she gave me a knowing look.

"I miss Holden. I want to be with him so much, Brynn. We tried, but I freaked out." I sank my teeth into my lower lip.

"You dealt with Dan, so do the same thing now. Try to compartmentalize, babe. The guard isn't any different."

I understood what she was saying, but I wasn't sure how to do it again. I'd had years of practice with Dan. This was fresh and raw in my mind.

"I have a feeling that things will move forward after you talk to Holden. Even though I know in my heart he won't see you any differently, you need to hear him say it yourself." She smiled at me, sadness in her features. "And when he tells you it's not your fault and to not ever blame yourself again, I imagine it will free you. You'll be able to reconnect with Holden again."

I stared at her, searching for any sign that she was trying to simply make me feel better. "I hope so. I love him so much. I'm scared things won't go back to the way they were."

"He knows how you feel about him. Holden's been through a lot of shit, babe. He can handle this. He's strong."

"Okay. I'll talk to him." I fidgeted with the hem of my shirt, unease blooming to life in my belly.

"Is there anything else you need to tell me?"

I shook my head no. "Not now. The rest are details of living in a dark hole for days beneath Barrett's house, then witnessing young kids being sexually abused and beaten. I'm not ready to talk about it, yet." I pursed my lips together, willing myself not to say Reid's name.

"Jesus. I can't imagine."

"I couldn't either, but I have to try to move on the best I can until they catch Opal and Kassandra." Realizing my slip, I quickly explained as much as I could. Holden had to tell her the rest. "They're the two women behind the sex ring."

Brynn gasped, her mouth moving up and down, but no words were coming out. "Women?" she squeaked.

"It's fucked up. But I'll save that for another day. I want to spend time with everyone without a ton of dark shit hanging over our heads." Plus, I realized once she saw Reid, there would be a lot more conversation. "How are you feeling? Are you tired?" I asked, changing the subject.

"No. I'm bored." Her soft laugh filled the area. "I'm off the chemo for a bit, so it should help."

I took her hand in mine. "I'm so sorry you're going through this."

"Don't." Her tone was firm and left zero room for negotiation. "I'm getting better. You're home, and I'm ready to have some fun with everyone. I don't want to talk about my treatment, or anything shitty. Hell, I think having as many orgasms as possible this week will help." A playful smile eased across her features.

"Well, you'll definitely have eye candy. Not only is Zayne with us but so is Vaughn. Holden booked the penthouse for all of us as well."

"Good. They're not prying us apart unless I'm asleep or with Chance and Jace." She winked at me.

The door opened, and a young nurse wearing pink scrubs rolled a wheelchair over to the side of Brynn's bed. "You ready to get out of here for a few days?" She smiled at Brynn.

"Hell, yes. My bestie is here to hang out with me. We're going to have our nails done along with a bikini wax. I want to be pampered and play." Her laugh echoed through the room, and my anxiety calmed. I assumed it would be one day at a time with cancer, but I was grateful to be with her again. We could talk more once we were settled in at the hotel. If Brynn wanted some pampering, then I would see if they offered anything at the hotel.

While Brynn was preparing to leave, I texted Holden about some appointments, and his response was almost immediate, assuring me that he would take care of it.

Almost as quickly as we arrived, we left the Knight Center, but with Brynn. Chance walked with Zayne as I stayed next to Brynn, my mind spinning with how she would react when she met Reid.

Suddenly, an idea occurred to me. "Is Catherine still in Portland? I thought your parents were here, too."

Brynn looked up at me, a faraway expression on her face. "My folks left early this morning. Work." Her words were clipped, angry.

"That's messed up."

"It's worse when they're around, so they did me a favor. Catherine is still here. She's in the same hotel as we are. I'm glad Catherine has been around. She's been really good to Chance and me."

My pulse skyrocketed. I wasn't looking forward to the conversation about Reid with her. Holden had been furious when it was confirmed that he and Reid were brothers. In my mind, there were too many possibilities, and I was determined to refrain from judgment until Catherine shared her story. My biggest fear? That Holden would lose his mom, and he would spiral. I was fucked up myself; I had no clue how to help him through this.

***

I glanced at Chance as we approached the penthouse. As far as I knew, Holden hadn't filled him in about Reid yet. Once they understood what was happening, they would be supportive, but there were still a ton of unanswered questions.

Chance knocked on the door, and Brynn bounced on her toes, grinning like a little kid. "I'm free for a week."

"We'll order anything you want to eat, binge Netflix, talk until the early morning hours." I grinned at her. "I think we'll have *plenty* to chat about." *Like as soon as we walk inside.*

Brynn squeezed my upper arm. "I understand what you're saying, but whenever you're ready to chat about the time you were gone, I'm here."

The door swung open, interrupting my response.

"There he is," Brynn said, smiling warmly.

Zayne remained in the hall with Vaughn as I followed behind Chance, who was blocking my view.

"I'm so glad you're here *with* River." Brynn said, excited.

"Me, too. She's the only person I know on the outside. I would literally be lost without her," a deep voice responded.

"Shit," I muttered, finally able to see everyone. *Goddammit, that's Reid. Where was Holden?* At first glance, I'd thought Reid was Holden, too. "Fuck!" *Where is my boyfriend?* "Babe?" I called out.

Brynn shot me a confused look, then focused on Reid again. "What do you mean on the outside?"

Chance stood next to Brynn and narrowed his gaze at Reid. "You're acting funny. Is the stress getting to you?"

Reid folded his arms, staring at them. A smile eased across Reid's gorgeous face. "You think I'm Holden, don't you?"

"I'm here." Holden flew out of the bedroom, regret twisting his features. "Shit, I'm sorry. I thought I would be in the living area when you guys arrived."

Brynn spun around on her heel, gawking at my boyfriend.

Chance rubbed his eyes with his large hands. "I'm exhausted, but I didn't realize I was hallucinating. There's two of you?"

Holden approached us. "You're not trippin', man." He grabbed Chance in a hug, then Brynn. "Chance, Brynn, meet my brother, Reid."

Brynn's attention bounced from Holden to Reid. "Brother?" she squawked. "Since when do you have a brother? Where did he come from? Where has he been? Can someone please explain to me what in the hell is going on?"

I chewed on my thumbnail, hating that this was how they were meeting Reid for the first time.

"Um." I squeezed Reid's arm before I closed the door and locked it. "Reid was in the cell next to mine." I peeked up at him. "It wasn't until the day the FBI arrived ... well I had no fucking clue that he and Holden were brothers."

"Not until a few hours ago when we got the DNA tests back," Holden added. "I didn't want to say anything until we had the results. Everyone has enough on their plate."

"Son of a fucking bitch," Chance placed his hands on his hips. "Do you think he's the kid in your nightmares and hypnosis?"

"Yeah, unless I've got another brother out there. At this rate, it's probable." Holden flashed us a sheepish grin. Although I appreciated that he was trying to make light of an intense issue, I understood he was rattled to the depth of his being.

Chance turned to Reid, then grinned. "Well, I have no idea how this all happened, but glad you're here, man. Welcome to the family." Chance shook Reid's hand, breaking the awkward tension in the air.

Brynn assessed the open floor plan, then strolled over and sank onto the Victorian cream sofa. Four additional chairs filled the living area and faced a large flatscreen television that rested on a dark brown entertainment center. The penthouse was beautifully decorated, but I was immediately drawn to the enormous window overlooking downtown Portland.

"You two are twins?" Brynn asked, still gaping at the brothers.

"No, I think I'm a bit older and clearly a little shorter than Holden," Reid said, finally joining the conversation. He stood next to Holden, allowing everyone to see the height difference.

"Holy shit!" She slipped off her shoes and tucked a leg beneath her. "How?"

Holden sat in a chair and pulled me into his lap. "We're not sure. I was waiting on the results before I said anything to Mom."

"Oh, shit," Jace said, entering the room. His dark hair and muscular chest glistened with droplets of water. "Apparently I missed the introduction." He tugged on the white towel he'd draped around his shoulders. His attention landed on Brynn, and a broad smile eased across his face. "Hey, gorgeous." He strolled over to Brynn and kissed her gently.

She ran a fingernail down his abs and to the waist of his low-hung jeans. "I've missed you."

Jace tipped her chin up. "I'll make it up to you, I promise." He winked at her, then grinned at Chance. "We both will."

I glanced at Reid, who appeared speechless. He'd seen it all, so I doubted that the three of them having sex would bother him. I think it was more the idea that *Brynn* was into that. Hell, I was jealous. If my life had been different, I would be playing with all of them too.

"We have a very discrete sex club, Reid. The guys and two other girls have been sleeping together for years. Well, Holden doesn't now. He's with River, but none of us are in committed relationships," Brynn explained.

Reid ran his fingers through his hair. "Wow. I wouldn't have ever guessed. I mean, I'm totally open to anything. I've seen and done it all. I've been a sex slave since I was ten."

A heavy silence hung in the air. Reid's words were so casual they screamed, and it ripped me into pieces. Brynn was the one to recover first.

"Now you don't have to do anything you don't want to. It's your choice when, where, and who you sleep with." Her gaze traveled from the top of his head down to his feet. "Jesus, you two sure do look like twins."

"We thought we were at the beginning," Holden added. "We still have to sort out the details, so if everyone would promise not to say anything to parents or friends, I would appreciate it."

"I think we need to talk to Catherine anyway and get her side of what happened before everything is public," I said.

"That's going to be one hell of a story." Brynn leaned back on the couch.

I peeked at Reid, sadness dancing across his expression. "I hope I can forgive her," he said, his voice hovering above a whisper.

"Me, too," Holden said. "Me, too."

Chapter Twenty-Two

"Fuck." I grabbed Brynn's arm, then cast a glance over my shoulder at Zayne. The hotel spa was on the other side of the door, and that's when it hit me.

"What's wrong?" Brynn shifted her weight from one foot to the next.

"I wasn't thinking this through. A stranger is about to touch me," I whispered, hoping that Zayne couldn't hear me.

"Dammit, I'm so sorry. Do you want to cancel?"

I shook my head. "No, I need to ... I need a wax. I've never had one before, and parting my legs and ass cheeks for someone I don't know ..." I chewed on my bottom lip, fighting the anxiety that was spiking through my body.

Brynn pulled me over to the corner for more privacy. Zayne had the decency to step back a few feet, but his alert gaze swept the area while we talked.

"What if we go in together and are in the same room? I would be right next to you. Do you think it would help? And there's nothing sexual about it. It hurts, but then you're all smooth and don't have to deal with it for a long time."

"Does a guy or girl normally wax you?" I gulped, trying to remain in the present moment, but Barrett's sneer returned front and center to my mind.

"Usually a girl. Would that work better for you?"

Shifting my weight from one foot to the other, I mulled over the options. "If it's too much, can I leave? You stay for your appointment, though. I'll skip that part and get my nails done with you."

"River, you do anything you need to. I'll love and support you no matter what." She took my hand in hers.

I sucked in a deep breath, then squared my shoulders and lifted my chin. "Okay, let's do this."

"After you." Brynn opened the door and ushered me through. "Just remember, babe. You have full control over this situation."

She was right, but I still needed her near me.

"Of course."

Brynn checked us in and easily arranged accommodations for us. She also ensured we would have female therapists. My fear settled into unease, which was a little better.

Once we'd changed into plush hotel robes, we entered our room. Waxing was first, massage, then our manicures and pedicures. I spotted two tables and waited for Brynn to pick one. She was a pro at this. I hadn't ever waxed any part of my body, much less my lady bits.

"Hi ladies," a cute blonde said, entering. "I'm going to take care of you today, then we'll have the masseuses come in next. Go ahead and get comfy." She flashed us a warm smile.

"Thank you for seeing us on short notice. We desperately need to be pampered," Brynn said. She dropped her robe and hopped up on the table. I hated and loved Brynn for her body confidence. Even though I tried to look the other way, I couldn't tear my eyes away from her. The only other time I'd seen Brynn naked was in the Master's Playroom, which had been dark.

Even sick, she was stunning—thin, curves in all the right places, perky breasts, and a great ass. One of her best assets was her long legs. What I wasn't prepared for was seeing her ribs. It was just a nasty reminder of her cancer. *What if this is the last time I have a spa day with her?* A shiver traveled down my spine. *Fuck that.* I swatted the dark thought away like it was a pesky fly on a summer day. I was bound and determined to make sure this was a good experience for her. Plus, we were in a public establishment. This wasn't the compound. I could pace the room, leave, come back, and do anything I wanted. I was free, and so was Brynn. We had an entire week together before she had to return to the hospital. Opal, Kassandra, Barrett, and Tim could choke and die. This was my life. *Game on, motherfuckers! I refuse to let you ruin me.*

I climbed up on the table but left my robe on. I would ditch it when I had to. Brynn yelped as her wax job began. Suddenly, I wasn't sure this was such a good idea. The thought of Holden touching me last night put things into perspective, though. I hadn't shaved since before I'd been kidnapped. I wanted to feel sexy and also have this done for him.

Forty minutes later, I was hair-free, and my skin stung like a son of a bitch.

"How are you doing over there?" Brynn asked. If we stretched out our arms, we could probably touch.

"I think having the massage after my pubes being ripped off was a good call." I rubbed my temples and giggled. "Fuck, that hurt."

"It gets better, I swear. Besides, you'll love not having to shave." She winked at me.

A few minutes later, two women joined us for the massages. Brynn was right. I did feel better with her next to me. I was also more comfortable with a female touching me than a strange man. It took a bit, but I finally relaxed as the tension left my muscles. Brynn had closed her eyes, but mine were on her the entire time. If I could see her, it helped tame my fear, and I knew I was safe. Maybe the trick was being able to look at someone. I wondered if it would help with Holden. I was willing to try anything to move forward with him.

The rest of the afternoon was filled with mimosas and giggles. The alcohol relaxed me, and I watched Brynn while she soaked her feet. The pedicure stations offered vibrating and warming chairs, and I wondered if I could talk Holden into buying one when we figured out a place to live. Realizing this was a perfect time to pick Brynn's brain, I took another sip of my second drink, then rested the glass on my thigh.

"Brynn?"

She turned her head, looking at me. "Yeah?"

"Something happened, and I wanted to see if maybe ..."

A wide grin split her face. "You have the hots for Reid, don't you?"

I balked at her, nearly spilling my mimosa all over my lap. "No! I love Holden. He's the only guy I want to be with."

Brynn covered her mouth with her hand, hiding her smile. "Sorry, babe. The way you and Reid looked at each other ..." She released a soft laugh. "River, it's okay to be attracted to someone even when you're in love with another guy. And good God. Cut yourself some slack. When you look at Reid, you see Holden. He is the spitting image of your boyfriend, only a bit shorter. Otherwise, I don't think we would be having this conversation."

"*We* aren't having this conversation, *you* are." I poked my bottom lip out, pouting.

"He's fucking hot as hell, but you know that already. Seriously, babe, think about it. You two went through a trauma that none of us will fully understand. Reid does, though. It sounds like he lived through it for years." Sadness flickered across Brynn's features. "You two are connected on a deeper—different level. You're attracted to who he is as a man—caring, compassionate, and not afraid to show it." She placed her palm on her chest. "I love him for being there for you. I honestly don't think you're attracted to him the way you think you are. It's only because your hot as hell boyfriend basically has a fucking twin. Not to mention the two of you lived through something horrible together."

I rolled my eyes at her. "They're *not* twins." I folded my arms over my chest, hating that Brynn could read me so well. "How did you know that it was screwing with me?"

"Because it would mess with me, too. We're human, and sometimes there's an attraction outside of a relationship. You won't ever act on it. Reid is a completely different story ..."

I whipped my head around, staring a hole into my best friend. "What's that supposed to mean?"

"That Holden has competition. Reid is in love with you, babe. The way he looks at you when your boyfriend isn't around, and the wistful expression when Holden *is* with you."

My nostrils flared, and I released an unattractive snort. "No. He's not. We just went through hell together, that's all."

"So you'll be all right if I ever ask him to play?" She wiggled her brows at me.

"That's not my decision. If he wants to be with you, fine. He's probably hella good in bed after ..." *What was I saying? How could I be so insensitive?*

"I think you need a threesome, River. Explore what it's like with Holden and Reid. If Holden isn't on board with uneven numbers, I'll be happy to join." She fluttered her eyelashes at me.

I searched her face for any sign that she was kidding, but I didn't see any.

"River, I'm not saying this to scare or guilt trip you, but I died. I flatlined. The doctors saved me, and now I don't want to waste time. I want to live, fuck anyone I want, travel, and anything else we can think of. If I don't beat this, at least I'll know that I lived life and I was happy."

This was the first moment I saw the doubt in Brynn. The fear that she wouldn't make it. I gritted my teeth together and gripped the arm of the chair so hard it shot pain through my hand. "You will fucking beat this. Don't ever say that again."

"All I'm trying to say is that I'm going to live my life. You should, too. Decide what works for you and Holden and do it."

I understood what Brynn was saying, but there was something

bigger she wasn't telling me, and I suspected it was a matter of her heart. Sometimes, it was easier to run from love than embrace it. From what I sensed, I figured my best friend was running as fast as she could.

She tapped the side of her head. "I was also thinking that maybe a vibrator could help you and Holden move forward again."

I leaned against the headrest. "I considered the same thing, but we haven't had a chance to go shopping."

"There's an Adam & Eve store close by. I'll send Jace over to pick some things up for us."

My cheeks blazed with embarrassment. I wasn't sure I wanted him to know what Holden and I were doing behind closed doors.

"I'll tell him it's for me, don't worry. And stop feeling bad about being normal." She winked at me, then the technicians returned, halting our conversation.

There was no way I'd ask for a threesome with Reid. I would never hurt Holden like that. He was sensitive about Reid anyway. Sex wasn't that important to me. Holden was.

***

By the time Brynn and I were finished with our nails, Jace had texted that he was in the penthouse and had the bag of goodies. Anticipation swirled in the pit of my stomach. I hoped this would help me relax and stop the flashbacks long enough for Holden and me to reconnect.

Brynn and I returned to the hotel room, pampered and relaxed. The guys were having drinks and schooling poor Reid on poker at the dining table near the bar and living area. It was nice to see them all bonding. I was well aware that we would have some tough days ahead, and I was quickly learning to take the good times and ride the wave for as long as it lasted.

Holden stood and wrapped me in his arms. "How are you feeling after your massage?"

"Better. Thank you." I kissed him, then pulled on his forearm. "I have something to show you. Do we have a room to ourselves?"

Holden's brows rose, and he nodded.

Brynn had stolen Holden's chair and had started playing his hand. She grinned at us. "I'll take over for a bit."

Holden laughed. "See if you can teach these fools a thing or two."

Brynn's gaze landed on Reid. "You're the big brother, so don't let him get away with calling you that."

Laughter and exclamations filtered through the air. I was home—with my family—and it felt damned good.

Brynn handed me the bag, then returned to the game, flirting with her favorite guys. It seemed like Reid would quickly be included in that circle. I hoped so. I knew how difficult it was watching from the outside, loneliness pumping through your veins.

I tilted my head in the direction of the bedrooms, and Holden led the way to ours. Anxiety fluttered in my chest as I closed the door and locked it.

"This is nice." I looked around the room, identifying the cream and baby-blue striped wallpaper, king bed, and matching dresser. A chair was nestled into the corner, and a television was mounted to the wall. I dropped the bag into the seat while I checked out my surroundings.

"We have a connecting bathroom, too." Holden pointed to the left. "The guys and I stayed here while you were gone. Chance has been staying with Brynn, and Jace and I flew down to help."

I sank onto the edge of the mattress and patted the spot next to me. "I need to talk to you, Holden."

Holden's body immediately tensed while he sat down and turned toward me. I looked around the room, everywhere but at him. Jumping off the bed, I paced, wearing a path in the plush tan carpet. "This is really hard for me, but I need to tell you if we're going to be able to move forward."

Fear flickered in Holden's eyes. "Take your time."

He didn't mean what he'd just said, and I knew it. I had to put both of us out of our misery and say it. "The first several days away from you were spent in darkness. I was naked, dirty, and hungry. I pissed in a corner so that I wouldn't step in it when I tried to walk around." I massaged my temples and took a long breath. "Everywhere I look, I think I'm trapped there again. I never understood that there were different intensities of flashbacks, but I do now. These are paralyzing, and they fucking suck. I'm hoping if I talk about what happened, they won't feel like they have as much power over me."

"Okay." Holden scooted back on the bed and stretched his long legs in front of him. I loved him for appearing calm and open to the conversation, but I hadn't missed the twitch in his jaw that indicated he was trying to hold it together.

"They kept me under one of the guard's houses. His name is Barrett. They have him in custody along with some others." My palms grew clammy, and I dried them on my jeans. Reminding myself that Barrett was behind bars, I barked out a nervous snort. The irony hadn't escaped me. "Sorry, I'm okay ... this is super difficult." I rubbed the back of my neck, wishing I was still getting a massage. "Anyway, I was finally able to eat and have some water, then a ... I was going to say shower, but that's not what it was. Barrett took me to a warehouse. There were drains in the cement floor and drawers and cabinets at the other end of the building. No one else was there except us. Barrett grabbed a hose and turned it on full blast ... It wasn't a garden hose. It was powerful, and the pain was excruciating."

Holden scooted to the edge of the mattress, both of his hands fisting.

"He allowed me to wash my hair and body, but I tried to stay hidden from him the best I could. I refused to wash ... to wash my ..." I felt like I was eleven years old trying to say the word 'vagina' for the first time. I pointed to my crotch.

"I understand." The tonelessness of his voice petrified me.

"He said that I could clean myself, or he would do it for me." Angry tears ran down my face, and I stared at the floor, attempting to control them. Once I found my footing again, I continued. "I fought as hard as I could, but I was weak from days of not having any food or water. He was a big guy as well, and easily overpowered me." I chanced a look at Holden. Rage rippled through him, and his eyes glowed with fury. If I ever wondered if he was capable of killing someone, I was clear now.

"He didn't rape me. It wasn't his agenda at the time. But ..." I wiped the moisture from my cheeks. "He ..." I sank to the floor, the guilt crushing me. My chin wobbled as I looked up at him. "I'm so sorry, Holden."

Holden knelt next to me. "Hey, it's okay. Whatever happened ..."

My tear-filled gaze connected with his. "You don't understand. When he had his hand between my legs, he made me ... I came, Holden. Some fucking stranger made me come."

Holden's expression morphed into shock, then white-hot anger danced across his features. He reached out to me, and I scrambled backward.

"Don't. I saw the way you just looked at me." Oh, God. I should have never told him. He hates me. I broke us. I'd shattered Holden's heart and mine along with it. I hid behind my arms, trembling.

"Babe, I'm not angry at you. You're misunderstanding. I want to fucking break him for what he did to you. Not only because he touched you, but he messed with your mind. This changes nothing except that he just signed his death warrant. You lived through absolute horror, and the games people play to break you ..."

I peeked at him through my fingers, watching his face fill with love. "I feel like I cheated on you. When it was happening, I tried to block it out and think about you. That it was your hand." I hiccupped, then wiped my nose with the back of my arm. "I love you so much. I was terrified to tell you. I can't lose you, Holden."

"Babe, I would never, ever hold that against you. The body has a mind of its own, and you had a normal reaction. I love you, and there's no judgement. None. I want you to heal, and I don't know how to help."

I rubbed my arms, attempting to soothe myself. "Are you sure? Are you sure that you're not going to wake up tomorrow and hate me?"

"That's not possible. I couldn't ever hate you, River. Please try and let the guilt go, babe."

I nodded. If he could forgive me, maybe I could, too. "I'll try. I talked to Brynn about it. She helped, too. She said I needed to tell you so that I could begin to heal."

"She's right. Don't ever blame yourself. Not for being taken, not for the assault. None of this was your fault."

I barked out a sarcastic laugh. "Holden, I was kidnapped because I ditched Zayne. It was *all* my fault."

Holden adamantly shook his head. "You're wrong. There was an investor in the club named Laura. She scouted 4 Play for people to kidnap and sell. The FBI linked her to the same sex ring as Opal and Kassandra. It was only a matter of time. Even if you'd stayed with Zayne, another attempt would have been made. Plus, it was personal —Becky ... Michelle, Opal, Kassandra. We all know that Michelle had it in for you the first night you two met. It wasn't your fault. If you're going to blame anyone, it should be me." His expression fell with his words. "I'm the one that's sorry, River. I never meant to bring you into this crazy, dark world. I love you more than you'll ever understand."

I crawled across the floor and took his hand in mine. "I'll make a deal. Stop blaming yourself for other people's actions, and I'll forgive myself about the assault and ditching Zayne."

Holden cupped my cheek, his thumb gently stroking my face. "Can you? Can you forgive yourself? Because I can. In my eyes, there's nothing to forgive. You did nothing wrong."

I leaned into his touch, craving more. "I'll do anything for you, Holden Alastair. I love you that much."

Holden leaned over and pressed his lips to mine. "And I'll do anything for you."

He began to pull away, and I grabbed the back of his neck and nipped at his bottom lip. Holden growled and kissed me as if he was suffocating, and I was the only air that could satisfy him. He swept his tongue deep into my parted mouth, tasting me, feeding me his need as though I was the only thing he lived for.

Breathless, I broke away and leaned my forehead against his. "Do you remember the first night you took me to 4 Play?"

Holden chuckled. "How could I forget? I thought I'd lost you forever."

I slid my palm up the inside of his thigh. "And after that, when you caught me using the vibrator?"

Holden shifted, and I looked down at his obvious erection. "Yeah." His voice sounded husky and sexy as hell.

"I want to try it again, see if we can be together without it throwing me into ..." I didn't have to explain it to him. He understood what I was saying.

"We can try, but the moment I pick up on any hesitation, we're stopping. Understand?" He tipped my chin up, forcing me to meet his gaze.

I tingled with his touch, with his possessiveness. "Yeah. I promise. I'd rather take it slow, anyway. I miss you so much."

Holden devoured my mouth again, flooding my body with heat. "Help me have new memories with you," I whispered against his lips.

Holden rose, held out his palm to me, and helped me off the floor. "What do you need?"

I pointed to the chair. "Do you want to watch? Brynn and I bought a few toys. Maybe just sit and let me see you jack off." I bit my lip, remembering how many times we'd watched each other. Typically, we ended up fucking, though. Spanking, nipple clamps, and anal beads. When we played, we played hard. When we made love, it was heart-to-heart. Nothing and no one existed in the world except us. They were the most intense and intimate moments I'd ever experienced.

My core pulsed with need. I was ready to do this—to try. It might take a while, but I was determined to take my life back.

Holden tugged his shirt over his head, then ditched his basketball shorts and boxer briefs. His thick, long dick bobbed free. He wrapped his fingers around his shaft, then handed me the bag and sat in the chair across from me. I discarded my top and jeans, revealing a waxed pussy. His focus transfixed on the clean skin.

Crawling onto the bed, I fluffed the pillows and propped up against them. The brown paper rustled, breaking through the silence of the room. I laughed as I removed a rabbit. Apparently, these vibrators were to die for. Ripping the package open, I located the batteries that were with the rest of the toys. It was then that I spotted the flavored lube. I tossed it to my boyfriend and smiled. Finally, I had everything ready. My attention returned to Holden as he opened the container and squirted the purple-colored liquid onto his palm. He stroked himself and pulled on the head of his cock. My tongue darted across my lower lip as I parted my legs for him.

I ran my fingers over my slit, watching his reaction.

"You're wet," he said, his eyes filling with need. "I've missed you." His hand traveled up and down the length of him, and I sucked in a breath. He was sexy as fuck.

I turned on the vibrator and massaged my clit. "Oh," I gasped as waves of pleasure coursed through me.

"Are you all right?" Concern flashed in Holden's expression.

"You can't keep asking me. It's breaking the mood, baby." I spread myself, allowing the toy to push against my opening. I focused on Holden's slow and steady strokes as I eased it inside me, watching him as I gasped. Heat licked beneath my skin like a fire, and I picked up the pace.

"You're so beautiful." His voice was deep and raspy and did strange things to my insides.

"Holden," I panted and pinched my nipple. "Can you ... help me?"

Without any hesitation, Holden climbed onto the bed and guided the vibrator in and out of me. I grabbed his hair, encouraging him to continue. I rocked my hips to the rhythm and dug my nails into his back. Not once did I take my attention off him. I took his other hand and placed it on my breast. He rolled my nipple between his fingertips, and I arched into his touch.

"I want to taste you so bad," he whispered against my ear.

I nodded.

"You gotta say it, baby. Tell me yes or no."

"Yes, I just need to be able to see you." That seemed to do the trick, and he paused while he moved to the end of the bed. His eyes darkened as his focus landed on my pussy. He guided the rabbit, then spread me apart with his fingers. He glanced up at me as he lowered his mouth to my bundle of nerves, then expertly sucked and nipped my sensitive skin.

Holden glanced up at me. "Seeing you writhe beneath me is making me crazy."

He flattened his tongue and licked me, sending my body into a crazed frenzy. All the wonderful memories of us together came rushing back, outweighing anything else.

"Oh, God." I bucked against him, clawing at his shoulders. "Harder."

Holden moaned against my flesh, his teeth grazing my clit while he pounded me with the toy. "Baby." My back arched off the mattress, and a raw, delicious heat spread through my body. Every part of me hummed with expectation and need, writhing and whimpering beneath his mouth. He thrust deeper and sucked harder.

I grabbed the pillow and bit the edge, stifling my scream as I shattered. Waves of intense pleasure drowned me as I came apart, my broken soul being remade at the same time. My heart was in Holden's hands, and he handled it with extreme care while he breathed life into me again. His love was the healing balm I so badly craved. Overwhelmed with the emotions ripping through me, I cried out. "Holden." A rush of tears consumed me as I shook beneath him.

He removed the rabbit and scrambled up the bed. "What is it?" He smoothed my hair, concern etched into his beautiful features.

I curled into him, sobbing. "Thank you. Thank you for not giving up on me," I hiccupped.

"Oh, babe, I love you so goddamned much." He wrapped his arms around me as I released the pain of Barrett's assault—the shame, guilt, and hatred for myself.

I peered up at him beneath my wet eyelashes. "I love you, baby. Don't ever doubt it." I paused, then asked. "Do you have a condom?" Under the circumstances, there was no way I wanted to risk another pregnancy.

"Yeah." Holden reached for his wallet on the nightstand and opened the foil wrapper.

He stroked my hair, then kissed my forehead. I threw my leg over him, feeling his erection. I rolled him onto his back and eased him into me. A moan escaped him as he slid in deeper. "If you're not ready—"

I placed my fingertips against his mouth, silencing him. I rocked my hips, my sensitive bud rubbing against him. He sat up and wrapped my legs around his waist, penetrating me fully.

"How does that feel?" He gently thrust inside me.

"Like I'm home." I smiled at him as we found our rhythm together. Taking and giving everything we had—every fear and every hope.

Holden looked up at me, tears in his eyes. I threaded my fingers through the back of his hair. "I love you, River. I've loved you since the first moment I saw you. I love your strength, your fight, your laugh, your compassion, your determination. Don't you ever forget that you belong to me."

I gasped, my core clenching his dick. His hot mouth closed over my breast, sucking on my nipple. He reached around and grabbed handfuls of my hair, gently pulling my head back and exposing my neck. His lips grazed the sensitive skin beneath my ear, and I shuddered. Holden reclaimed my body, reminding me that no matter what happened, I was his. He was mine.

"Jesus, you feel so good," he whispered. He nipped me lightly with his teeth, moving his hips faster. His fingernails dug into my back, then trailed down to my ass cheeks. I wanted more. I wanted him to touch and lick every part of me, but I was afraid to push it. We were together, making love, savoring each other. There was plenty of time to play rough.

As if he could read my mind, Holden bucked as he tensed and moaned, pouring himself into me. He slipped his fingers between us, massaging my clit while he continued to move even after his release. Seconds later, I buried my face in his neck and muffled the noise as I climaxed. We sat still, holding each other, unwilling to let go. I pressed my palm to his muscled, hard chest, and felt his heart racing beneath my touch.

He covered my hand with his. "It beats for you," he whispered.

I lifted my head and pressed my lips to his. "Your smile and laugh kept me sane while I was gone. All I could think about was telling you who was behind my kidnapping. My desire to protect you was stronger than anything. I've never felt that way about anyone. Ever."

Holden pressed his lips to mine, and I smiled.

I draped my arms around his shoulders and kissed the tip of his nose. Hesitating, I realized I should bring up the conversation before Brynn did. "By the way, don't be surprised if Brynn invites Reid to the sex club. I just didn't want you to be taken off guard."

"Fuck, are you serious?" Holden's head hung down. "I don't think that will go over well."

"What do you mean?" I asked, massaging the back of his neck.

Chapter Twenty-Three

H e turned toward me, a dark curl flopping into his eyes. "While you were gone, Chance told Brynn that he's in love with her."

"What!" I scrambled off him, plopping down on the bed. "She didn't mention anything to me at all!" I fell back onto the mattress, exasperated. "What did she say? Why didn't she ..." I smacked my palm against my forehead. "I knew it. I knew she was holding back about something. It must have been about Chance."

Holden laid down, then rolled to his side and propped his head up with his hand. "I love seeing you like this." He trailed his fingertips between my breasts and down my stomach.

I snapped my fingers and grinned at him. "Stay on topic, Holden. Focus up here." I pointed to my eyes and laughed.

His chuckle rumbled through his chest. "Chance never told us what she said."

I scrunched up my nose. "Holden, from what she shared with me today ... even if Brynn is in love with Chance, she has no intention of settling down. She wants to fuck, eat, travel, and have fun. She doesn't want to have to make decisions for anyone else except what makes her happy. Honestly, I don't blame her. She died, and if she needs to plan and play to help her beat cancer's pathetic ass, I'm going to support her."

Holden blew out a sigh. "We all will. We'll give her anything she wants ..." Holden held his hand up, his lips pursing. "I should clarify that statement. I won't give her anything. I haven't slept with Brynn in a long time." He ran his fingertips down his body. "This is off limits to anyone except you." He wiggled his brows at me, laughing.

I released a full-on belly laugh. There wasn't any doubt in my mind that Holden loved Brynn, but he wasn't in love with her. I had that piece of his heart. I did appreciate him clarifying, though.

"I trust you." I toyed with the idea of telling him what Brynn had said about the group sex, but I chose not to. Unless I was asking to be with all of them, there wasn't any point. "Brynn dropped her robe in front of me at the spa."

"Doesn't surprise me. She's very confident with her body."

"She's beautiful. The only time I saw her was the first night you introduced me to the Master's Playroom, and I couldn't see her well. But today ... I could see her ribs. She's lost weight. We need to feed her as much as possible. Maybe some edibles or something. I hear pot is legal here."

"It is. I'm sure we can have someone pick up some for her. She used an edible before she ended up in the hospital and it definitely worked." Holden chuckled. "She ate a ton of food, then fucked Chance and Jace."

"I wish I'd had more experience the way you all do. You've tried everything, including each other." I snickered. "I feel a bit vanilla compared to everyone."

"We've done a lot of things most haven't." Holden's gaze dropped to the white-and-blue striped bedspread, and he pulled on a small thread. He looked at me again. "Do you want to experiment eventually?"

"I don't know. I mean, I've wondered what it would be like to have a threesome. Brynn's gorgeous and I love her, so if I mess around with a girl, it will be her. But Holden, I'll never cheat on you. Please know that I'm simply talking this over with you because you've lived this full, exciting life that I haven't. After Brynn talked about not settling down and doing what made her happy, it made me think. The one place I've not fully allowed myself to explore is with sex, but I'm not sure I want to, either. After everything I saw ..."

Holden remained quiet as he rubbed my arm. "I know we're at different places in that area, so if you decide you want to try a three-some, we can talk about it."

"What if I wanted to be with Brynn? If she's dying ... I would want to grant her wish." I swallowed, suddenly uncomfortable with what I'd shared. I could feel the blush creep up my neck and across my cheeks.

Holden reached over and plucked my nipple. I glanced down, his dick hard again. "Tell me what you want, baby. Would you want her to touch you here?" His hand worked between my thighs, and I parted them, allowing him better access. He massaged my bundle of nerves with his thumb. "Have you ever had a girl eat your pussy?"

"Baby, I didn't say I would be with her, just that I was thinking about it because she might be dying." As soon as I said it, I realized Holden was enjoying a fantasy. "No, I've never tried it."

He pinched my clit. "According to Payton and Sariah, Brynn knows how to use her mouth. The girls are straight, but they were first in line to mess around with Brynn." My eyes widened as he inserted a finger into me. "Tell me what you want to try, River."

I arched against his touch, turned on way more than I wanted to admit. "I want to kiss her, feel her mouth on my tits while she strokes my clit." A small gasp escaped me when Holden moved his finger from my pussy to my puckered hole. He pushed against it, easing inside. I squirmed beneath his touch.

"Can I watch as she licks and sucks you?"

I nodded, breathless. "I want to suck your dick while she's tasting me." I moaned. The thought of the threesome made my body burn with an animalistic desire.

"I need to watch first. If you're on your hands and knees and she's under you, you can sit above her face. I can see her tongue as she fucks you."

"Oh, God!" I gasped, grinding against him.

"Let me show you. Roll over, babe."

Without hesitation, I rolled onto all fours, then Holden slid beneath me and lowered my core over his mouth. I watched him as he dug his fingers into my thighs, pain and ecstasy pumping through me. He shoved a finger into my ass, and I buried my face into a pillow, muffling my cry of pleasure as I rocked against him.

Desire licked every inch of my sensitive skin. My muscles tightened. Seconds later, I released, clawing at the bed with the most intense orgasm I'd ever experienced. I whimpered as his mouth left me. Holden took care of a condom before he rolled me onto my back, then slid his cock into me. Thank God my birth control pill would kick in the next day.

I wrapped my legs around him. "Fuck me hard, baby."

Holden grabbed my wrists and pinned them over my head. He thrust into me so hard, the headboard bounced and knocked against the wall.

"That's it, baby."

He released me, lifted my leg, and pushed it, my knee hitting my chest. Holden placed a palm on the mattress and shifted, his new angle sending me into a frenzy.

I scraped my nails along his sweat-slickened skin while he pumped me harder, my breath ragged and my body greedy.

He let out a harsh growl, gripped the back of my thigh, and began plowing into me. "Fuck," he said, then his mouth parted. The entire bed shook as he slammed into me one last time, then he tensed and jerked as he released. Before I realized it, he pulled out and slid down the mattress until his mouth was on my clit. He fucked my ass with his finger, his tongue lapping at my bundle of nerves. Stars danced behind my eyelids as I exploded again.

Panting from the workout, I went limp as my arms flopped to my sides. "What the hell did you just do to me?"

Holden chuckled, then made his way up the bed. "It's called a fantasy, babe. You don't ever have to act on anything, but it can be fun as hell to pretend." He kissed the tip of my nose, grinning. "I know you love Brynn, and sometimes our emotions are a little confused. From what you've told me, you weren't close to anyone other than Addison. Now you're exploring your sexuality. You're attracted to a lot of people and things, but it doesn't mean you want to sleep with Brynn. Relax and enjoy it."

"I love her, Holden. If her last wish is me, I would give it to her. Not because I like girls, but because I love *her*." I massaged my forehead. "I'm not sure that's making sense."

"It makes a lot of sense. One thing I've learned from owning 4 Play ... so many people deny themselves their fantasies because they're afraid they'll be shamed. River, there should never be shame in learning who you are. Straight, gay, bi ... Our bodies are made for pleasure. People are attracted to who they're attracted to. I just wish everyone's fear and judgement would take a backseat to love and happiness."

Although I heard what Holden was saying, I wasn't taught the same way. After being raped over and over again by Dan, I hadn't ever allowed sex to be positive, loving, and fun. I'd rejected my body for being too curvy ... too seductive, even though I tried to wear baggy clothes and not attract attention ... until Holden.

"I think we'll sleep well after that workout." He turned to me, his expression growing serious. "Honestly, I think I'm afraid to close my eyes."

My brows knitted together. "Why?"

"I'm terrified I'll wake up and you'll be gone."

That made way too much sense to me, and I wasn't sure how we would heal except to fall asleep and wake up next to each other every morning.

"Just hold me, then." I rolled over and flung my leg over his while I nestled against him, listening to the rise and fall of his chest.

"We should shower and grab something to eat. Brynn's not the only one that's lost weight." He patted my back, implying that I'd also dropped a few pounds. He kissed the top of my head, then we laid still—neither of us in a hurry to pry ourselves apart.

***

Once we showered, we joined everyone else in the living room. Brynn was stretched out on the couch, curled up next to Jace, softly snoring. Chance and Reid were watching a basketball game, and Chance was teaching Reid the rules. I wondered what this big world looked like to him.

Before Holden ordered Chinese from a restaurant that delivered, he poked his head into the hall and took Vaughn and Zayne's order as well.

I glanced at Chance as he studied Brynn, and internally, I struggled. There was no mistaking that she held his heart. Unfortunately, she had no plans to settle down any time soon. I understood where she was coming from because I'd promised myself if I made it out of the compound, I'd embrace life and live. Never again would I take a day of freedom for granted.

"Can I sit with you guys?" I asked, pointing at the seat between Reid and Chance.

"Of course," Reid pulled out the chair for me and flashed a sexy as hell smile at me. The same one Holden had.

"Chance, are you going to teach Reid to play basketball?" I hadn't seen the guys play, but I bet it was competitive as hell. Brynn and I could sit on the sidelines as we watched the sweat glisten off their bare chests and ripped abs. "We should find a court. Brynn and I can cheer while you guys play and teach Reid." I looked at Reid. "What do you think?"

"If he wants. Jace is better than I am, but Holden is the king."

Chance ran his hands through his blonde hair, his blue eyes studying Brynn while she slept.

"I'm all about some exercise. Plus, it looks fun." Reid's attention returned to the muted television.

Holden strolled over and took an empty chair at the table with us. "I just got off the phone with Mom." He leaned back, stretching his long, muscular legs out in front of him. My gaze traveled from his thighs to his gorgeous face, and my stomach plummeted to my toes. The ability to ignore his mom much longer wasn't an option.

"I didn't realize she'd gone home to Washington for a few days. She returns tomorrow and wants to see everyone. She burst into tears when I told her you were here, babe."

Wide-eyed, I stared at him. "You didn't tell her when you texted everyone that night?"

Holden laced his fingers behind his neck while he stared at his brother. "No. I wasn't convinced that she hadn't been a part of your kidnapping. It didn't seem like a good idea until we knew for sure that she wasn't involved. Not to mention, I think I was in shock and trying to process Reid."

I understood Holden's hesitation. "Thank you for protecting us." I patted the back of Reid's hand. "I don't think the conversation with Catherine is going to be easy."

Reid's shoulders tensed, then he rubbed his stubbled chin. It was eerie as hell that even his mannerisms were similar to Holden's.

"I'm not sure what to say to her. I mean how is this going to go down?" he asked Holden.

A small smile pulled at Holden's mouth. "Normally, this would be your problem, since you're the big brother, but ..."

Reid chuckled. "Give me some time, bro. I'll be bossing you around and making up for the lost years."

I giggled, enjoying the brotherly teasing.

Chance drummed his fingers on the table. "Well, what are you wanting to achieve? Do you want to take Catherine off-guard, so you have a better chance of learning the truth? Or are you going to talk to her, then decide if you believe her or not?"

I offered a forced shrug, trying to be casual when I was actually freaking out inside. This whole thing could go terribly wrong, and I wanted to protect Holden from any more pain. Even though he had his brother back, he'd lost Reid and Hannah, and Tim had turned out to be a real piece of shit. Mallory and Catherine were his only family left, and I couldn't speak for Mallory, since I hadn't met her.

"I think catching her off-guard would work best. That way she doesn't have time to change her story. Mom doesn't rattle easily, and when it comes down to it, her poker face is exceptional. The only way we're going to get a true reaction is for me and Reid to show up together. River can help us look for any signs Mom is lying."

I nodded. "I hate to throw someone off guard like that, but I think it's necessary. However, this isn't only about Catherine, it's about Reid, too. He needs to feel comfortable with the plan."

Holden cast a lingering glance my way.

"I don't think any scenario you all play out is going to be easy, but it should be up to Reid. He's the one meeting his mother after all these years," Chance offered.

"Yeah, it all sucks," Reid shoved his fingers through his hair, leaving a section sticking straight up.

I resisted the urge to flatten it. Reid wasn't Holden, and I needed to be careful with how comfortable I allowed myself to be around him.

"Let's get it over with, then. She'll be returning to the hotel early. She continued paying for the room even while she was gone." Holden leaned forward and propped his elbows on the table. "Reid, whatever happens tomorrow, whatever Mom says, I'm on your side. From the details that I was able to remember, you and I were close when we were little. Rebuilding our relationship is my first priority. Other than River, I mean."

My chest warmed with his confession. Even though he'd made it clear I was the most important person to him, sometimes it was nice to hear. Hopefully, he and Reid would end up close. I suspected that Holden missed that with Hannah.

"I appreciate it. I feel as though I'm swimming in shark-infested waters. I have no fucking clue what I'm doing, and I need a life vest," Reid said.

"Dude, if sharks are around you, a vest won't do shit. You need a helicopter to pull your ass out of that water." Chance grinned at him. "Regardless, we've all got your back."

"Thanks, man."

"Well, that's settled," Holden said as Vaughn opened the hotel door, carrying several bags of food.

My mouth watered as I caught a whiff of the sweet and sour chicken.

Brynn woke as well.

"Holy hell, I'm starving." She grinned at Jace and gave him a peck on the lips. "I've missed you."

"You, too." Jace kissed her again, then helped her off the couch.

Over dinner, we all kept the conversation light and fun. I didn't miss Brynn's hand under the table. Jace seemed like he was trying to keep a straight face and eat, but whatever was going on, he was having a hard time. I almost snickered, but then I realized Chance might not think it was funny. They'd all been together for years, and nothing had changed except for Chance's feelings for Brynn, but that was a big deal. I wondered how this would all play out in the end, or if Brynn was right in not settling down until she knew how the cancer was treating her.

My heart somersaulted and plummeted to my toes. She had to beat the disease. She fucking had to.

Chapter Twenty-Four

I shuddered as the cool air brushed against my bare skin. After hours and hours of screaming, I'd eventually conceded and spent my energy trying to stay warm, but it was difficult to see in the dark. The odor of the soil told me it had been freshly dug. Clumps had clung under my nails as I'd searched the small area, hoping to find a way out.

Finally, a trap door opened above my head, and a ladder eased down into the hole. Waiting to see if I was being let out or ... A large man began to descend the steps. Once his feet touched the ground, he focused on me, his tongue darting over his lower lip.

"Please, let me out." I used my hands to cover my bare breasts the best I could.

With a wicked grin and glint in his eye, he closed the gap between us. He jerked my head back by my hair and forced me to my knees. He fumbled with the button and zipper on his pants, then freed his cock. "Suck me off, bitch."

"Fuck you," I seethed.

His fist smacked the side of my head so hard it sent me flying backward. "Fine." He pinned me down on the unforgiving ground, then crawled between my legs, forcing them apart.

"Get off me!" I screamed. "Stop!" Tears streamed down my dirty face as I fought with all the strength I had.

"Babe, it's me, Brynn. River, can you hear me?"

My chest heaved, and my vision burned as the room came into focus. "Brynn?" My voice cracked, an agonizing ache in my throat.

Brynn knelt, her fearful gaze even with mine. "River, you're at a hotel with Holden, the guys, and me. You had a nightmare, but you're safe."

Trembling, I forced myself to look around. Holden, Reid, Jace, and Chance were all staring at me, fear flickering to life in their expressions. Blood trickled its way down Holden's cheek, revealing four scratch marks. I peered at my nails. "I hurt you?" My legs wobbled.

"He's okay, hon." She reached her hand out, and I stared at her, puzzled how all of this had happened. I was fine when I went to sleep, then I recalled the night terror with Barrett.

"Barrett," I tried to explain. It was all that needed to be said. They both knew he was the guard that had assaulted me.

"It's okay, babe. Let's wash your face, then we can snuggle and talk while Holden orders some hot tea. It will help calm you down. Hopefully somewhere around here is open."

My attention landed on my boyfriend. "I'm so sorry," I whispered.

"I'm fine, baby. Let's get you feeling better." He didn't step forward or offer to help me off the floor.

I took Brynn's hand, a bubble of nausea erupting in my stomach. A cold sweat rippled over me, and my pulse pounded in my head, making me feel like I was going to pass out. Brynn slipped her arm around me and led me to the bathroom, where I washed up before we made our way to the living area. The guys were right behind us. Brynn and I settled in on the couch, then Holden covered us up with a blanket before he took a seat in one of the chairs. He was bare-chested and in basketball shorts. It was then I noticed more claw marks on his side. I slapped a palm over my mouth, tears welling in my eyes. I'd hurt him. Afraid to look at him directly, I forced myself to do it.

"You don't need to worry. I'm okay, River. I'm more worried about you." He leaned forward and propped his elbows on his knees.

Every cell in my body burned with guilt and a desire to protect him. "You're the one that should be taken care of. I'm fine."

Brynn patted my leg. "You were screaming and attacking Holden. That's not fine, babe."

"Shit." I placed my other palm against my forehead, wishing that I was invisible. "Goddammit."

Chance sat next to me and took my feet, placing them in his lap. I laid my head on Brynn's thigh, stretched out, and let Brynn smooth my hair. "Holden is fine, he's a tough guy. A few scratches won't hurt him."

Jace and Reid grabbed the other chairs, their attention remaining on me. I hated this. I hated that I had a nightmare and hurt Holden. I hated that I couldn't escape Barrett and the compound.

Reid's brows furrowed. "It's going to take a while. At least, that's what I'm guessing."

"Are you having flashbacks or nightmares?" I asked Reid.

"All the time," he confessed. "Nights are the worst. I spent a lot of years alone in that cell ... until you showed up."

I glanced at Holden to see how he was dealing with the conversation. Pain flashed across his features the minute Reid mentioned the cells.

"I still don't really understand why they put me next to you. At one time, you'd said the compound was nearly full and more people would arrive in our building, but ..."

Reid shifted in his seat, appearing uncomfortable. "Not long before we were released, I overheard a conversation. I only recently wrapped my head around it, so I decided to keep my mouth closed."

Frowning, I sat up. "What did you hear?" The anxiety infiltrated my veins, slithered into every part of me, and I squeezed Brynn's hand for support.

Reid's lips pursed together. "The compound had a lot of employees, and one day I overheard a few guys talking. Our situation had been planned, River. Apparently, they were counting on us becoming close. It was all part of the plan for when I trained you, broke you. I'd never trained anyone before, so they were gambling on the fact that I look like Holden."

My mouth hit the fucking floor. "What?" I whispered.

"When I'd eavesdropped, I had no idea that I had a brother and how similar we looked. But you would have seen me and freaked. It was all head games. They excelled in breaking you mentally, then physically. That way they owned all of you."

Holden shot out of his seat and across the room. The penthouse door slamming ricocheted in my ears. Jace hurried after him.

I rubbed my face. "It would have worked, Reid. The moment I saw you, it would have been like Holden hurting me. It would have broken both of us." I closed my eyes, willing the tears not to fall.

"Maybe some of those details shouldn't be shared with Holden," Chance said. "I'm not trying to be an asshole, but Reid, River is the love of his life. He'd kill for her. The thought of what almost happened ... it's crushing him."

Reid tossed his hands up in surrender. "It's late, and I'm struggling myself. My social skills are lacking, unless it's asking what you want sexually. I didn't mean to mess with his head. I swear."

"I know, man, but it takes a friend to tell us to think before we open our mouth sometimes." Chance stretched his arm along the back of the couch.

Sitting up, I whispered in Brynn's ear. "Holden is going to think our sex is to blame for my nightmare."

A wistful expression twisted her beautiful features. "Dammit. I hate to say it, but it probably is."

I shook my head, refusing to believe her answer. Holden and I had made progress last night. I refused for a stupid nightmare to rip it away. "I should find him." I rose from the couch, dropping the blanket on Brynn's lap. I hurried into our bedroom and grabbed one of Holden's hoodies to wear over my pajama tank top. I swapped out the short bottoms for jeans, then slipped my shoes on.

Heading to the exit, I glanced at everyone. "I'll be back. I'll take the other bodyguard, so if someone knocks, don't answer without checking who it is."

"Yes, Mom." Brynn gave me a playful salute and grinned. "Love you."

I halted right before I left, my attention sweeping over my friends. "I love you guys, too. More than you'll ever know."

Chance blew me a kiss, but Reid remained still.

I flung open the door and stepped into the hall. "Hey, Vaughn. Do you know where the guys went?"

"No. Zayne said they would be back, and to stay with you," Vaughn replied while his mismatched eyes landed on me.

"Can you help me find Holden? I need to talk to him."

"Give me a minute." He removed his cell from the inside pocket of his jacket, his fingers dancing across the screen. It was one of the few times I'd seen him in a suit instead of black pants and a West-brook Security polo shirt. His phone vibrated within a few seconds. Vaughn focused on me. "They're on the way back."

"Okay. I'll wait here with you." I rubbed my arms, warding off a sudden chill even with the sweatshirt on. For whatever reason, when I was seriously stressed, I got cold. I leaned against the wall, thinking of what to say to Holden. I'm sorry was a given. Groveling was a given. Cutting my nails was even a good thing to do. I glanced down at the French manicure with pink tips, regretting my choice to get them.

Holden's deep voice traveled down the hall, and I watched him, Jace, and Zayne walk toward us. Holden wore a green T-shirt, and I guessed he'd borrowed it from Zayne because when he'd hauled ass out of the hotel room, he hadn't been wearing one. I chewed my lip, willing him to look over and see me. My pulse pounded in my ears.

He was upset. I could tell by the rigid set of his jaw and the slump of his shoulders. Finally, he glanced up, his gaze focusing on me.

Holden said something to Zayne, then broke into a jog toward me. I hurried to him, stopping before I reached him. I wasn't sure what to expect.

"Babe." He gently kissed me. His lips left mine, and he cupped my chin, peering deep into my eyes, his expression determined and sincere. "I'm sorry I lost my shit. It had nothing to do with you. It fucking guts me to hear what you and Reid lived through."

"I'm so sorry that Reid said that in front of you. Chance asked him to be more careful." I reached up and touched the scratches on his face. "I must have thought you were Barrett." My throat ached with regret. "I'll have the nails trimmed tomorrow. I don't want to hurt you again."

Holden grabbed my hands and kissed my knuckles. "It's okay. I know that Reid wasn't trying to be a dick, but it's hard to hear." He tapped the tips of my fingers. "Don't take the nails off. You really didn't hurt me. I was more surprised than anything, and I couldn't break through to you." He wrapped his arms around me. "Let's go back to the room. Even if we don't sleep, we should at least try. Tomorrow is going to be a big day."

Once we returned to the bedroom, I removed his hoodie and flung it on the chair. "We're still having sex." I climbed into my side of the bed. "For whatever reason, I'm horny as hell, and I need you. The more I see you, the more I associate a touch with you, the faster I'm going to move forward."

Holden sighed while he slipped under the sheets next to me. "I'm afraid it might have triggered you. Maybe we moved too fast."

"No. I refuse to believe that, just like I refuse to allow those monsters to come between us." I placed my palm against his chest, smoothing his dark hair. "Please, Holden. Don't pull away from me."

He glanced down at me and played with a strand of my hair. "I don't know what's best for us, River. I don't want to hurt you but reconnecting with you meant everything to me. When I'm stressed,

I'm horny as hell, and I'm guessing that's what's happening with you, too. What you can't do is use sex to hide from the real issues. You were kidnapped and assaulted. You have to give yourself some time to process."

"What's wrong with that, though? Being with you reminds me that I'm really home again. You're my anchor, Holden. Don't take it away from me."

"I don't want it to get in the way of you moving forward. That's all. I know after I lost Hannah, I used sex to escape the pain."

"As long as I'm with you, I don't see a problem with it. If you won't be with me, I can always use the vibrator, though." I smirked at him.

"If you're going to push the issue, then I won't say no." He smiled, but I didn't miss the worry in his expression.

"Oh, shit." My eyes widened as I pointed to the toy on the floor. "Everyone saw it." I slapped my hand over my face, slightly horrified.

Holden chuckled. "They've seen it all before, don't be embarrassed."

"That's easy for you to say." I leaned my head against him again.

"Did you like it? The rabbit, I mean?"

I gazed at him and smiled. "Very much. In fact ..." I hopped out of bed, retrieved the toy from the floor, and took it to the bathroom, where I washed it. I removed my pajamas, then leaned against the door frame, focusing on my boyfriend. "If you think making love to me triggered my nightmare, then this time you can't touch me." I sat in the chair and draped a leg over each arm.

"No touching at all? It's hard not to lick your pussy, babe. Jesus, you're hot. I think you're enjoying torturing me."

I wiggled my brows at him. "I would have to agree with that. I'm definitely having fun."

Holden flipped the covers off and removed his clothes. He grabbed his cock and rubbed it.

"I miss the Master's Playroom." I turned the rabbit on, rubbing it against my swollen clit. "Are you going to rebuild it?" I tweaked my nipple for him.

"If you're on board, yes." His eyes darkened with need as he watched me slide the toy inside me. He moaned as he stroked his shaft.

"I want to try the vibrating anal beads. Will you fuck me with them?"

He gripped the sheets, bunching them beneath his fingers. His attention was glued to me as I picked up the pace with my new friend. Feeling more and more in control, I pinched my nipple. "I miss the clamps. I miss you spanking me like you did in the voyeur room." I could feel the flush creep up my neck and cheeks. "Do you want to do that again, baby? Did you like spanking me while we watched the couple fuck?"

"I loved every minute of it. You were so fucking sexy bent over my lap, your ass pink from my hand."

"I want to watch our friends next time ... suck your cock while the guys fuck and lick Brynn."

"God, that sounds good."

I sank my teeth into my lower lip, imagining we were there again. Holden scooted to the edge of the bed while he tightened his grip on his dick.

"Holden," I panted, squirming in my seat. "I need you to finish me off baby, then come on my tits."

"Are you sure?"

"Very."

Holden walked over, then knelt on the floor, taking control of the vibrator. He spread me apart, then licked my clit, sending delicious waves of ecstasy through me. "Your touch is fucking magic." I gasped, surrendering to him.

Within seconds, glorious shivers wracked my body. I gripped the arm of the chair and chewed my bottom lip in order not to scream his name. As soon as I was finished, he straddled me. I grabbed his dick and sucked him, my tongue swirling around the tip.

"River, I'm going to lose it."

I cupped his balls, glancing up at him. He grunted, and I popped him out of my mouth and stroked him as he came all over my tits. I licked the drop of come off his swollen head. I smiled at him. "I think I can sleep now."

Once we cleaned up, we climbed back into bed and snuggled up. My eyes fluttered closed, the rhythm of Holden's chest rising and falling relaxing me. I didn't have nightmares the rest of the night.

***

The next morning, Brynn, Chance, and Jace left the hotel room to shop with Vaughn. After discussing it more, Holden had decided to have his mom come to the penthouse instead of meeting somewhere else. I would greet Catherine, then Holden and Reid would join us in the living area. A part of me felt terrible for her. Little did she know she was about to be ambushed, but I had to support Holden's decision. Catching her off-guard was the best way to see her reaction and if she was being truthful or not.

Even though I was expecting it, the knock startled me. Holden kissed me before he and his brother disappeared into one of the bedrooms.

Although a bodyguard was in the hall, I still peeked through the peephole, verifying it was indeed Catherine.

I inhaled deeply, then opened the door. "Hey, Catherine." I stopped myself from flinching when she stood in front of me. Even though Zayne was next to her, and I was safe, I searched her face for the beauty mark Kassandra had, but it wasn't there.

Catherine's red blouse and cream slacks were paired with black Louboutin heels. She'd removed her wedding ring but wore a large teardrop diamond on her middle finger. She clutched her classic Chloe purse that hung from her shoulder.

"River," she said breathlessly, then flung her arms around me, hugging me tightly. "I'm so glad you're back." She released me, then placed her hands on my arms. "Are you hurt? Are you okay?" A frantic expression twisted her features.

"I'm fine." That question was impossible to answer. If I said no, people would want details, and other than my group of friends, I wouldn't explain anything. At least not right now.

Catherine patted my cheek. "Welcome home, honey."

My chin felt wobbly just like my insides. I was well aware that Catherine might have a good reason for what happened to Reid, but meeting her son was about to turn her world upside down.

"Thank you. I'm glad you're here." I took a chair and motioned for her to have a seat. My job was to watch her reactions while Holden and Reid asked the questions.

Before we had a chance to settle in, Holden and his brother strolled into the room.

Chapter Twenty-Five

The color drained from Catherine's face as she stared at Holden and Reid. Her chin trembled as she stood rooted in place, clearly in shock.

"Catherine?" I asked, encouraging her to say something.

Her attention bounced between each of us. She approached Reid slowly, then she gripped his shoulders. "Garrison?" Tears streamed down her cheeks. "Is it really you?"

"I don't know anyone named Garrison. My name is Reid." He gently removed her hands.

"How?" Catherine glanced at Holden. "How?"

"Let's have a seat, Mom." Holden remained near Reid, and for the first time in their adult life, I witnessed a brotherly allegiance taking place.

Catherine stumbled to the couch, still pale. Hell, I was afraid she was going to have a fucking heart attack. I stood, then collected a box of tissues and poured her a glass of orange juice. "Here." I gave her the drink. "Please take a few sips. You're not looking so good." Resisting the urge to sit next to her, I set the Kleenex down, then returned to my seat. Holden was stone-cold rigid while Reid seemed a little bit more relaxed, but he'd had years of practice detaching himself from reality. *Shit. I hope he is going to be all right.* This entire situation sucked.

"How is this possible? The police told me you were dead." She looked at Reid, Holden, then me. "The only way I know who you are is that you're the spitting image of your brother." She held her palms up. "Wait, are we sure? I mean sometimes people have a doppelganger. It has happened."

"Mom, I had the DNA tests run before I reached out to you. Reid is my older brother."

Catherine fell back against the couch, tears in her eyes.

I cleared my throat and glanced at my boyfriend. He nodded for me to tell her my part of the story. "Catherine, Reid was at the compound where I was held. We were in cells next to each other. Reid was kidnapped when he was small and has worked as a sex slave since he was ten."

Horror filled Catherine's expression. "What?" Her hand flew over her mouth as she struggled to hold it together. "Please, River. Please tell me that you weren't ... oh, God, ten years old, Reid? My baby?" Catherine's shoulders shook, her cry echoing through the room. It sounded like fury melded with sadness and torment.

I couldn't fucking take it anymore. She clearly had nothing to do with Reid's disappearance. I hopped out of my seat, sat next to her, and wrapped my arms around her. "He's home now, Catherine. Both of your sons are home." I rubbed her back as she continued to cry. I looked at Holden, at the pain evident in his features. Reid sat motionless, detached from the situation.

Finally, Catherine regained her composure, dabbed at the mascara beneath her eyes, and straightened up. She plucked a few more tissues from the box and patted her cheeks.

"Actually, all three of my kids are home. That includes you, River." Catherine gave me a tired smile. "I owe you boys an explanation." She sniffled and bunched the tissue in her palm.

"We're listening." Holden's tone was clipped, his anger simmering beneath the surface.

Catherine blanched, then cleared her throat and looked at Reid. "You were four. Before Mom died, the entire family was at my mother's house for Thanksgiving. Tim and I were packing up to leave when Hannah flew into the kitchen, screaming. She was hysterical, and it took me a while to calm her down enough to learn what was wrong." Catherine gave me a tight smile, regret flashing in her gaze.

"All of the kids were downstairs in the playroom. The home was huge, and Opal had over a hundred acres. When she died ... she left it all to my sister Kassandra." She swallowed, then took a sip of her juice. "I've not seen or spoken to Kassandra since Opal passed. We're actually twins. Hannah and Mallory remember her, but Holden, you were three when our lives were changed forever."

I looked at Holden and discreetly nodded. So far, what she was saying lined up with what Opal and Kassandra had told me.

Holden rubbed his chin but remained quiet.

"There was a door downstairs, and Mom always kept it locked, but for some reason it wasn't that night. According to Hannah, Mallory was in the bathroom when a strange man walked into the playroom, snatched up Garrison—Reid—and ran. Hannah took off after him, but she was only six. When she turned around ... Holden, you were right behind her, crying and reaching out to Reid."

Holden hung his head. "I fucking tried," he whispered, clutching his brother's arm. Reid took his hand but continued to remain quiet.

"Holden, you were inconsolable for months. You would run around the house calling for your brother ..."

Holden sniffled, then raised his head, his eyes bloodshot from his tears. "Why didn't you ever talk about him? Why didn't Mallory or Hannah say anything to me?" Holden shot out of his chair. "I don't understand how everyone just pretended that this didn't happen! Pretended that my brother wasn't stolen right under our goddamned noses!"

200

Catherine flinched. "I'm so sorry, Holden. Reid, there wasn't a day that went by that I didn't think about you."

Reid folded his arms across his chest. "I'm not sure sorry is good enough, Catherine." His voice was soft but firm.

Holden paced behind the chairs, rubbing his neck as waves of frustration and pain rolled off him.

"We called the police and reported what had happened," Catherine began.

"Say it out loud, Mom. He was *kidnapped!* This wasn't something that *happened.* He was sold into slavery when he was fucking ten. He's been raped, beaten, tortured. Goddammit." Holden rubbed his face, tears streaming down his cheeks. "You have five minutes to explain the rest, then you're leaving—for good. I don't want to talk to you or ever see you again." He held up his wrist and looked at the watch. "I highly recommend you start talking now."

Catherine trembled beside me, then sucked it up and continued. "Months later, the police didn't have any leads until one afternoon someone rang our doorbell. I knew something was horribly wrong. When I answered, they said they discovered remains of a little body and they identified it as Garrison." Catherine stared at Reid. "I was told you were dead. I had no idea you were alive, or I would have scoured the earth until I found you. Please ..." She balled her hands into fists. "That's the truth, please believe me."

Holden glanced at his watch again, then at his mom.

"Your father was at work when this happened, but as soon as he came home, I gave him the news. We clung to each other and sobbed. But the police said something to me that shook us to our core."

I knew the guys were upset with her, but my heart was in fucking pieces. I took her hand in mine. I'd fallen apart that I'd lost my baby, but this ... this was horrible. I couldn't even begin to imagine the stress it put on Tim and Catherine's marriage.

She clutched my fingers. "The detective told me that they'd been trying to catch the man that was stealing and killing children." Catherine pursed her lips, then sucked in a breath. "He said to count myself lucky, that the killer normally took a boy and a girl at the same time. Whoever this sick man was studied families for months and always chose a family with a boy and girl. I was terrified he might come back for Hannah or Mallory. Tim made me swear we would never speak about it again. Then he called the girls in and explained that this monster might return and take them if they ever said anything. I fucking hated him for doing that. *Hated him.* It was the beginning of the end for us." Catherine broke down crying, and I peeked over at Reid.

He leaned forward in his chair, his attention on Catherine, tears clinging to his eyelashes. Even for just a moment, she was reaching him. I looked at Holden, my gaze pleading with him to believe her. She was too broken to be lying. I saw how her family could lie, and Catherine wasn't made from the same cloth. She had a conscience and felt her emotions very deeply regardless of if she shared them or not.

Holden sat back down and steepled his fingers together. "So, it was Tim that terrified everyone into not telling me?" Holden's tone held less anger, but the hurt and defeat were evident.

Catherine looked up. "Yes. And it worked for a while. Although Mallory and Hannah swore to protect you and never say a word, Hannah began poking around when she was older. It tormented her. She started using drugs ... I don't think she could deal with the lies and fear anymore. One evening Hannah waited until you'd left to spend the night with Chance and Jace, then she confronted Tim about what he'd said to her and Mallory, Garrison, and the monster coming back for them. There was a huge blowout. Tim got in her face and Hannah wouldn't back down. She was feisty and full of spunk." Catherine gave us a heartbreaking smile. "She had so much potential, too. Smart, funny, beautiful. She had a real gift for reading people, even the first time she met them."

"I don't remember any of that," Holden said.

"You were so traumatized after losing Garrison ... sorry, Reid, that you were a walking zombie. I took you to therapy when you couldn't remember little things like where you'd left your stuffed bear, Barry. You loved that toy, and never went anywhere without it. Eventually the psychiatrist diagnosed you with dissociative amnesia."

Holden straightened in his seat. "I had nightmares of a small kid calling out to me, begging me not to let them take him. When River was kidnapped, I had Jace help me with a form of hypnosis we'd used in the past. After a few sessions, I knew whatever had happened to River was horrific. It wasn't until I came face-to-face with Reid that the suppressed memories made sense, though."

Reid looked at Holden. His jaw twitched, his expression revealing zero emotion again. "Even after all of that, you remembered me."

Holden nodded. "I still failed you."

"Holden, no," Catherine interjected. "You were only three."

A heavy silence blanketed the room. I was pretty sure the five minutes were up, but Holden didn't make a move to show Catherine out. Catherine must have realized that, too, because she continued. "After the huge argument with Tim, Hannah left that night. She started to stay at her friends' houses, skipped school, and her grades dropped. The crowd she ran with was different and into partying. I knew she was trying to cope with her little brother dying and Tim's blatant lie to silence the family, but I couldn't seem to reach her. I scheduled therapy sessions, but she just sat there and refused to talk. As she got older, she became obsessed with finding Reid's kidnapper. One evening I found newspaper articles, notes, and a map. She was attempting to track the kidnappings. She also learned that there weren't many bodies, which didn't make sense if Reid was taken by a serial killer."

Catherine stared at her feet, then at the guys. "Hannah got too close," Catherine whispered. "She didn't overdose, Holden. She was murdered like you thought."

Holden shattered in front of me. He dropped to the floor next to his chair and broke down, sobbing. Catherine sprang off the couch and gathered Holden in her arms, rocking him as he clung to her. Unable to control them anymore, tears streamed down my cheeks.

I waved Reid over. He joined me on the couch, and we held hands, comforting each other like we had when we were at the compound.

Finally, Holden pulled himself together, but instead of standing, he leaned against the chair and slid his arm around Catherine's shoulders.

"I always knew something was off about Hannah's death." Holden rubbed his eyes.

"I suspected it. It was Mallory who found proof. She took it to the police, but they brushed her off. Your sister confided in me, then said she was leaving for Spain. I asked her for the evidence she found, but she refused to share it with me. Mallory insisted I would be in grave danger, and she couldn't have that on her conscience. She said that she couldn't deal with the secrets anymore. Mallory was desperate for a fresh start without us in it. Who could blame her?"

"I'll call her," Holden said. "She needs to know her brother is home." Holden looked at Reid. "Let me know when you're ready to meet her."

Reid nodded, the crease in his forehead indicating he was struggling to wrap his head around the new information. I wasn't sure how to help either of them process what Catherine had shared. He was lost in a new world with no tools to cope.

Catherine rose slowly, releasing Holden. "I've overstayed, but I wanted you to hear what happened."

My anxiety spiked. I had to tell her a hard truth as well. "Catherine, before you go, I need to talk to you about something."

Chapter Twenty-Six

"By the look on your face, I suspect I should sit back down." Holden remained on the floor as Catherine sat in the empty chair next to him.

"Holden, does she know Becky?" I asked.

Regret flickered in his gaze. "Yeah."

"Becky isn't really Becky," I said to Catherine. "Her real name is Michelle. Not only is she an FBI agent, but she worked for two women on the side. Michelle's job was to talk to underaged children and befriend them, then she kidnapped them and sold them to ..." Reid squeezed my hand, encouraging me.

"She sold them to the sex ring that Opal and Kassandra ran." I paused, waiting for the names to sink in with her.

Confusion clouded Catherine's expression. She glanced at Holden, and he nodded at me to continue.

"Opal isn't dead. She admitted that she faked her death when the FBI was getting too close to the family business." *Fuck, I did not say that!*

My bad choice of words didn't seem to faze Catherine at all, thank God. "Alive? My family is behind the sex ring?" Her attention landed on Reid, then me. "You met them, River? This isn't just a rumor? You actually saw them and talked to them yourself?"

"I did. The day I was taken, I'd found out I was pregnant." A lump caught in my throat, and I swallowed hard. "I was nearly raped by a guard, but I begged him to stop and explained that I was pregnant." Agony stabbed me in the chest as I recalled the details. "Barrett, the guard, reported it. No one tried to hurt me after that, but ... I was cleaned up and presented to Kassandra and Opal. I have to admit that, when Kassandra stood in front of me, I thought it was you. I had to look really hard for the differences." I touched the corner of my eye. "She has a beauty mark here."

Catherine nodded, clearly in shock. "She does have a mole. Kassandra always hated it when we were little girls." Catherine shook her head. "But ... you're going to have a baby?"

I shook my head, my gaze connecting with Holden's. He mouthed, 'I love you,' and I placed my hand over my heart.

"No. Not anymore. I'll explain, though." I squirmed in my seat, choosing my words carefully in order not to cry again. "Opal and Kassandra pretended that I was family since I was pregnant with Holden's baby. They fed me, took me to the doctor there, and had her run blood tests to confirm. I never even knew that the results had come in. The last thing I remembered was eating dinner with your sister and mother, then I felt drowsy and dizzy. I woke up after the procedure." I hesitated. "Opal and Kassandra aborted the baby without my knowledge." I bit my lip, attempting to hold the tears back.

"Those fucking bitches!" Catherine hissed. "How dare they hurt you and my grandbaby!" She slammed her fist against the arm of the chair. "They disgust me. Where are they now? Are they in custody?" Catherine jumped from her seat and grabbed her phone from her purse. "I want to see them both. I ..." She tossed her arms in the air, choking on her cry. "I don't even know what to say ..."

"No. The FBI is looking for them. Until then, Reid and I are laying low, and we have two bodyguards," I explained. "But it's plausible that Opal or Kassandra had Hannah killed if she was getting too close to the truth."

"I don't know what to say other than I'm sorry. They've stolen so much from us. Hannah, Reid ..." She picked her purse up from the floor. "My family has caused all of us so much pain. I had no idea they were behind Reid and River's kidnappings. I never saw anything illegal going on when Mom ... Opal was alive. Kassandra and I broke off our relationship when she began dating an abusive man and refused to leave. I couldn't see her go through that. She was my sister. My twin." Catherine shook her head. "I'm so sorry. Holden, I understand that you no longer want to have me in your life. Maybe not having me around will protect River and Reid." She turned to Reid. "I've always loved you, son. I should have continued to search for you, but I truly thought you were dead. I hope that eventually you can forgive me." Catherine took my hand in hers. "River, you're an extraordinary young woman. Beautiful, strong, determined. You remind me of myself at this age. But more than that, you're so good for Holden. He started smiling and laughing again after you arrived. He loves you so much. I'm so sorry that you lost the baby. Maybe someday you and Holden will have a child, but first you need to heal."

She turned back to Holden. "I'm afraid my mistakes have devastated our relationship beyond repair. Please know that I love you more than words can ever express. Take care of River and Reid." She leaned down and planted a kiss on his forehead, then she turned and headed for the door. The turn of the bolt screamed in the silence. I looked over my shoulder, wishing things could have played out differently.

Catherine glanced at us with regret in her expression, then stepped into the hallway. Reid bolted off the couch. "Mom, don't go!"

Catherine turned to see who had called her name. She and Reid stared at each other.

"Don't go, Mom. I believe you. Please stay."

Holden rose from his seat and joined his brother. "Reid's right, Mom. Don't leave," Holden said, his voice raw with emotion.

"Are you sure, Holden?" Her hand trembled beside her as she searched his face for the truth.

"Absolutely." Holden grabbed Catherine in a big hug.

Once Holden released her, Catherine dropped her purse on the floor and ran to Reid, throwing her arms around him. "Oh, my God. My baby is home."

Reid wrapped his arms around her and finally broke down crying.

Holden sank into his chair, I crawled into his lap and kissed him, then wiped away his tears. "I'm so proud of you, baby." I smoothed his hair. "I didn't think it was possible, but I fell more in love with you today."

He pressed a sweet kiss to my mouth, his lingering tears tasting salty on my lips.

Over the next several hours, Reid opened up to Catherine and his brother. He answered their questions honestly, but he also asked about his new family. He had a sister he didn't remember at all. Catherine's phone was loaded with pictures of all the kids and a few of Reid when he was little. If anyone asked, she had told them it was Holden. It was easy to play off since they looked so much alike.

I had a front-row seat, watching wonderful people in my life cry and heal. It was the most amazing thing I'd ever witnessed. Granted, they had a long way to go, but this was a huge step in the right direction. Out of all of them, I was most concerned about Reid. With his past, I wondered how it would affect him in his relationships. Would he choose the wrong people and open up quickly? Or would he have so many walls in place he wouldn't be capable of truly growing close to anyone? Only time would tell.

At least I realized where I stood with Reid, and maybe I could help him navigate the muddy waters of his new world. I owed him that. Holden had believed in me and given me a new life, but Reid had been my rock at the compound. No matter what, he had my love and loyalty. The tricky part, though? Not sending the wrong message to Reid and helping him manage his expectations as we all moved forward. The guys were making strides already, but there was definitely contention between the two.

Exhausted, Catherine left that afternoon. She gave me a huge hug and whispered a heartfelt thank you before she walked out of the door. I think all of us were in an emotional crash, but at least it was good to have learned the truth, finally.

"Baby, I need a drink. Probably a strong one." I pushed up on my tiptoes and kissed him, hooking my fingers in the waistband of his fitted, low-hung jeans.

"I'll make us something. Reid?"

Reid had stretched out on the couch and turned the television on. He'd discovered the remote, and I was pretty sure he would never surrender it again. I grinned at him as he flipped channels. In some ways, he was like a little kid, exploring and seeing things with the innocence of a child.

I ran over and snatched the control away from him.

"Hey!" He sat up, scowling at me.

A giggle slipped free. "You're so focused on the television you didn't hear your brother ask if you wanted a drink."

Reid gave me a sheepish grin. "Sorry, it's just all new."

I gave him the remote back. "I know, and I'm going to tease you, so get over it." I put my hand on my hip. "Drink or not?"

"What's available?" he asked Holden, who was already working on ours.

"I'm making some Long Island iced teas. Have you ever had one?" Holden glanced over at us before he returned his attention to the glasses.

"Nope, but I'm game." Reid winked at me, then focused on the program he was watching.

I laughed before I turned away.

"Hey." Reid grabbed my wrist, and I faced him.

"Yeah?"

His eyes misted over. "Thank you for today. I'm not sure it would have ended well if you hadn't been there with us."

I smiled at him. "I'm glad it did. It will take everyone some time to adjust, so please be gentle on yourself."

Reid kissed my knuckles before focusing on the basketball game again.

I smiled and joined my boyfriend. "It's been a hot minute since I've had alcohol. I'm ready to relax. Everything with Catherine was a huge fucking deal."

"No shit," Holden responded quietly. His heated gaze fell on me. "I couldn't have done it without you."

"Sure you could have, but I'm glad that I was able to be there for you. For Reid, too." I peeked over at the couch, grinning at how immersed Reid was already. "How are you feeling about having a brother again?"

"Good. Hopefully, we can reconnect and make up for the lost years." Holden handed my drink to me, then plucked a straw from the bar top and shoved it in my glass.

I took a long pull of the Long Island and sighed. "That's so good."

"But you need to know that, if he steps out of line with you, I won't hesitate to check his ass." Holden's expression was stern, the muscle in his jaw twitching.

"You have nothing to worry about. I promise. First, *I* will check his ass if he steps out of line, then you can have at him. Second, I understand him better than anyone else here. He wouldn't ever cross that line with me. He knows who I belong to. I talked about you the entire time I was at the compound."

Holden's brows shot up to his hairline. "You did?"

"Why would that surprise you? I love you." I placed my palm against his chest, gazing into his dark brown eyes.

"Aren't you two just the sweetest," Brynn said as she waltzed into the penthouse, Jace and Chance on her heels. Brynn's and the guys' arms were loaded with bags. "Got us a few things, babe." She sauntered over to me and kissed my cheek. "We should change, then model for the men."

"Umm, maybe not?"

Brynn took my wrist, and we laughed as she dragged me to her and Chance's room. She closed the door behind me and set the bags on the bed.

"How did it go?" She plopped down on the mattress and patted the place next to her.

"In-fucking-sane. Holy shit, it was so intense." I sat down, then stood again. "Wait, I want to get my drink. Do you want one? Can you have alcohol while on chemo?"

"No, it might make the side-effects worse, but ..." She rummaged through a few bags, then produced a little box. "I have some edibles. I'll eat a part of one. If I have an entire piece, I'll be so stoned I can't follow a conversation." She opened the package and removed an orange gummy. "I haven't had this particular edible before, but most of the time, I get the serious munchies, then I get horny as hell." She took a bite and winked at me. "It's going to be a really good night."

I laughed, then left to get my drink, returning a few seconds later. "Okay, are you ready?" I sat next to her. "So, Holden told Catherine he never wanted to talk to her again after today."

"What? Holy shit."

"He came around, though. Once he saw Reid's reaction, I think he came to terms that he wanted his mom in his life as well. Now Catherine has her sons back."

"Oh man, I bet that broke Catherine at first. Holden has always been her favorite."

"Oh, I didn't know that. Interesting. And who knows, Reid might have been her favorite if he hadn't been stolen." I took another pull on my straw, relaxing a little. Apparently, drinking on an empty stomach made the alcohol hit you faster. "Let me back up. I honestly thought Catherine was going into heart failure when she saw her sons standing next to each other. And ..." I grabbed her arm and shook her slightly. "Get this. Reid's given name is Garrison."

Brynn's eyes narrowed. "I like Reid a lot better. It fits his sexy, fine ass." Brynn giggled.

I snorted, then we laughed even harder. It took another half hour to update her on the rest of the story. She stared at me, astonished. "How was everyone when she left?"

"Oh, man. Girl, I fucking lost my shit. Catherine told us goodbye, opened the door, walked into the hall, then Reid yelled at her to stop. He asked her to stay." I fanned my face, attempting not to cry. I glanced at Brynn and the big, fat tears running down her cheeks.

"Oh, my God." She placed her hand on her chest. "That's poetic. Like, fucking heart wrenchingly poetic. I'm so glad he asked her to stay. And what about Holden?" She frowned. "Oh boy, I think this edible is stronger than I thought it would be. You better talk fast before I can't follow the conversation."

"Are you okay?" I looked at her, noting her pupils were already dilated.

"Yeah, my head is a bit fuzzy. Keep going. Tell me how Holden handled Reid wanting her to stay."

I slumped forward, then slurped the last of my drink down. "I need another one. You, however, don't need any more of that edible. Your pupils are huge. How ya feelin', hot stuff?" I nudged her with my elbow, and she flung herself on the mattress, knocking a few shopping bags onto the floor.

"Hungry. Horny." She bit her lip and looked at me. "I really want to take Reid for a test ride."

"Brynn ... I'm not sure that's a good idea."

She covered her face with her hands. "Holden told you, didn't he —about Chance?"

"That's not why I said it's not a good idea, Brynn. Reid is ... he's like a lost little boy. He needs some time to get on his feet. I love you tons, but I'm not going to budge on this one." I slurped the last remnants of liquid from my glass. "And yeah, he talked to me about Chance, but Chance never told the guys what you said when he confessed that he was in love with you."

Brynn peered up at the ceiling, her leg bouncing. "I don't want to give up what I have and settle down. That probably makes me a real bitch, doesn't it?"

"No! Not at all. But while you're in a vulnerable and stoned state, I'm going to take advantage of it."

"Not cool, babe." She pointed at me, a silly grin on her face.

"I'll ask for forgiveness later." I rubbed the condensation on the outside of the glass with my thumb, scrambling to put my words together. "Who are you waiting for, then? If it isn't Chance."

Brynn quirked a brow at me. "I don't like where this is going, River Collins."

"You don't have to, but I need to know. You have something great with both of the guys, and you would be lucky to settle down with either of them."

Her green-eyed gaze narrowed at me. "Isn't it acceptable to not commit to anyone or anything right now? I'm young, I'm dying. I think I've earned the right to do what I want and be happy."

I blanched. "You don't have to be dying to deserve to be happy, Brynn ... but what are you not telling me?"

Brynn sat up and tucked my hair behind my ear. Before I realized it, she leaned over and pressed her soft lips against mine. She broke the kiss and peeked up at me. "The doctors don't think I'm curable, River. I only have a small chance of beating it. The guys don't know yet."

I stared at her, my surprised and buzzed brain refusing to comprehend what she'd said. "Was this our goodbye kiss?" I choked on my words.

"No." She leaned in and kissed me again, nipping at my bottom lip. "That was. I do love you, River. So much."

I grabbed her wrist and panic seized me. "I love you, too, Brynn. I'm just not in love with you."

"I know, babe. But if I don't make it ..."

I closed my eyes as our foreheads pressed together. "You needed to tell me like Chance told you," I whispered.

"Yeah." She pulled away. "I need to live like I'm not going to make it, River. Please, help me do that."

"Brynn." My chin wobbled, and I tugged her to me. "You have to fight. For me. Please."

She nodded against my shoulder, clinging to me. "Don't get me wrong, River. I do love Chance. Eventually, I could see myself settling down with him, but I don't think eventually is something that exists in my world anymore."

The dam of grief broke—the final blow to my beaten and broken soul.

I stroked her red hair, cherishing these moments with my best friend. "What can I do to help, Brynn?"

She sat up, wiping the moisture from her cheeks. "You have to make me a few promises."

"Anything."

Chapter Twenty-Seven

"You can't tell anyone what I shared with you, not even Holden."

"Brynn, you're asking me to keep a huge secret from him. We talk to each other about everything." I took her hand in mine as the guilt stabbed me in the chest. I wanted to support her, and seconds ago I told her I would give her anything she wanted, and now I was taking a step back on my word. The pain in her expression broke me a little more.

"I know. I can't tell them yet. Please give me the rest of this week. When I return to the hospital, I'll have another round of chemo, then they'll evaluate to see if it's working or not. Please, it's only a few more days."

I nodded. I could give her that. "All right. What else?"

"Let me talk to Reid, and see if he wants to join in. He's used to a lot of sex. For him, it might be a coping mechanism. Giving him a choice is helping him take his life back."

"It's not my decision, Brynn. He's a grown man. I'm just protective of him is all." I took my straw and stirred the remainder of the ice cubes in my glass. "Brynn, would you have told me if you weren't stoned? I mean, about the chances of surviving?"

"I'm not sure. I wasn't going to tell anyone at all, but you're my best friend. It's easier to talk to you." She pulled at a thin thread on the black comforter.

"I get it. I feel that way about you as well." I slid off the bed and stretched, attempting to wrap my head around what was happening. "I need another drink. Do you want to join us in the living room, or do you need some rest?"

"I'm good. I'll sleep when I'm dead."

I whirled around on her. "That shit is *not* funny. There is still a chance that you can beat this. Knock it off, or I'm going to beat your ass. You're an amazing, strong, feisty woman and you need to be reminded of the badass bitch you are." I glared at her for extra emphasis and poked her in the shoulder with my finger.

Her face fell as she stared at me for a moment. With a sniffle, she threw her arms around me. "Thank you. Oh, my God. Everyone stopped reminding me of that. I became Sick Brynn. Let's take care of her, coddle her. No one has said, 'you've got this.' " She hiccupped, and I returned her hug.

"That's what best friends are for."

We released each other, smiled, and held hands as we left the bedroom with the unopened bags, then entered the living area. What Brynn didn't know was that I'd left my heart on the fucking floor.

Once Holden made another drink for me, I sat in his lap while Brynn snuggled up to Reid and Jace. Chance sat in the other chair, pretending it didn't bother him. Maybe if he understood that her odds of beating cancer were slim, he wouldn't take her behavior personally. Brynn admitted she could see herself settling down with him, but if she didn't have a future ... Black clouds rolled into my thoughts, and I kicked them to the curb. Brynn was one of the strongest women I knew. She could fucking beat this.

"Are you okay?" Holden whispered against my ear, stroking my hair.

I couldn't lie to him, but I couldn't betray Brynn's trust either. "Brynn and I had a heavy conversation. I'm just chewing on it. It's been a big day."

"Do you need to talk?" Concern weaved through his words.

"Not yet. I'll let you know when I do." I kissed him. "By the way, Brynn ate an edible and she's pretty stoned."

The corners of Holden's lips turned up. "Oh yeah?"

"Mmhmm." I took a long drink, allowing the alcohol to relax me even more.

"So, Reid, when 4 Play is rebuilt, do you want to join the sex club?" Brynn asked.

My drink spewed from my mouth, spraying my boyfriend's shirt. "What the hell, Brynn? Shouldn't you have talked to the guys before you asked Reid?" I asked, choking. I stood and searched for something to use to dry him off. I hurried to the bathroom, then handed Holden the towel. The room was stone-cold silent, Reid's expression unreadable.

Finally finding my voice, I sat back down. "It's not like the compound, Reid. It's all consensual with playrooms. It was actually a lot of fun."

Reid leaned forward, then back again. He placed his long finger over his lip. "Why does it need to be rebuilt?"

Holden peered around me. "Because our father, Tim, burned it to the fucking ground. There was the main club, then the lower floor was for exclusive clientele. Each person had to apply, I ran a thorough background check, and they had to sign consent and nondisclosure forms when they used a room."

"Huh. Sounds like my kind of place. Are you definitely going to rebuild?" Reid took a sip of his drink.

"I'm considering it, but it also depends on River. She was kidnapped from there, and we haven't decided yet."

"If anything, we definitely need to rebuild the Master's Playroom," I added. Everyone chimed in, agreeing.

"What's that?" Reid asked.

217

Brynn winked at me. I understood what she was doing, but it wasn't cool to bring it up like that. I hadn't ever seen Brynn behave like this, so I was going to blame the edible.

Holden cleared his throat. "Two other girls, Payton and Sariah, along with Brynn, Jace, Chance, and myself formed a secret group when we were in high school. We didn't sleep around like most everyone else. We kept it within our circle, but anything was fair game as long as everyone was on board."

Reid let out a low whistle. "Was there a reason behind forming the elite group?"

Jace cleared his throat, looking at Holden. "It's a long story."

I twisted in Holden's lap and quirked a brow at him. "I don't know why you started it, either."

Holden rubbed my back. "It's not just my story to share. It also belongs to Brynn, Jace, and Chance. They're the only other people who know the truth."

"I don't care if Reid and River know. I'm not ashamed of how it went down," Brynn said.

"It's not only about you, though," Chance added, his tone short.

I hadn't heard Chance cop an attitude with Brynn before, but he was clearly irritated with her. I was sure it had happened before, but I hadn't ever seen it.

"If Reid is one of us, then we should tell him." Brynn stretched her long legs in front of her, eyeing Chance. "I mean, River should know as well."

"Brynn, they would be implicated and spend time in prison if anything happened. You're not thinking this through." Chance rubbed the back of his neck, and I nearly snickered. Brynn was definitely being a pain in the ass right now. I wasn't sure those edibles were worth it.

Then Chance's words hit me like a freight train. "Wait. What?"

"We're all in it together, so if one of us goes down, we all do," Jace said, crossing his arms over his muscular chest.

I sat up straight, my attention sweeping over Brynn, Jace, and

Chance. "Reid, I want to know what the hell happened, but you don't have to be involved. Maybe hang out in the bedroom for a while so you can't overhear the conversation. Or stay but understand the consequences." I didn't think that Reid would take me up on the suggestion, but he needed to know he had a choice.

Reid shifted in his seat and stretched his arm along the back of the couch. "I'm in. You have my word that I won't repeat anything to anyone. It's not like I know anyone outside of the room other than Mom."

My chest warmed with his use of the word Mom, and I smiled at him.

"What about everyone else?" Holden asked.

Jace tossed his hands up in the air. "I trust everyone here except Reid, and that's only because I don't know him yet. Sorry, man. I call it like it is."

"No offense taken," Reid replied.

"Chance?" I asked.

"I'm with Jace, but I have a feeling Brynn is going to talk regardless of what our opinion is," Chance said, clenching his jaw.

"Well, shit." I rubbed my forehead. "I don't have an opinion because I have no idea how it all started, so I'm just here to listen."

"Well, since we're split, I'll make the decision. It all started with Emerson," Brynn began.

I jumped off Holden's lap. "Brynn, you can't do this. You guys, Brynn ate an edible and it's making her horribly obnoxious."

"That's what's going on?" Chance asked, shaking his head. "Thanks for letting me know. She normally doesn't react like this, but the edibles aren't regulated very well and different types can encourage different behavior."

"At least we know. I was going to haul her to the bedroom and spank her." Jace shoved his fingers through his hair, frustrated as hell. "And I don't mean that in a fun way, Brynn."

"I'll step out of the room and let you all figure this out." Reid stood, a dark curl flopping over his forehead. "Maybe it's best that I don't know. Down the road, you can decide if you want to include me. For now, it's all good."

I stared at Reid as he strode out of the room, then I nearly gave myself whiplash as my attention landed on Brynn again.

"I love you, but you're acting like a brat right now." I returned to Holden's lap, and he slipped an arm around my waist.

Brynn smirked, then apparently realized that I wasn't kidding. "You're taking things too seriously, babe."

"And you're not taking things seriously enough!" Exasperated, I leaned back against Holden.

"Fine. I'll be serious. Real serious, actually." Brynn straightened up and tucked a leg beneath her. "As I said, it all started with a girl named Emerson."

Chapter Twenty-Eight

"Who is Emerson?" I asked.

"She was a girl we went to high school with, Brynn's best friend at the time," Holden explained.

I glanced at Jace and Chance, who remained quiet now that Reid was out of the room. Jace stood and excused himself to use the bathroom, but I suspected he was making sure that Reid wasn't eavesdropping. He returned a minute later and sat down next to Brynn.

Brynn twirled a strand of red hair around her finger, then began. "It was a Friday night, and Emerson was on a date with a college guy named Steven. I'd warned her not to go, but she ignored me like always. He took her to the lookout on the mountain, and he got touchy real fast. Emerson sent me a text that she needed a ride home. I was only ten minutes away, but when I arrived, things had escalated. He was in the process of trying to rape her on the hood of his Mustang." Brynn paused and looked at Holden. "When I hopped out of my car, Emerson was fighting him off. Her shirt was torn open, and her skirt was shoved up. She managed to kick him in the thigh and stand. She must have been disoriented because she ran to the side of a cliff.

"I tried to reach her fast enough, but Steven punched her in the face ... Emerson lost her footing, and she went flying backward over the edge."

"Holy shit," I muttered.

"I've never raged like that before, but I did that night. I jerked Steven around, then slammed into him. I guess what they say is true because when my adrenaline kicked in, I was a lot stronger. I shoved him a few times, then he lost his footing on the loose gravel, and seconds later he disappeared over the cliff, too. I peered over the side, but I didn't see him. Honestly, I didn't care about him anyway, I had to find Emerson. I called Holden to bring the guys to help, and he reported the incident to 911."

"We arrived before the paramedics," Chance said, his voice haunted. "I had a flashlight in my truck, and we were able to spot Emerson down below us. It was too dark to see if she was breathing or not. When Holden spotted Steven ..."

"His neck was twisted in the wrong direction. He was dead," Holden said quietly.

"I killed him," Brynn admitted through clenched teeth. "And I would do it again if a motherfucker was trying to rape someone."

An emotionally charged silence filled the room, then Jace spoke up. "Emerson is in a wing in the hospital for long term patients. She's alive, but has been in a coma for years."

I gasped, then slapped my hand over my mouth. "That's horrible. Will she ever wake up?"

"We don't know," Chance added. "It's been a hot minute already."

Jace drummed his fingers on the arm of the couch. "I still have hope. Every once in a while, you hear of a patient waking up years after being in a coma. I would think it would be disconcerting as hell, though."

"What happened afterward?" I asked.

Chance leaned forward, propping his elbows on his knees. "I told Brynn to get out of there. Jace and Holden climbed into the car with her. Brynn was hysterical, so Holden drove while I stayed behind and talked to the EMTs and cops. I told them I saw Steven push Emerson off the edge, then when I yelled at him, it must have startled him because he stumbled and fell, too. In a nutshell, I lied to protect Brynn. Otherwise, she could have been charged with murder."

My eyes widened as it all sank in. They were all in this together. Brynn killed a guy, and they helped her cover it up. *Holy fucking shit.*

"I'm still confused with how the club started, though." I focused on my boyfriend, a new respect for him bubbling to life inside me. If I'd ever doubted how far he would go for the people he loved, I didn't anymore.

"Steven tried to rape Emerson," Holden began. "After that, with our small group, we didn't even date. We hung out and fucked each other. It was a safe place to experiment and have fun. The girls were protected, and it worked really well. We all tested for STDs once a month, but we were always clean since we didn't have sex outside of the club. It was peace of mind. That's why I started it, River. To protect Brynn and the others."

"Wow. Did the police ever ask questions or anything? Was Brynn ever a suspect? They had to have seen the text to Brynn from Emerson's phone records." I tucked my hair behind my ear, thinking this through.

"Emerson and Brynn were on the phone or texting all the time. They never questioned her, or any of us. Chance drove over Brynn's car tracks where she'd pulled over. People went there often, so chasing down a tire track by the next day was useless," Holden explained.

"I covered any evidence of her being there before the police arrived." Chance stared at Brynn. "And I would protect you again if I had to."

Brynn blew him a kiss. "I know. You've proven over the years how loyal you are. I love you for it."

"I don't think Reid really needs to know any of this. What if he went to the cops or slipped up?" I asked.

"It's a big burden to carry when you've barely met someone," Jace said. "I think it would skew how he saw us—saw Holden. It might put a wedge between them," Jace said.

"So, are we in agreement that we don't tell Reid?" Chance's gaze narrowed on Brynn. "I know you've had a gummy and probably said some things tonight that you didn't mean. But I need your word, Brynn. We all do."

Brynn's edible must have started to wear off since she finally seemed like she was taking this seriously. "I should have kept my fucking mouth shut." She rubbed her face and stifled a yawn. "I'm not sure that particular edible is good for me. Holden, I kissed your girlfriend ... twice. I wouldn't have done that normally."

Holden and Chance gaped at her.

"Oh, boy," Jace muttered. "I'll see what you bought. It's definitely a no-go moving forward."

My lips pursed. I glared at her in warning, and I shook my head. "Apparently, you're still stoned, so why don't you go eat some food before you get into more trouble?" I asked, scolding her.

"We need to talk," Holden said, patting my hip.

I rose from his lap and frowned. Why did I feel like a little kid heading to the principal's office?

Holden took my hand and led me to our room, closed the door, then whirled me around, pressing my back against the wall. His palm moved over my shoulder, and his eyes searched me with a fierce intensity.

I swallowed excessively, attempting to clear the lump in my throat. He had to be upset about the kiss. My nostrils flared, ready to defend myself since Brynn had also kissed him.

"I know that you've been drinking, but do I have your attention?" he asked.

Delicious shivers wracked my body at the huskiness in his voice and the conviction in his tone.

"Yeah, but what is this about?" I attempted to fold my arms across my chest, but Holden was standing too close to me.

"I realize she's your best friend and you won't betray her trust, so I want to make sure I get a good read on you when I ask this next question."

I stilled and stopped breathing, waiting to hear where this was going.

"Was Brynn's kiss a goodbye kiss?"

I froze. Dammit, Holden wasn't upset she kissed me. He understood the meaning behind it. She'd kissed everyone goodbye when I was gone.

"Shit. You don't have to answer, babe. You look like a deer in fucking headlights." Holden backed away and sunk to the edge of the bed.

"I can't confirm your suspicions." I shoved my hands into my jean pockets, realizing I hadn't said a word that had betrayed her, but I definitely needed to work on my poker face around Holden.

I sat next to him and slipped my arm through his. "I know she's been obnoxious tonight, but we need to make sure she has the best week of her life. It sounds like Jace is taking care of the edible fiasco, but she has every intention of fucking Reid. And honestly, if he's into her, then let them have fun. If Chance understood the situation fully, I think he would be supportive of her choices." I focused on the floor for a moment.

"Is it a for-sure thing? The doctors can't do anything else?" Holden's voice caught in his throat.

I leaned my head against his shoulder. "You're going to have to guess, Holden. I can't betray her. Especially now. Besides, I feel like I already have."

"You've not said a word, River. I've known Brynn for a long time. The moment she said it, I knew. I'm not sure Jace and Chance picked up on it. They might have looked at the kiss differently."

"She did admit that she's in love with me." I peeked up at him. "I told her I loved her, but I wasn't *in love* with her. And for the record, the kiss was sweet, not hot and heavy."

The corner of Holden's lips kicked up. "That's too bad. If you had liked it ..."

I sat up and playfully punched him in the arm. "I did like it, but I wasn't going to tell you about it."

"Oh, really?" Holden laid back on the bed, and I straddled him.

"Eventually, I probably would have. I don't like secrets between us." I followed Holden's gaze and laughed. He had a full view down my shirt.

"I love the black lace."

I rocked my hips against him, feeling his erection through his jeans. "It seems as though you do. Since you've figured out what Brynn was talking about, I move that we change the subject. I can't deal with it right now. My mind is blown, and I desperately need to hop off the emotional roller coaster, even if it's just for a little while. I vote that you distract me."

He slipped his hand beneath my top, his fingertips skimming my skin. An uncontrollable shudder traveled through me. Holden cupped my breast through the material of my bra, his tongue darting across his bottom lip.

I raised up, pulled off my top, then released the clasp on my bra. He slid the straps down my shoulders and tossed it on the bed. He sat up, his mouth sucking on my nipple as he caressed the other one. I arched into him as my fingertips danced beneath his shirt and over his washboard abs and up to his chest.

"You should ditch the shirt and jeans. They're in the way." I giggled against his lips, then hopped off him, allowing us to wiggle out of our clothes. After he rolled on a condom, he laid back on the bed, and I crawled on top of him, positioning the tip of his cock at my entrance. Our eyes locked as I slid him inside me. His hands landed on my waist as I began to grind against him. Holden sat up and wrapped his arms around me, burying himself deeper inside of me.

"I love you, River." He pressed his lips to my lips, silencing my response. His kiss grew more aggressive as we clung to each other, raw emotions revealing themselves once again. His mouth discovered my neck, his scruffy jaw gliding over my sensitive skin. Holden held my hips and slowly eased out and back in.

We found a gentle rhythm as we kissed and whispered, "I love you." Losing myself in him, I focused on his touch and his citrus and wood scent. In those precious moments, I knew it was more than making love. It was healing my heart of the past, encouraging me to move on. Move on with him. There wasn't anything in this world that I wanted more.

Holden's pace quickened, and he dug his fingers into my back, triggering my release. My core clenched around him as I tensed, then gave in to the tidal wave of pleasure. Seconds later, Holden's body tightened, and his eyes slammed closed as he climaxed inside me. I watched as he came down. "I love you, baby. More than you'll ever know."

He kissed the tip of my nose. "This is what I wish for Brynn. What we have. I don't care who it's with, but there's nothing better in the world than having someone to share your life with and to love."

I melted. "I feel the same about you." I cupped his cheek and stroked his face with my thumb. Feeling happy that we'd connected without any flashbacks creeping into my mind, I grinned at him. I balanced my knees on the mattress, allowing Holden to slide out of me, then I giggled. "Looks like you've got the wet spot this time."

Holden smacked me on the ass, laughing. It was the best sound I'd heard all day.

Chapter Twenty-Nine

I curled up in the corner of the penthouse couch, staring out the window, watching the rainfall. The rest of the week had flown by, and Brynn would head back to the hospital that day. The guys were all talking in our bedroom. I wasn't sure about what, but I trusted that Holden would clue me in if needed.

"Hey," Brynn said, the usual cheeriness missing from her tone.

"Hey." I patted the seat next to me. "How are you doing?"

She plopped down and leaned against me. I put my arm around her.

"I'm scared," she whispered. "And I'm so sorry for acting like a total bitch the other night. I should have never kissed you, and I had no right to drag Reid into hell with me. He seems like a great guy. He deserves a chance to live his life without being implicated in a murder."

"It's over. You've never ever acted like that before, so it was easier to let it go. Besides, that wasn't the Brynn we know and love. I knew it, and so did the guys. Once I mentioned the edible, everyone understood what was wrong." I wrapped a strand of her red hair around my finger. "Are you in love with me or were you stoned off your ass?"

Brynn sat up. "I'm confused, actually. I have feelings for you, but I think having a best friend as close as you are ... Maybe I've misunderstood some of what I feel. I've never loved a girl like I do you. Our relationship is special, and I trust you. That's all new to me. It's always been the guys I've felt that way about. Am I making any sense?"

"Yeah. It's new for me, too. Addison and I couldn't ... didn't talk about boys or clothes or kidnappings." I grinned at her, trying to inject a bit of humor into an intense conversation.

"Well, I wish we hadn't discussed kidnappings either. I wish it hadn't happened." Her expression twisted with grief and guilt. "So, are we good? You're not pissed at me anymore?" A deep sadness filled Brynn's green eyes.

I covered her hand with mine. "No Brynn, I'm not mad at you. I was only irritated that evening. The following morning, you were your normal, loving self. I know you're terrified that the chemo won't work, and so am I, but I refuse to give up on you. You're going to beat this. I'll be your rock until you can believe it for yourself. We all will."

Brynn nodded. "We should have an answer next week. I'll talk to the guys before I leave. I asked you to not say anything for a few days, and you granted me that. Thank you."

I stifled my cry, grief tearing through me like a hurricane, leaving my soul in a million pieces. What if this was over, and I never saw her face to face again? "Can't I stay? I'll rotate with Chance so he can have some sleep. We all will. I don't want to go back to Spokane without you." I hiccupped and pressed my lips together, swallowing the resentment that was lodged in my throat. *Fuck cancer.*

"You need to be with Holden and Reid. Chance will be here with me. I'll be in good hands, and we'll talk on the phone every day. Now that you have a cell again, we can text and Snapchat as well."

"Brynn, please. We should be here with you." Begging had never been my style, but I had no shame when it came to Brynn.

She tucked my hair behind my ear and smiled. "River, I don't want you to see me like this. I need you to remember me looking

229

somewhat normal. The next round will kick my ass. My hair will begin to fall out, I'll lose more weight. I don't want you to remember me like that."

I pulled her in for a tight hug as we cried together. "I love you. Don't you ever forget it," I whispered to her. "Be good to Chance. Tell him the truth, Brynn. He needs to know that you're in love with him, too."

She sat up and wiped her face. "I definitely owe him an apology. His feathers got ruffled with Reid, but he doesn't get upset with Jace at least. But our friendship is different."

"Do what feels right. If you don't want to tell him, don't. But let him know how special he is. He deserves that."

Brynn nodded. "I'll see you soon." Brynn covered her mouth as her shoulders shook with her cries. "I refuse to say goodbye to you."

I nodded. "Same. In fact, we're going to plan the next trip down. Let's do something fun. Celebrate the good results."

"Okay." She reached for my hand and squeezed it. "Love you, babe."

"Love you, beautiful." I sniffled as Chance and the guys joined us in the living area. We exchanged hugs and kisses, then Chance and Brynn left the penthouse. I curled into a ball in the corner of the couch and sobbed. Holden scooped me up into his muscular arms and carried me to the bedroom. He held me for the next few hours, allowing me to fall apart.

Once I'd settled down, I smacked my palm against my forehead. "Shit. Brynn didn't tell the guys about the chemo most likely not working." I pushed up into a sitting position. My nose was stuffy, and my eyes felt like sandpaper.

"She didn't need to. It was probably too much for her to deal with after saying goodbye. But she gave it all away when she said she kissed you. The guys just needed confirmation. It's what we were talking about before Brynn left."

"So Jace and Reid understand it might be the last time we see her?" A stabbing pain dug its claws into me, slicing me open and ripping my heart out. I blinked several times, breathing in, hoping to fill my lungs with much-needed air.

"Yeah. We'll talk to her though. Chance promised he would keep us all up to date."

I nodded, pulling my knees to my chest. "She's scared of settling down right now. Her main focus is living the remainder of her life if she can't beat the cancer. She also apologized for kissing me, as well as the 'I love you' confession. It all happened after her edible."

"Man, she's never allowed to have that kind again. It certainly wasn't our Brynn who was talking that night."

"I agree. It was an alien talking out of their ass."

Holden chuckled and sat up, combing his fingers through his hair. "Are you ready to go home?"

"No. I don't want to leave her, but she made me promise." I wiped my cheeks, hating that she was making us go back to Spokane. We should stay here with her. "Plus, we're not going to our own place. We're going to Chance's."

"I know. I've been thinking a lot about what that looks like for us. Why don't we visit the property in Sandpoint and see what you think?"

"When?" As far as I was concerned, the sooner the better. I needed to have some stability with Holden again. My life had drastically changed, and I was spinning from the last several weeks at the compound, the situation with Reid, and Brynn's battle with the cancer monster.

"We can go this afternoon if you want to. Zayne can drive us there from the airport."

"I would really like that. And, baby? We need to have dinner with your mom. She needs us. So much has happened, and she's still trying to pick up the pieces like we are."

He smoothed my hair and kissed my forehead. "Already ahead of you. We're all going to her place tonight. She has something to tell us."

I froze, fear twisting my stomach into knots.

"Hey, babe. It's okay. She promised it was good news."

I released the breath I hadn't realized I was holding. "Okay, I can deal with some good news."

***

Holden and I showered and changed before we'd checked out of the hotel. Holden had mentioned it was cooler on the water, so we'd opted for jeans instead of shorts. He grabbed a jacket in case we were there after dark.

The flight to Spokane was quick and easy. Zayne drove Holden and me to the property while Vaughn took Reid and Jace home.

I stared out the window, remaining quiet and deep in thought on the way there. I hadn't seen these parts of Spokane and Idaho. It wasn't much different except that it wasn't in the city.

It was good to have Zayne around again. I'd missed him when he had been on hall duty. It was sweet that Brynn had hugged him and Vaughn goodbye before she left. If she survived the cancer, I wondered if she would invite Zayne to play. She'd wanted to since the first evening she'd met him. I couldn't blame her. He was hot as hell.

The sun had begun its descent as Zayne drove the Mercedes onto an open field. The golden rays bounced off the smooth, glass-like water, and I immediately fell in love. Before the car had fully stopped, I opened the door and hopped out.

"Hey, don't do that, River," Zayne barked, clearly irritated with me.

I laughed and took off running, leaving both the guys behind. The clean, fresh water tickled my nose, and I sucked in a deep breath. The oak, aspen, and maple trees had grown their summer leaves, painting a brilliant splash of green against the crystal-clear blue sky. It was heaven, and I wanted to stay forever.

Twigs snapped and rocks crunched beneath footfalls, alerting me someone was drawing near. I glanced over my shoulder.

"I wasn't expecting that reaction." Holden chuckled as he approached and wrapped his arms around me, pulling my back against his chest. "It's stunning, isn't it?"

"It's so peaceful. Was it like this when you saw it?" I peeked up at him, the sun accentuating his long, dark eyelashes.

"Yeah. There are neighbors, but a lot of trees in between. We can plant more if you would like to. If you want the property, then let's talk about starting our future here." He kissed the top of my head.

"What does that look like to you? Honestly? What do you really want?" I closed my eyes for a moment and concentrated on his deep voice as he shared his heart with me.

"A log house, a boat, to rebuild the club, but in town where Chance would manage it, and we'd stay there only a few nights a week. Summer parties and barbecues, then a sitter when we wanted to travel."

"It sounds wonderful. Maybe I could go back to school once we settle in. I want to help with the club like before ... I mean, if the offer is still open. And what about New York?" I shivered as the cool air blew off the lake, causing soft ripples across the top of the water.

"It's not the right time. I want to stay close to Brynn until we know what's happening. Plus, I don't want to throw you into the nightlife environment right away. It will take a while to find the perfect location, rebuild 4 Play, and build a place to live. We have plenty to do to keep us busy: planning, working with the architect, making decisions. And no, you can't have your old job back."

I whirled around, frowning. "Why? I loved working with you, Holden."

He kissed the tip of my nose. "You're so cute when you're irritated."

I smacked him lightly on the chest. "Be nice."

He tilted my chin up and tenderly brushed his lips against mine. "I want you and Chance to be my business partners, babe."

My mouth opened and closed like a fish out of water. Scrambling for something to say, I shook my head in shock. "Partner? Holden, that's huge. I understand Chance because you two have grown up together. You trust each other implicitly. If anything ever happened between us, though, it would be a hell of a legal battle. Or you would be stuck with me in one way or the other until you were old, bald, and using a cane."

Holden chuckled, then grew serious again. "I know it's a big deal. While you were gone, I talked it over with everyone, then contacted my attorney. If we split up, which we won't, you could sell me your third of the club."

"Mm, that's not fair. Aren't you buying a part for me now anyway?"

Holden grinned. "No. You are. It's going to be yours fair and square. You've been preapproved for a loan if this is what you want to do. I knew you'd have objections and want your share to be yours and not given to you. We'll each have a salary so you can easily afford to pay the loan off early if you want."

Overwhelmed, I stepped away from him. "Holy shit, Holden. Like, holy shit. This isn't big, it's fucking mammoth." I placed my hands on the sides of my head and took a breath of the fresh air. Closing my eyes, I imagined what life would be like here with Holden. Our own log home, a successful club, friends, family ... and the sound of little feet pitter-pattering on the hardwood floors. It was a life I hadn't dared to dream about, much less with a man as amazing as Holden. Looking at him, I nodded. "Yes. I want this with you." A jolt of excitement shot down my spine, and I bounced up and down on my toes, clapping. Seconds later, I launched myself at him. I wrapped my arms around his neck and my legs around his waist. "I love you."

He grabbed my ass, lifting me. "I love you more." He kissed me deeply, and I moaned as his hot tongue swept across mine.

Breathless, we pulled away. "We should get to Mom's. She hates it when people are late for dinner." He set me down, my feet meeting the ground that would hopefully be ours soon.

"I'll call my realtor on the way and let him know I want to put in an offer. It's been on the market for a few months due to the price, but it's worth every penny to me."

I beamed up at him. "Let's do it."

***

An hour and a half later, Zayne pulled up next to Vaughn's Mercedes at Catherine's house. Reid hopped out when he saw us.

This time I waited until Zayne had turned off the car to climb out. "Hey," I said, hugging Reid. "You should have gone on in."

Reid gave me a nonchalant shrug. "It seemed easier to wait for you and Holden."

I rubbed his biceps. "She doesn't bite ... much."

Holden chuckled as he slipped his arm around my waist. "River didn't think that when she first met her."

"Yeah, she was rather intimidating, but not anymore." I laughed at the reminder of meeting Catherine in the kitchen for the first time. She'd asked if I needed birth control, and I'd nearly passed out cold. A mother sticking her nose into her son's sex life wasn't okay with me.

Holden rang the doorbell, and we waited for Catherine to answer. Seconds later, the door swung open wide, and Catherine stood there with a huge smile on her face. "Hi, kids."

We entered the foyer, and she gave me a big hug. I remembered Holden had mentioned that Catherine wanted to redecorate eventually, but the white marble floors, the wood staircase that led downstairs, and the chandelier were stunning. I wasn't sure how it could look better. "I hope you get to meet Mallory soon. You two will get along great."

I glanced at Holden and Reid. "I would love to meet her. Maybe she'll be open to visiting now that Reid is here."

Catherine hugged and kissed each of her sons on their cheek. "I hope you're hungry."

"Starved," Reid immediately replied.

Holden chuckled. "I don't know about River, but I'm definitely ready to eat. What's for dinner?"

Catherine motioned for us to follow her. It had been a while since I'd seen the formal dining room. The first time I saw it, I recalled gawking at the large chandelier hanging over the center of the cherrywood table. I would have to ask Holden if we could find a hutch and table similar to Catherine's for our new home. It would look amazing with the right logs in the house.

A woman in her early forties appeared with a bottle of red wine. She began filling our glasses as we sat down.

"Thank you, Leena." Catherine picked up the glass and swirled the liquid around before tasting it. "Mm, excellent. It's a Caymus Cabernet Sauvignon. I hope you all like it."

Reid took a sip, and his brown eyes narrowed, then he took another drink. "I've not had a lot of wine, but it's very smooth."

Holden and I took a drink, and to my surprise, I loved it. "Wow, I'm impressed. I'm like Reid, I haven't tasted a lot of wines, but that's really nice."

Holden stretched his arm out on the back of my chair. "It's one of Mom's favorites. Tim hated it, so Mom kept it in stock." He winked at Catherine.

"Mallory was also a fan, so I didn't do it just to irritate him. Although I'll admit, it was one of the reasons."

I glanced at Reid, who was wearing a faraway expression.

"Reid? Are you okay?" I placed my hand on Holden's knee under the table.

He ran his fingers through his dark hair, frowning. "I understand why Tim isn't on our list of all-time favorite people, but I don't know this man. Did he have any good qualities? Did he think about me after I was taken? If possible, I would like to hear about both sides of him."

Catherine's face paled. "Of course. I'm sorry, I should have thought about it."

"He's smart. It was ... Dad who helped me with my calculus homework when no one else could," Holden added.

"He's a wonderful businessman." Catherine peeked at Holden. "From what I learned recently, he has another job that I don't know much about, but we built our financial company from the ground up. He could rub elbows with anyone, regardless of if they were one of the wealthiest people in the world or just beginning their journey."

"Can I ask what your business is?" Reid asked.

"Honey, you can ask anything you want. You have a right to know. It's part of your inheritance when I leave this earth. I'll split it between Mallory, Holden, and you."

Reid stared at her, shocked. "Really? People do that?"

Pain twisted Catherine's features. "Yes. As parents our hope is to leave our children with a better financial status than what we had. For a long time, my mother and father were poor, but I've managed to build a very successful company. When your father and I divorced recently, I kept the business, since he had another one." Catherine grimaced and lifted her glass to her lips. "Anyway, we help companies invest and grow, purchase, take over other ones. There's a strategy to it all. Tim and I have an excellent reputation of helping businesses large and small propel to the next level and above. It's a numbers game, but I've also built a lot of important relationships all over the world."

"Numbers, as in money?" Reid asked, curiosity clinging to his question.

I leaned into Holden's side, watching Catherine and Reid get to know each other better. Hell, I wasn't sure any of us understood what she and Tim really did in the business. When I'd asked Holden, he'd shrugged it off. Now that I looked back at it, I think he was trying to protect his heart from becoming too invested in his mom. Even before Hannah, he sensed something was wrong, but little did he know he was missing a brother.

Catherine continued to answer Reid's questions with a smile on her face. She was thrilled that he was taking such an interest in the company.

Half an hour later, Leena brought in the prime rib, mashed potatoes, gravy, green peas, and fresh rolls. My mouth watered as she set the table. A moment of sadness tugged at me. Brynn should be home and able to hang out so I could fill her in on how the evening went. I'd have to settle for calling her, but I still hated her decision.

After we ate, Leena refilled our wine glasses. Catherine dabbed the corners of her mouth with the white linen napkin, then set it near her plate. "I have an announcement."

Thank God Holden had mentioned this was good news, or I might have crawled under the table and hid.

"First, I wanted to show you this, Reid." Catherine rose from her seat and gathered a manila envelope sitting on the hutch. She placed it in front of him and patted his back before she returned to her chair.

Clearly puzzled, Reid opened the flap, then slid out a piece of paper. "What is it?"

"It's your birth certificate. You were born in Spokane County on August 6th ,1998. Your legal name is Garrison Marcus Alastair. If you want, I can help you change your first name to Reid. It's your choice. With everything that's happened, I wasn't sure if you knew the day you were born or your age. I was hoping this would be helpful."

"Thank you, Mom. I had no idea when my birthday was, and they didn't lie to me about how old I was, I just lost track ..."

"Holden is nine months younger than you are."

Holden squeezed my hand as we watched Reid stare at the document that gave him a piece of his missing history. I couldn't imagine what he was feeling, but at least he was here with us and rebuilding his life.

Catherine dabbed her tears, then continued. "I've decided to take some time off. My family is more important to me, and I'd rather build a relationship with my children. I'm including you in this as well, River. You're already a daughter to me, regardless of what the future holds for you and Holden. I would also like to offer the house again. There's plenty of space while everyone decides their next step. It's, of course, rent-free. I do ask that you clean up after yourselves. If you go out, take one of the bodyguards with you."

"We will, Mom. Reid and River are still in danger until Opal and Kassandra are caught."

"Yes," Reid blurted out, interrupting his brother. "But I need something else, too."

Catherine's face lit up like a Christmas tree. "You'll move in?"

"I will. I would like to live here and spend time with you. We have a lot of catching up to do."

Catherine clutched the napkin, tears welling in her eyes. "What else do you need ... son?"

Reid returned her smile. "I don't have a formal education. I don't even know where to start. I'd like to work on that while I'm here. Can you help me?"

Holden smiled, widely. "Dude, that's awesome. I can help, too. Mom knows some really good tutors, if they're still around. It's been a few years, but they helped me after Hannah died."

"Yes! Gina was wonderful. I'll contact her." She turned her attention to Reid again. "As you get your GED and begin your college education, maybe we should talk more about the company. If you excel in math and business classes, who knows? Maybe you can work with me for a few years before I retire."

Holden wadded up his white linen napkin and tossed it on the table. "Damn, Mom. I see how this is going to work. Reid is already the favorite son."

"Holden Matthew Alastair. You've never expressed one iota of interest. Plus, you have your own billions, so don't get sassy with me."

Holden threw his head back and laughed. "I'm teasing, Mom. If Reid has found his purpose, I'll do everything in my power to help him achieve success. I'm clear on my path."

Reid burst out laughing. "I thought you were serious for a minute, Holden." Reid rubbed his chin, eyeing his brother. "I'm starting to see how this sibling thing works. We give each other a lot of sh—crap." He gave his mom a sheepish smile.

"I swear around her all the time. She's used to it. And yes, we're going to give each other shit, but we'll also be best friends."

I bit my lip, trying not to cry.

"I hope so. I really want to make this family thing work. I've never had a chance before."

"You do now," I said.

"It's crazy how our lives look so different after a few weeks." Catherine sipped her wine. "So, Holden and River, what about the two of you? Would you be interested in moving home for a little while?"

"Let us talk about it. River just got back, and I know Chance needs someone to stay at his place for a while. It might be after Chance and Brynn return to Spokane. I'm not sure if she'll want to live with her parents again or not."

That's assuming she beats this. There was no way I would say that out loud, and both the guys understood the stakes.

"Let me know." Catherine folded her hands in her lap, smiling like a little kid on Christmas morning.

Holden glanced at me, then to Catherine and Reid. "I put in an offer on a piece of property this afternoon. We'll know in a few days if it's accepted. River and I want to build a log house."

"That's wonderful! Where is it?" she asked.

"Sandpoint. There are five acres on the lake. Those opportunities don't come around often. We've also agreed to rebuild the club. The next several months will be busy, but we'll have a lot of good things to look forward to."

We all toasted to a new beginning, then Holden's cell rang. He fished it out of his back pocket and frowned, then lifted it to his ear.

"What's up, man? Is everything all right?"

The color drained from Holden's cheeks. "Are you sure?" He

paused, frowning. "Yeah, of course. We'll meet you there." Holden rose from his chair before he even hung up the phone.

"What's the matter, son?"

"I can't believe it." Shock and disbelief twisted Holden's features.

"Babe, you're scaring me." I tugged on the hem of his shirt. "Is it Brynn?"

Chapter Thirty

"It was Jace. Emerson woke up from her coma earlier today."

Catherine's silverware clinked on the edge of the China plate before it tumbled to the wood floor. She scooted her chair back in a hurry. "What? *Our* Emerson? It's been years."

"Jace said he was absolutely positive. Her mother just called him. She's asking for us."

Holy fucking shit. "I can stay here while you go, babe. Emerson doesn't know me, and I don't want to overwhelm her."

"No, I need you there. Plus, she'll ask about Chance and Brynn most likely. Reid, I'll drop off your belongings tomorrow. Mom, maybe you can take him shopping. He didn't come home with anything except the clothes on his back. Jace took him out a few days ago, but he needs more."

"Of course, I'll take him. It will be fun."

If things hadn't been so serious, I would have laughed. From Reid's expression, I didn't think he agreed with Catherine, but at least they would have some time together. I hurried over, hugged Catherine goodbye, and thanked her for dinner. Reid stood, then embraced me and kissed me on the cheek.

"I'll call you later." I kissed him on the cheek, then Holden and I hurried out of the house and into Zayne's Mercedes.

"We need to pick up Jace, then head to the hospital," Holden explained.

Zayne's concerned gaze appeared in the rearview mirror.

"No, someone just woke from a five-year coma." Holden buckled up, and I slid across the smooth black leather to the middle seat and fastened my seatbelt.

Zayne's brow lifted, but he didn't ask any additional questions as he shifted into gear and eased onto the street.

"I assume that you guys have talked about how to tell her what happened?" I rubbed my palm along Holden's thigh, wishing I could help him.

"Yeah. It's ingrained in my brain." He took my hand and stared out the window at his mom's street. "It's kind of crazy that Maxwell hit you with his car and broke your leg. I knew the minute I saw the damage that you would be stuck staying with me."

"I hate to admit it but getting hit by him was the best thing that ever happened to me. It brought us together." I kissed him, then snuggled.

"If I hadn't forced you to stay with me, I might have stalked you anyway." He grinned as he rubbed my leg, and we fell into silence. I suspected he was playing a million different scenarios in his mind concerning the situation with Emerson.

Hopefully, Emerson would be able to heal and piece her life together. It sucked that Brynn wasn't here to see her, but maybe the good news would give her something else to live for.

An hour later Jace, Holden, and I were shown to Emerson's room. We were finally at a hospital for something other than a trauma. No chemo treatments, no broken limbs, just the guys visiting a friend.

Emerson must have had a private space since there was only one bed. The white walls were bare other than a whiteboard with the nurse and doctor's name on it, dietary needs, and medications. A small television was mounted on the wall, muted.

Feeling awkward with the situation, I attempted to hide behind Holden, but he wouldn't have it.

"Holden, thank you all for coming," an older woman with grey, shoulder-length hair said as she hugged my boyfriend. "Jace." They embraced, then she turned to me. "Hi, I'm Peggy, Emerson's Mom."

"Hi, I'm River." I shook her hand, feeling out of place. It didn't matter though. Holden needed my support, and I would move heaven and Earth to give him anything he needed.

Peggy stepped out of the way, revealing a gorgeous blonde in a hospital bed. Her large blue eyes lit up when she saw us.

"Hey, Emerson," Jace said, approaching her. "It's good to see you."

"Jace?" She stared at him. "Thank you for coming. Wow, you look different, but still the same." Her gaze darted across the room. "I can't mistake Holden. He looks the same, only hotter." Emerson's attention fell on me. "I don't remember you." Her forehead creased slightly with confusion. "The doctor said I might have some memory loss, so I apologize. Please don't take it personally."

"It's okay. You haven't met her yet, Emerson. This is River, my girlfriend," Holden explained.

"You settled down?" Emerson attempted to smile at me, but without years of movement, it would take a while for her to regain muscle control. "These two ... well at least when we were in high school, were so full of trouble, but they were some of the best friends I could have ever had."

"We still are." Holden took her hand. "It's really good to see you awake."

"It's so freaking weird. I look different ... everyone is older, but I have no idea what's happening in the world today. When Mom told me what year it was, I freaked. I mean how am I going to wrap my head around all of this?" Fear and excitement flashed in her eyes.

"We'll all help you," Jace said. "We've got this."

Emerson searched the room. "Where's Brynn? Chance? Are they not living in Spokane anymore?"

"They are, but they're in Portland right now."

"Oh, together? As in they're married?" Emerson asked eagerly.

"No ..." Holden rubbed the back of his neck. "Brynn has cancer. She's being treated at the Knight Center."

Emerson's blue eyes filled with tears. "That's awful. Is there hope?"

"Always," I whispered. "Plus, she's strong and feisty. She's going to beat this."

Holden took my hand in his. "River's right. Brynn's got this, and she will be ecstatic when we tell her that you're awake. I'm sure she'll want to call you."

Over the next half hour, Emerson plied Jace and Holden with a million questions. She reminded me of Reid, absorbing everything like a sponge.

The more they talked, it became clear that they were all close. I wondered what she would think if she found out about the club, how the guys had protected Brynn and lied for her—saved her. The pact they'd made had been proof that they would do anything for each other. My breath stuttered, and I stopped breathing for a moment. These were *my* friends now. *My* life and family. Overcome with gratefulness, I dipped my head and looked at the floor. I refused to get emotional in front of a stranger.

Emerson released a soft giggle, appearing in awe of how her voice sounded. She was a breath of fresh air, and I hoped I had the opportunity to get to know her better.

***

Holden and I crawled into Chance's bed at nearly midnight. We'd called Brynn and told her about Emerson. Everything inside of me wanted to see Brynn's beautiful face light up with the news, but she refused to FaceTime. Sometimes she was a stubborn ass.

Yawning, I realized how exhausted and on emotional overload I was, but I assumed Holden was as well.

I looked at my boyfriend and propped my head up on my fist. "What do you think of moving in with your mom?"

He placed his thumb on my lower lip and stroked it gently. "I don't know. A part of me thinks that Reid needs to have Mom all to himself. She definitely needs him around. Not once has she ever taken time off work, and now I understand why. She'd lost two children, and being a workaholic was her coping mechanism."

"Makes sense, but now she's trying to do the right thing by him. By you, too. I just wonder ... ya know ... if Brynn comes home, where will we live?"

"*When* Brynn returns, she'll most likely stay here with Chance. You and I can have the guest room that Reid was using. I was there before you both got here. We could also stay with Jace if we wanted to. His place is bigger. We have options. Most importantly, I want you to feel safe."

I looked into his chocolate brown eyes and melted. "How did I get so lucky?" I smoothed his dark brow with my thumb, then kissed him. "I guess for now, we'll play it by ear and hope that Brynn has good news next week."

"It's the best we can do at the moment." Holden rolled over, and I snuggled up to him. The soft rise and fall of his chest lulled me to sleep in no time at all.

Chapter Thirty-One

"Are you ready?" Holden's attention bounced between Reid and me as we sat around the kitchen island in Chance's house. He reached in the back pocket of his jean shorts and retrieved his cell. He'd selected a dark green polo, a color that looked amazing on him, but not one he wore often.

I looped my arm through Reid's and nodded. "Are you?" I tugged on Reid's black V-neck designer shirt Catherine had bought for him. It turned out that he and Holden had similar taste in clothes, too. Once Catherine had introduced him to shopping and all of the available choices, he'd taken pride in how he presented himself. He consistently wore designer jeans and shorts that fit his butt and thighs as well as they did his brother's. He'd also discovered tank tops. I thought Holden was cut, but Reid proved to have more muscle definition. I'd mentioned that little tidbit to Brynn during one of our phone calls, and I was pretty sure she'd started drooling.

"Yeah, let's do it." Reid blew out a sigh and ran his hand through his hair. "Man, I'm nervous."

After a few things were moved into place, including the acceptance of Holden's offer on the lake property, we'd all decided it was time to call Mallory. She deserved to hear all the good news. Maybe someday, she would even consider visiting.

Holden tapped the FaceTime app on his iPhone and tilted the camera to show only him. He wanted a chance to explain before Reid appeared.

"Hey, little brother," Mallory said, her soft voice filtering through the phone.

"Hey, yourself." Holden's smile lit up his gorgeous face. "How are things in Spain?"

"I really like it here. The time off to focus on what I want has been really helpful. Are you coming to visit soon?"

"I would love to, as long as I can bring my girlfriend."

Mallory burst into giggles. "You settled down? No way."

Holden gave her a sheepish smile. "Yeah, it's been about six and a half months, or close to it."

"No fucking way! She must have a hell of a pussy if she got you to settle down."

Holden shot me an apologetic look, and I covered my mouth, stifling my laugh.

"I'm going to ignore that comment. Her name is River. She's smart, stunningly gorgeous, and feisty. You'll love her. I know I do."

A fierce blush crept across my cheeks. Reid nudged me in the side and winked at me.

"Where did you meet?" Mallory asked, eagerness in her tone.

"Well, you're not going to believe this, but she was sleeping in the recycling bin at Mom's house."

"Eww. What the hell?"

I could picture Mallory's nose scrunching up in disgust. My head hung down, ashamed of my past. I hadn't wanted to share it, but Holden insisted that she would love me for my strength.

"She was homeless, Mallory, don't be a bitch." Holden narrowed his gaze briefly. "She broke her leg and stayed with me while she healed. She's gone back to college and works with me at the club ... well, she will when the new one is ready."

"Okay, wow. That's a lot, dude. What happened to 4 Play? She was your baby."

"Tim burned it to the ground, so I would work with him."

Silence filled the room. "Watch your step, Holden. There are things you don't know about our father."

"Yeah, I got a pretty rude awakening. We'll talk about him later, but I would love for you to meet River first."

"Oh shit, is she right next to you? Holden, you did *not* put her and me on the spot like that." Her tone was stern.

Holden adjusted the phone, adding me to the screen. "Hey, Mallory." I offered her a friendly smile. Honestly, I didn't have anything to lose if I wasn't her favorite person. She was in Spain, and we were here. From what I could tell, she didn't have a lot of influence on Holden or his decisions.

"Hi," she squeaked. "Sorry about the recycling bin comment." She squirmed in her seat, adjusting her navy shirt. She flipped her dark hair behind her shoulders, her hazel eyes sparkling with curiosity. She and Holden definitely shared physical similarities. It would have been a shame if she'd looked more like Tim than Catherine. Unlike Holden and Catherine, Mallory had a small beauty mark near her left eye, exactly like Kassandra. My stomach twisted into knots, the reminder slapping me. I wiped my sweaty palms on my jeaned thighs.

"For the record, I agree with my brother, you're gorgeous. I'm glad someone has tamed this guy. Hell, I respect you simply for that feat." A beautiful smile spread across her tan face. "Holden, you two need to visit me over here. It would be a lot of fun showing you guys around."

I peeked up at Holden. "I would love to see Spain."

Holden gave me a sweet kiss. "We have a full schedule building the club and new house, but as soon as we're done, we'll book a trip. It would be great to see you."

"Oh, a new place to live, huh?"

"A log home on waterfront property in Sandpoint," I added,

trying to join the conversation. Although I sensed a bit of sisterly protectiveness over Holden, it didn't throw me off. I'd met girls like her before at school. They hadn't fazed me, and she wouldn't either. I had nothing to be ashamed of. I squared my shoulders and tilted my chin up.

"That sounds amazing! River, you'll have to send me pics as everything falls into place. If you need a second opinion on anything, I would love to help." She gave me a warm smile, and my defensiveness relaxed a little.

"I think that would be fun. I will."

Mallory stifled a yawn. "It's been a long day and my ass is tired. Maybe we can talk tomorrow evening?"

"Sure, but I have one more thing to share with you ..." Holden paused, and I rubbed his back, encouraging him. This wouldn't be an easy conversation. "Mal, I know about our brother, Garrison."

The color drained from Mallory's cheeks. "How?" she asked, her voice hovering above a whisper.

"Because I met him," I said. Holden and I had rehearsed exactly what we were going to say. I had nothing to hide. "We became really close after I was kidnapped and held at a training compound for sex slaves. Reid was in the cell next to mine."

Mallory shook her head, disbelief written all over her expression. "This isn't funny, Holden. You shouldn't ever joke around about something like that. Garrison was found dead not long after he was taken." She shot him a scathing look that would have peeled paint right off the fucking wall. She definitely had shades of her Aunt Kassandra in her.

I stepped closer to Holden as Reid joined us. "I'm very much alive."

Mallory gaped at Reid, and I took his hand in mine.

Holden glanced at his brother. "I had the DNA test run before I even told Mom. We had to be sure."

Mallory gawked at Reid, but it didn't seem to bother him. "What the hell? But how? Garrison?" Tears streamed down her face, and she swiped at them. "I thought you were dead."

"I know. Please call me Reid, though. It's the name I've used since I can remember. Mom told me about the man that took me, and that the detective told everyone they found my body."

"Mom knows?" Mallory's dark brows knitted together. "How long have you been home?"

"About a week and a half."

She planted her hands on the sides of her head, then she made the sign that her mind was blown. "Oh fuck. I just realized what you said, River. Cells? Reid ... you two were held in captivity?" Mallory covered her mouth, muffling her painful cries.

"One day I'll answer your questions. Right now, I'm grateful to River for giving me a new start and a family. I'm trying to focus on my future."

Mallory nodded. "Of course. I understand. Will you FaceTime with me now that you're ... back?"

Reid offered her a warm smile. "I would love to. I can't wait to get to know my older sister."

Mallory beamed at him through her tears. "Holy hell, I wasn't expecting that one. Shew!" She laughed while swiping her thumb beneath her lower eyelashes, removing the black mascara smudges.

"I probably should call Mom. We have a lot to talk about, including the possibility of coming to Spokane for a while. I don't want to waste any more time away from you, Reid. It will take some time to wrap things up here, but would that be okay with you? I don't want to crowd you in any way."

Reid chuckled. "Get your ass here as soon as you can. I'll be waiting."

I leaned into Holden, happy that the conversation had gone well. If I were Mallory, I would want to come back, too. She'd just learned about a missing piece of her heart.

"Mal, we'll call tomorrow. River and I have a meeting with the architect this morning. We're designing the new 4 Play and the house with him. We're pretty stoked."

"Congrats to you two. I feel like I've missed so much. I can't wait to stay up all night, drinking and catching up." Mallory blew us a kiss. "I'll talk to you all later."

We all said goodnight, then Holden disconnected the video call.

"Under the circumstances, that went well," Holden said, looking at his brother.

"It seemed like it, yeah. She's going to be full of questions that I'm not sure I can answer." Reid tapped his finger against the black granite countertop.

"You're not in this alone. I'll help you figure things out." I pushed up on my tiptoes and kissed his cheek.

"I'm not sure what I would do without you guys." He reached around the back of me, then pulled his brother in for a hug. "Thanks for everything, man."

"Thanks for coming home," Holden replied.

There wasn't a dry eye left when Holden and I were ready to meet the architect. I was on the same page as Reid. I needed to look ahead. The lingering nightmares were enough of a reminder of what I'd lived through. Fortunately, I hadn't attacked anyone again. It appeared that, as I felt safer, the flashbacks had eased as well.

Holden and I climbed into the back of Zayne's Mercedes and buckled up. As soon as Zayne shifted into drive, Holden's phone buzzed. He reached around to his back pocket and removed it. He frowned, looking at me. "Babe, it's Brynn ... on FaceTime."

Shit. This couldn't be good.

Chapter Thirty-Two

I grabbed Holden's arm and hung onto it for dear life as he answered the video call. Brynn's face filled the screen, and I couldn't help but smile.

"Hey, beautiful," I said first.

"Hi, babe. I sure do miss you." She winked at me, then smiled at Holden. "Hey, Holden. How are things going?"

Confusion clouded my thoughts. Had she just decided to video chat after all? She'd made it clear that she would only talk on the phone or Snapchat with a filter.

"We're on the way to meet with the architect. I bought the lakefront property, plus we're designing the new 4 Play."

"Oh my gosh. I can't wait to see it. I bet the lake will be so much fun next summer. We'll have to have a housewarming party, too!" She clapped her hands, nearly giddy with excitement.

"Wait, *we*? *Next* Summer?" I blinked several times, putting the pieces together. "Brynn, is the chemo working?"

Tears streamed down her cheeks. "Yeah. In fact, it's working better than the doctor had hoped. Next, I'll be moved to a less aggressive treatment center in Spokane. I'm coming home, you guys," she announced, nearly squealing.

"Really?" Hope filled Holden's words.

"Really. I'm going to beat this." She wiped her face and laughed. "I really don't know what I would do without all of you. I love you guys so much."

Unable to control it anymore, I started to cry. This time, tears of joy and relief. "I'm going to be stuck to your side. You're going to be tired of me."

Holden slipped his arm around my shoulders while he held up the phone. He sniffled and wiped the moisture from his eyes. "I never doubted you. You're a badass, Brynn. I'm so happy you're sticking around longer."

"Please, you're not getting rid of me that easy."

She laughed, then Chance stuck his head next to hers. His smile was infectious. "Hey, guys."

I waved at him. "When you get here, you're going to sleep. I'll take care of our girl."

Brynn nodded her agreement. "I'll be there in a few days. They want to run a few more tests before they release me, but the important ones are showing a bunch of positive improvement."

"I'm so fucking relieved," Holden said. "I'm so fucking relieved." He hung his head for a minute, then looked at the screen again.

"Are you and River going to stay in one of the guest rooms for a while?" Brynn's expression pleaded with me.

"Chance, is it okay?" I chewed my bottom lip while I waited for Chance to respond. "That way you can rest, and I can stay with her. You should get some fresh air and sunshine, too. Both of you have been cooped up in the hospital. The temps are already warming up here, and your porch is a perfect spot for us to hang out."

Holden twirled a piece of my hair around his finger. "We can give you two a break and stay at Jace's some, too. Once we get the house designed and the materials ordered, the construction for both 4 Play and our home will start. When we get to a certain point, I'll hire twenty-four-hour crews. River and I are ready to settle into a new routine."

"There's no question that you two will stay. Plus, when the club is ready, I'll be managing most nights, so that will take me away from Brynn. But by then, hopefully she'll be in remission." Chance smoothed the hair from Brynn's forehead and kissed her.

Zayne pulled into the parking lot and shifted the Mercedes into park.

Holden squeezed my knee, grinning. "We're at our appointment, but we'll call later. Super happy you guys are coming back."

I blew them a kiss and waved goodbye. Since the car had stopped, I crawled into Holden's lap and buried my head in his neck. "She's going to be okay," I whispered against his ear.

"Yeah, babe. She is." He held me for a minute, then we climbed out where Zayne was waiting for us.

A huge grin eased across his face. "Excellent news. I can't wait to see her again."

"I know, me too." I gave Zayne a brief hug, then took Holden's hand in mine as we approached the building.

***

The rest of the day was filled with planning and selecting the color of the logs, chinking, rafters, floors, and ceilings for the main level of our home. Holden and I had both agreed on a contemporary rustic style. Neither one of us wanted a moose head or antlers anywhere. Thank God we both had good taste.

After the meeting, we swung by Catherine's to tell her the news about Brynn and Mallory. She was elated and immediately called the hospital to see what Brynn would need at Chance's to continue her care. Catherine also hired a full-time nurse to be able to administer any medications and to monitor her closely. Catherine wasn't leaving any room for a mishap, and I loved her for it.

Reid joined us for dinner. He and Jace had taken off to play some basketball at the gym while Vaughn kept watch. For the most part, we were lying low, but sometimes we had to blow off some steam. Vaughn did a great job at sneaking Reid through the side or back door where no prying eyes could see him. If someone did recognize him, they would most likely think he was Holden as long as my boyfriend wasn't around. Reid was okay with that. It helped him not have to hide as much.

Catherine busted out more expensive wine, and we polished off a few bottles that evening, celebrating Brynn and Emerson. Both of the ladies would be home the same day. Although Emerson would have a ton of physical therapy, her parents had the money to have someone come to their home most days to work with her. Even though Brynn wouldn't have a lot of energy or get out much, I assumed she would want to see Emerson.

"River, how are you feeling about the club reopening?" Catherine asked.

"Good, actually. We have a lot more security protocols in place. It will also look different. We're making a lot of upgrades and the layout won't be the same. I think it will help. Plus, it's going to be near the river, so a new location."

"Chance will also be managing. River and I will be at 4 Play a few nights a week. I want to ease into it. We have plenty to do from the house. I think that change will make a difference as well." Holden stretched his long legs under the table, and I rubbed his muscular thigh.

"If you ever need to stay here instead of the club, you're always welcome," Catherine offered. "The drive to Sandpoint can be long late at night. If the weather is bad, there's no use driving to your place and risking an accident."

"Thank you. I'm sure we'll take you up on it," I said, offering her a grateful smile.

Reid and Holden played some pool while Catherine and I chatted details about the home. Catherine had recently stocked up on interior design magazines, so we leafed through them and picked out things we both liked.

"Have you talked to Mallory lately?" I turned down the corner of the magazine, marking a page I wanted to show Holden. The furniture was similar to the style I wanted.

"She called this afternoon and told me she met Reid. That sounds funny, doesn't it?" Catherine leaned back in her chair, taking a break from looking at the magazines. "I can't believe he's really here, River. Now Mallory wants to return. I'm not sure for how long, but is it crazy to think that my family is finally healing? The only one missing is Hannah."

I shifted in my seat, facing her, and crossing my legs. "No, it's not crazy. It's wonderful. I have a feeling that Hannah is somewhere watching all of this, too."

"I hope so. I miss her so much. She had such a bright future ahead of her, but she couldn't handle the secrets and she blamed herself for not protecting Reid. Mallory blamed herself for using the bathroom when he was taken. She swore that Reid wouldn't have been taken if Hannah and she had attacked the man when he walked into the house. What she didn't seem to understand was that she and Hannah were tiny. He would have hurt them, too." Catherine took a drink of her wine, then set the glass back on the table. "Hannah wasn't strong like you are."

I quirked a brow at her. "I'm not strong, Catherine."

She waved me off. "The hell you're not. You're one of the strongest women I've ever met. You survived a horrible life with your guardian and a kidnapping. You're doing everything to heal and move on. One of these days, you'll realize that you, River Collins, are unstoppable."

She raised her wineglass to me, and I lifted mine as well. "To strong, unstoppable women."

We clinked our glasses together, then took a sip. "Thank you for believing in me."

"Thank you for bringing my son home." Catherine leaned over and hugged me.

This was the first time I'd really felt close to her. Almost mother and daughter close. I wasn't sure where our relationship would go, but I was happy to have her in my life. I hadn't had these experiences with my own mom, and I wanted to cherish every minute I had with Catherine. At first, I wasn't sure if she was a good person or not. Then, I realized that she simply handled her grief differently. Once she came out of her shell, I quickly saw her strength and vulnerability. I absolutely adored her, and I hoped she would be in my life for a long, long time.

Chapter Thirty-Three

"**Y**ou look hot enough to eat," Brynn said, grinning at me. We'd decided to prepare for the night at Catherine's house. First, the bathrooms were larger than at Chance's, and second, we wanted to get ready together for the opening of the new club. It had been a hectic six months, but it had all come together beautifully.

"Yeah?" I wiggled my brows at her as I smoothed my palms over the navy evening dress I'd bought for that night. It reminded me of the one I wore when Holden took me to 4 Play the first time. I'd been in a trance the entire night, falling more in love with him as the evening continued.

"You know I like teasing you, right?" Brynn peered at me from the corner of her eye as she applied a deep pink lipstick. She'd opted for a silver dress with a deep V in the front, revealing her cleavage. That was actually an understatement. The material covered her nipples, and that was about all. Once Brynn had completed chemo and had gone into remission, she'd gained her body back quickly, along with her confidence.

A soft knock pulled my attention away from the mirror.

"Come in," I yelled.

"You look absolutely breathtaking, River." Holden's heated, lust-filled gaze traveled over my face, breasts, and legs as he joined us.

"See? Good enough to eat," Brynn said, replacing the lid on her lipstick and smacking her lips together.

"I'll be the only one eating River, Brynn." His voice was stern, but he smiled at his longtime friend.

"Well, don't mess it up. If you do River will be asking me to show her how it's supposed to be done."

We all burst into laughter. Brynn could have any male or female she wanted, but she loved teasing me. I didn't mind. I was actually flattered.

"I'll give you two a minute." She grabbed the bag containing her clothes and the rest of her makeup, then excused herself.

Holden closed and locked the door, smiling at me.

"You look damn good in that tux, Mr. Alastair. Definitely good enough to eat."

He stood behind me. "I have something for you." Holden brushed my hair to the side, then held up a choker necklace with an H on it. But this one had several rows of diamonds, then the H was in emeralds.

Breathless, I glanced up at him. "It's stunning."

"And so are you."

I turned and lifted my hair as he slipped it around my neck. He nipped at my ear, his eyes connecting with mine in the mirror. "Do you remember what this is for?" His hands gripped my waist, and I nodded.

"You're marking me as yours."

"Do you understand to always wear it at our club or any other club?" The possessiveness in his voice had my core throbbing already.

"Yes," I said breathlessly as he leaned his hips against my ass. His fingers trailed up the back of my leg and beneath my dress.

"You're mine, and tonight I'll remind you of that over and over." His other hand wrapped around my neck and tipped my head up.

"Spread your legs." He tugged on my G-string until it was around my ankles. "You won't need this."

Jesus, why is this so fucking hot?

Holden knelt and flipped my skirt up. He smacked my ass cheek and I gasped at the pain, my pussy growing wetter by the minute. His fingers ran up and down my slit, then he shoved his tongue so far into me I almost came on the spot.

"Holden," I whimpered, bending over the bathroom vanity. Suddenly a soft hum reached my ears.

"Sit on the counter."

I did as he asked. He stood, his gaze on my wet core. "You'll keep this in until I tell you." He held up a little silver bullet. I moaned as he slipped it into me, then turned it on. It buzzed inside me, reaching all my pleasure sensors at once. I wiggled around, gasping. "Holden, oh, my God."

He dipped his head between my thighs, sucking my clit until I came all over his mouth. When he was finished, he stood, grinning. He switched off the bullet and shoved the remote in his pocket. "That was just the first time you'll come for me tonight. Whenever this is on, remember that you belong to me." He pointed at the toy that was still inside me. "I'll remove it later. If you take it out, I *will* spank you. Understand?"

I sank my teeth into my lip, realizing that he could turn the bullet on whenever he wanted. He was in control. I was at his mercy, and I loved everything about it. But he also knew me well enough to know that I would push him. "You know me better than that Mr. Alastair. I don't behave for anyone." My tone was challenging, egging him on.

He closed the gap between us, his breath tickling my ear as he spoke. "Don't disobey me, River. You won't like the consequences."

A small gasp escaped my lips. Holy hell. I thought I was going to come again. His voice was deep and gruff, leaving me putty in his hands.

"I bet I would love the consequences, actually." I cupped his erection through his slacks, ready to suck him dry.

He reached in his pocket and switched the bullet on.

My back arched with the pleasure coursing through me again, then he switched it off. By the time he was done with me tonight, I would be begging for him to fuck me.

I hopped off the vanity and adjusted my skirt. Picking up the G-string, I defied him and slipped it on. "If I don't wear something, I'll have juices running down my leg." It wasn't up for discussion as I walked past him. I unlocked the door and strolled out of the bathroom, leaving him alone to wash up. Before I even made it halfway down the hall, the bullet turned on. I placed my palm against the wall, gasping. How in the hell would I make it through tonight? I was going to orgasm in front of everyone. I would fucking die. Maybe he wouldn't torture me too much. With that thought, the toy quieted again. I straightened up, wondering if I could handle the buildup to the mind-blowing release at the end of the evening.

A few minutes later, we all said goodbye to Catherine and piled in the back of the limousine. Reid, Chance, and Jace all wore tuxes, looking hardcore gorgeous. Brynn was one lucky girl.

My nerves fluttered in my chest. Not only was it opening night, but the lower floor was booked with extremely wealthy clients paying a premium price for the playrooms. Not only had Holden built six more rooms, but the Master's Playroom was also open for us.

Zayne and Vaughn closed our doors, then hopped into the front and raised the privacy glass. Both bodyguards would be with us all evening, plus additional security. Also, Brynn and I each had a container of mace tucked into a hidden pocket of our dresses. Mine was near my breasts, hers ... hell, I wasn't sure where she could hide anything in hers, but she looked beautiful. As soon as Reid, Chance, and Jace saw her, their expressions said it all. Holden's attention remained on me, which I loved. Brynn was gorgeous, and on occasion, I wondered if he missed being with her.

"We should toast," Brynn said. Chance popped open the bottle of champagne, and we laughed as it spewed everywhere.

"To new beginnings and love for a lifetime." Brynn held up her glass, and we all toasted.

The bubbles tickled my nose as I took a drink, then kissed Holden.

"So, River and Reid. You've never been with us when we've had a big celebration. We like to pre-game a little, so to speak."

I glanced at my boyfriend, frowning. A spark of lust gleamed in his eyes, and jitters bloomed in my stomach.

He leaned over and whispered, "Remember, you're mine."

Goosebumps peppered my skin. I wondered if this was going where I thought it was. My question was quickly answered as Brynn lifted her dress, and Jace slid his hand between her legs. She reached for Reid and kissed him while he palmed her breast. Brynn moaned into Reid's mouth. *Holy shit.*

Chance unbuttoned his tux pants, releasing his thick, hard dick. He stroked himself as Jace dropped to his knees and buried his head between Brynn's thighs. He lifted one of her legs over his shoulders, and she shifted on the seat, allowing him better access.

My core buzzed as Holden turned on the toy. I gripped his forearm, my focus glued to my friends. Brynn undid Reid's pants and freed his dick. It was long and thick, just like his brother's. My tongue darted across my bottom lip as I leaned over and undid Holden's slacks. Keeping my attention on the four of them, I slid Holden's cock into my mouth. He lifted his hips, and I cupped his balls.

Moans filled the back of the limo as Reid and Jace changed places. Reid dipped his head between Brynn's thighs, and I almost came. I peeked up at Holden, but he was watching too. I focused on my boyfriend, my gaze cutting over to Brynn and Reid occasionally.

Although I wouldn't ever cheat on Holden, I watched all three guys stroking themselves. It was hot as hell and even better than the voyeur room at the club. Holden grabbed my head, guiding me as I took him deeper until he touched the back of my throat. I squirmed as the bullet vibrated inside me. I finally understood more of Holden's plan. It wasn't just about control for the evening; it was to get me off without allowing our friends to see me naked. *Well played, Holden.*

Reid and Chance changed places next, and Brynn arched off the seat as Chance took his turn worshipping her pussy.

Holden caught me off guard as he switched the mode on the toy, and I released a cry. "Oh, God."

"That's it, River. Come for me." He dug his fingers into my ass cheek, the short skirt on my dress riding up dangerously high.

Glancing at Reid, his focus was on me as he squeezed his dick. My lips parted as I watched him jerk off. Looking at Holden, I followed his focus. Brynn's hips were squirming beneath Chance's mouth. Although I couldn't see everything, it was enough to turn me on.

I wrapped my hand around Holden's shaft and pumped him fast and hard as I gave in to the hot wave of desire that consumed me.

"That's it, baby."

"Holden," I called as I tensed and released.

He glanced down as I sucked on the tip of his dick. Seconds later, I swallowed as he came, then I licked the remaining sticky, white fluid off his cock.

Brynn threw her head back and moaned as Chance got her off, then Jace and Reid followed. Holden turned off the toy with the remote control, and I attempted to regain my composure. Holden had definitely caught me off-guard, but I was ready to take playtime to the next level. Even if he didn't want anyone else to touch me, watching Brynn and the guys had been intense in the best way.

"How do you like the bullet I picked out for you?" Brynn said while she flipped up a seat compartment and grabbed a container of baby wipes. She handed us all one as we wiped off, then readjusted our clothes.

"You chose it?"

"It's one of my faves." She winked at me. "By how flushed your face is, I'm guessing you really like it."

Holden chuckled, then kissed me hard. "This is just the beginning of the night, babe."

My eyes widened, and I laughed. "I'm going to sleep *good* tonight."

The limo filled with laughter and chatter the rest of the way downtown. A few months ago, I wouldn't have been ready for what had happened, but I'd been in therapy for a while, working through the abuse from Dan and Barrett. Maybe some girls wouldn't have hopped back into the sex, but I was a fighter. I loved Holden with all my heart, and our sex life was important to me. Not only did the sex and play help me heal, but it was also a big fat fuck you to Opal and Kassandra.

Although those sick bitches were still on the run, Pierce had let us know the instant Becky-Michelle had been taken into custody. I didn't think she'd survive long, especially not after selling children. Worst case scenario, she would serve the rest of her life in a cell behind bars. The irony hadn't escaped me. Honestly, I was fine either way.

The evening was a rush as I was introduced to investors and clients. Every man at the club glanced at my necklace, gave me a slight nod, then moved on. The choker provided a sense of security, which I needed.

Holden turned on the bullet several more times. It was an all-new challenge to hide what was happening. He liked to mess with me and flip the switch on the remote when I was in the middle of a conversation. Over the evening, I was able to control my reaction better. Once I had to walk away and pretend that I had to use the restroom. Holden had met me near the bathroom, slipped his hand beneath my dress, and massaged my clit until I lost it. He was loving the power play, but I was, too.

After ordering drinks, Brynn and I sat down at a table in the corner of the room.

"Hey," I said, tapping her on the leg. "Isn't that Sutton and Pierce?"

"It is! I'm so glad they made it!" Her expression slipped, and she grabbed my arm. "Oh. My. God. It's Hendrix and Gemma from August Clover." Brynn squealed. "They're both drop dead fucking gorgeous."

"No shit. I wonder why they're here, though." It appeared that I was about to get my answer.

Pierce, Sutton, Zayne, Vaughn, a stunning blonde next to him, and a few others waltzed over to our table.

"You look amazing, and the club is incredible!" Sutton yelled over the DJ.

I stood and hugged Sutton, then Pierce. "I'm so glad you all made it!" Sutton wore a gold, glittery, fitted dress and black heels. She had legs for days, just like Brynn.

Sutton leaned in near my ear. "I would like you to meet a few people."

I waved at Brynn to get her ass closer to hear the introductions.

"This is Cade, August Clover's guitarist and his fiancée, Mackenzie."

"Mac for short," the pretty, petite girl said.

"Nice to meet you both." Cade stuck out his hand, and Brynn, then I, shook it.

"You two know Vaughn, and this is Claire, my sister and Vaughn's fiancée."

Before I could react, Claire bundled me up in a big hug. "I can't wait to get together sometime. Sutton has told me a little about what you went through. I'll give you my cell number."

With building the club and our home, it had been hit-and-miss trying to get together with Claire and the others Sutton had wanted me to meet.

I grabbed my clutch from my seat and gave her my phone.

"Call me any time, day or night." She waved as she stepped away.

"Thank you! I will." I offered her a warm smile.

"And don't forget. We're no longer victims or survivors. We're strong women that pieced our lives together after assaults. We're queens." She winked at me, then she hugged Brynn.

"I'm sure you both know Hendrix and Gemma from August Clover," Sutton said.

I full-on gawked at them. Glancing at Brynn, I laughed. I hadn't seen her speechless before, but it appeared she was at the moment.

Gemma hugged me. "I know Claire said for you to call her. I would love for us all to get together, too. It helps so much to talk to other women who have lived through something similar." She squeezed my shoulder.

"I can't wait." Tears welled up in my eyes. Gemma Thompson was absolutely gorgeous *and* sweet.

I was super grateful Holden wasn't next to me when Hendrix Harrington smiled and shook my hand. I almost dropped to the floor and bowed at his feet. Hot wasn't even the word for it. Thank God I didn't have to choose between Holden and Hendrix. I was afraid I wouldn't be able to. My legs wobbled with nerves and excitement at the same time.

I giggled as Brynn gushed over Hendrix. She wasn't inappropriate in any way, but she held onto his hand longer than normal. I glanced at Gemma, pointed to Brynn, and laughed.

"I'm used to it," she said over the music, grinning.

"Gemma has nothing to worry about. She has Hendrix whipped. He'll never screw around on her," Mackenzie chimed in.

I threw my head back and laughed. "I like you already," I said and hugged her.

"Omigosh, I can't wait for us to all get together. It will be so amazing. We'll order pizza, have some wine, and gush about our guys," Mac said.

"I'll catch you later, we need to set up," Gemma said, patting my arm.

"For?" I asked, confused.

"Didn't Holden tell you? He hired us to play tonight." Gemma tucked a strand of her long, red hair behind her ear.

I fist-pumped the air. "Hell yes! That's my man."

We all chuckled, then everyone waved goodbye. Brynn and I sat back down, grinning at each other like two stupid teenagers.

"I would have fucking killed Holden if he'd turned on the bullet while I was talking to them." I rolled my eyes and took a drink of the white Russian Brynn had ordered me.

"I would have giggled so hard I wouldn't have been able to breathe." She crossed her long, lean legs, showcasing her toned thighs.

"We have a great turnout," Brynn said, her attention sweeping the large crowd.

Suddenly overwhelmed, my fingers white-knuckled my glass.

Zayne must have seen me tense up because he moved closer to me. "Are you all right? I can have Vaughn next to you as well. Say the word. At the moment, he's on the other side of the room, talking with Pierce. I guarantee you that Pierce, Sutton, and Vaughn have men all over this place."

I sucked in a breath, placing my hand on my heart, which was galloping in my chest. He was right. I was safe. Even when I'd run to the bathroom earlier, Holden had met me before I reached the restroom. I hadn't been alone the entire evening.

"Welcome, everyone! On behalf of Holden, River, and Chance, welcome to 4 Play!" Hendrix's voice boomed into the microphone.

The crowd erupted into loud applause, and I stood in order to see Hendrix. The band had set up in the back corner of the room.

"I'm Hendrix Harrington, along with my beautiful wife, Gemma, my guitarist Cade, and our amazing drummer, Asa, from August Clover. I hope you enjoy the music tonight."

Gemma's voice filled the area, then Hendrix joined in. Their harmony was to fucking die for.

"I never thought I would see them in concert, much less performing at a club I partially owned. Like, is this really my life, Brynn?"

"You bet your ass it is, and you deserve every amazing thing about it, babe." She looped her arm through mine.

"You, too, beautiful."

The music reverberated through 4 Play, and Brynn dragged me onto the dance floor, where Claire, Sutton, and Mac joined us. We danced in a group, giggling and cutting up.

Brynn's face lit up as a dark-haired, tall, pretty girl joined us. Her red cocktail dress fit every curve perfectly. Her long hair flowed down her back, and her manicured fingers sported several diamond rings. "Mallory!" Brynn threw her arms around her neck and kissed her cheek. "Welcome home."

Mallory turned to me, grinning. "It's nice to finally meet you in person, River." She hugged me, and I smiled at her.

"Welcome back. I can't wait for you to meet Reid. He's amazing." Once the hugs were exchanged, she joined us, dancing and chatting.

After several upbeat songs, August Clover dialed it down a notch. Gemma took the microphone and started to sing "Simple Things" by Teddy Swims.

Holden parted the crowd on the floor, making his way to me. His gorgeous smile made my pulse skip a beat. He took my hand in his, then slid the other one around my waist. We swayed to the music, staring at each other. Words weren't necessary. The lyrics were beautiful and spoke for us.

Holden placed his forehead against mine, and everyone else slipped away as we lost ourselves in each other.

The song ended, but instead of the band kicking off the next song, everyone moved off the dance floor except Holden and me.

Holden dropped to one knee and produced a black velvet box. He flipped the lid open, and I gasped at the diamond and emerald ring.

"River Collins," he started, then looked up at me, love and adoration in his eyes. "The day you strolled into my mom's house, scared and determined, I knew there was something special about you. It took me a while to realize that I'd given you my heart in those first moments, but it was the best thing I've ever done. Those days without you were torture. It was as if the better part of me was gone, and I couldn't breathe. You make me a better man. You taught me to live again. You taught me to fight for what I wanted, and you're who I want ... for the rest of my life. River, I don't want a future without you in it. Would you do me the honor of becoming my wife, so every day is the best day of my life?"

My legs trembled, and I grabbed his shoulder, terrified I would drop to the floor, unable to get up. He would have to carry me in front of everyone.

Silence filled the room while they waited for an answer. This man was my everything—the air I breathed and the light in my darkness. "Yes, I would love to be your wife. I'm ready to start my forever with you, Holden Alastair."

He rose and took my hand, slipping the huge diamond ring on my finger. Holden tipped up my chin and kissed me passionately. I wrapped my arms around his neck as the crowd cheered behind us.

"I love you, Holden." I ran my fingertips across his clean-shaven jawline.

"I love you more, babe." He kissed me, then threw his head back and let out a loud whoop as he lifted me and spun me around.

Holden led me off the dance floor and grinned at me. "I have a surprise for you."

"Another one? I'm not sure I can handle any more." I laughed, staring at the beautiful ring.

His arm slipped around my waist as we headed to the door of the elevator, and he stood still as the retinal scanner did its job. He pushed the button for the fourth floor, remaining quiet. This time our offices, as well as the conference, game, and break rooms, were all on the top. Other than us, the area was restricted.

The elevator whooshed open, and Holden guided me to the conference area.

I stood rooted to the spot and gasped as my attention landed on Shirley and Ed. I looked at Holden. "I don't understand."

"While you were gone, Shirley and I had a few conversations. They had nothing to do with the tracker, babe. Shirley even helped me do a bit of digging to find out who did. Logan had another girl put it in, then she turned up dead."

I stared at Shirley and Ed, memories of that night rushing at me like a fucking linebacker. At the time, they'd been so good to me, but when we found the tracker, I'd lost hope that they were decent people.

"Hi, River. You look absolutely beautiful." Shirley glanced up at Ed, tears in her eyes. "Congratulations on the engagement. We watched from the side of the room, then came here so we could talk."

Holden rubbed my back, then in a few steps, I closed the gap between us and hugged Shirley, then Ed. "I've missed you guys. How are you?"

Over the next hour, I plied them with questions, and they asked some as well. Holden had thought ahead and had snacks, wine, and beer for us. It was wonderful to see them and get off my feet.

Finally, we said goodbye, with assurances that we would meet them for breakfast at our new place the following day. I couldn't wait to spend the night next to Holden as his fiancée, but with the view of the lake.

"Thank you, Holden. Thank you for finding out that Shirley and Ed had nothing to do with the tracker. It means the world to me."

We entered the elevator and Holden pushed the main floor. "Shirley had left a message on your phone, and I called her back. She clearly had no idea where you were or that you'd missed your stop in Idaho. Lucky for me, you landed in Spokane." He pressed his mouth to mine. "I can't wait to take you to our new house."

"Same."

The rest of the night was busy with congratulations from everyone. Holden stuck to me like glue, kissing me every chance he had.

Brynn, Chance, Reid, and Jace also stayed with us. I glanced around at their smiling faces while I leaned into my fiancé's side. He wrapped his arm around me, and I snuggled against him. The events that had led up to that night had been insane, and although I was still healing, I knew I was exactly where I'd always wanted to be. Home.

Chapter 34

Epilogue Holden's POV

"Are you sure, man? This is a big deal. Once it's done, you can't ever undo it." Zayne hesitated, his grip on the handle of the door.

"It needs to be taken care of and there's no time like the present." I ran my hand through my dark hair. "It's my job to protect River."

I took a step back, taking in our surroundings. It was a warm day, and the leaves rustled in the breeze. Zayne and I had hiked a few miles into the forest, and I had no fucking clue where we were. But I trusted Zayne with my life.

"I didn't have a chance to congratulate you and River last night. Thanks for letting me help with the proposal."

I patted Zayne on the back. "Thank you. I hadn't even thought of having the band play. Brynn and River nearly passed out when they met Hendrix and Gemma. I was off to the side, watching it all." I chuckled, appreciating the change in the conversation for a minute.

"Gemma and Hendrix are really good people. Those kinds of friends are hard to find, but you found some, too."

I nodded and sucked in a breath. "Any word on Opal or Kassandra?"

"No. Pierce and Sutton are still searching for them. They'll find them. I promise."

"I sure as hell hope so. You'll call me as soon as they hear something?"

"Yup. I told you I was in this when you asked, and I meant it."

Through the nightmare of River's kidnapping, Zayne had ended up a damn good friend.

I squinted at Zayne, blocking out the afternoon sun. "Swear to me that River will never know about this."

"I'll never repeat this to anyone. Not River, not her friends, not my boss. This is between you and me. I'll take this to the grave." Zayne patted his chest.

"All right, let's do this."

Zayne pulled on the handle. The steel door creaked and scraped the dead leaves on the ground as it opened. I stepped into the small building as he closed it and flipped on a light switch. The power and water for the small space were strictly solar operated. When Zayne mentioned his buddy had an abandoned bunker, I took him up on the offer. I had to agree to make the drive blindfolded and never attempt to figure out where this place was.

"Holy shit, it stinks in here." I covered my nose as I took in all the details of the space. Finally, my attention landed on what I was looking for. "Thanks, man. I'll only be a minute."

"Take your time." Zayne stepped back outside, leaving me in the room. I pulled up an old, rusty metal chair and sat down.

Terror twisted the man's face in front of me. A dirty gag was shoved in his mouth, and it was clear that he'd lost weight. His eye was busted and swollen shut. His clothes were filthy, and he smelled of urine and shit.

"Hello, Tim." I folded my hands in my lap. "How's Zayne treating you?"

Tim violently trembled, just a shell of the man he used to be.

"Do you know why I'm here?" I crossed my legs and stared at him. Every fucking thing about him repulsed me.

Tim shook his head, attempting to talk behind his gag.

"I wanted to tell you that your months of living in a cell are over."

His reply was muffled, but his gaze was full of hope.

"River is home and we're getting married soon. I've rebuilt 4 Play, and we have a future ahead of us. But ..." I pointed at him, "there's something stopping me from moving forward." I tapped the side of my head as if I were thinking hard. "My job as River's fiancé and husband is to protect her. It also means that everyone that hurt her will be hunted down and killed. Normally, the thought of ending someone would bother me, but not this time. Anyone who would kidnap, beat, and sell children as sex slaves doesn't deserve to live. That includes you, Tim."

Tim's muffled cries filled the room as he rocked back and forth in his chair. I assumed he was begging for his life, but I didn't care. I'd begged for River's life, too.

"I did want to let you know that Garrison is back."

Tim's eyes nearly bugged out of his head.

"He wasn't dead. Opal or Kassandra had him kidnapped. He's worked as a sex slave since he was ten. *Ten.*" I glared at the man who was supposed to keep his family safe. The man I had once adored had become nothing more than a sperm donor to me. "He's been beaten, raped, and tortured by men and women. We suspect that Hannah got too close to the truth, and Kassandra or her piece of shit mother ordered a hit on her. Not to mention threatening Mallory, terrifying her for years." I held up three fingers. "That's three children you let down." I stood, pacing the small space, wondering if this was how River and Reid had lived. In a small cell, dirty and terrified.

"Then you let me down when you didn't come straight to me when you knew who had taken River. She was gone for three horrifying weeks. She lived in a hole underneath a house for the first several days with no light, no food, no water, and naked." I clenched my teeth, the anger I'd buried until now burning a fire inside me, begging to be released. "For the record, I fucking hate you. You're a pathetic piece of shit, and I'm going to make sure that you never hurt anyone again."

My pulse kicked into high gear as I walked over to the bucket that was turned upside down. I lifted it up with the toe of my hiking boot and peeked beneath it. It was there like Zayne had said it would be. I owed him big time. Bending down, I clutched the handgun, the cold metal cool against my skin.

Tim's cries became louder as tears streamed down his dirty face. He shook his head, his eyes pleading with me.

"A little too late to make things right, old man." I wrapped my fingers around the handle of the gun and raised it, standing back like Zayne had taught me. I took in a deep breath and held it for a second.

"See you in hell," I said, then squeezed the trigger.

Dear readers: **Do you think Holden killed Tim or just scared him? Post your thoughts in my reader's group and join the discussion! Click Here or copy and paste https://www.facebook.com/groups/JAOwenby

Also by J.A. Owenby

OTHER BOOKS BY INTERNATIONAL BESTSELLING J.A.
OWENBY

Bestselling Romance

The Love & Ruin Series

Love & Sins

Love & Ruin

Love & Deception

Love & Redemption

Love & Consequences, a standalone novel

Love & Corruption, a standalone novel

Love & Revelations, a novella

Love & Seduction, a standalone novel

Love & Vengeance, a standalone novel

Love & Retaliation

Wicked Intentions Series

Dark Intentions

Fractured Intentions

The Torn Series, inspired by True Events

Fading into Her, a prequel novella

Torn

Captured

Freed

Standalone Novels

Where I'll Find You

About the Author

International bestselling author J.A. Owenby grew up in a small backwoods town in Arkansas where she learned how to swear like a sailor and spot water moccasins skimming across the lake.

She finally ditched the south and headed to Oregon. The first winter there, she was literally blown away a few times by ninety mile an hour winds and storms that rolled in off the ocean.

Eventually, she longed for quiet and headed up to snowier pastures. She now resides in Washington state with her hot nerdy husband and cat, Chloe (who frequently encourages her to drink). She spends her days coming up with ways to torture characters in a way that either makes you want to throw your book down a flight of stairs or sob hysterically into a pillow.

J.A. Owenby writes new adult and romantic thriller novels. Her books ooze with emotion, angst, and twists that will leave you breathless. Having battled her own demons, she's not afraid to tackle the secrets women are forced to hide. After all, the road to love is paved in the dark.

Her friends describe her as delightfully twisted. She loves fan mail and wine. Please send her all the wine.

You can follow the progress of her upcoming novel on Facebook at Author J.A. Owenby and on Twitter @jaowenby.

Sign up for J.A. Owenby's Newsletter:
BookHip.com/CTZMWZ

Like J.A. Owenby's Facebook:
https://www.facebook.com/JAOwenby
J.A. Owenby's One Page At A Time reader group:

https://www.facebook.com/groups/JAOwenby

A note from the author:

Dear Readers,

If you have experienced sexual assault or physical abuse, there is free, confidential help. Please visit:

Website: https://www.rainn.org/

Phone: 800-656-4673

Made in the USA
Monee, IL
27 May 2022

97148887R00173